THE ADMIRER

THE ADMIRER

KARELIA STETZ-WATERS

SAPPHIRE BOOKS

SALINAS, CALIFORNIA

The Admirer

ISBN - 978-1-939062-42-0

Cover - Christine Svendsen

Sapphire Books
Salinas, CA 93912
www.sapphirebooks.com

Printed in the United States of America
First Edition – December 2013

Dedication

For Fay

Acknowledgements

Thank you to the P & C Committee – Paul Hawkwood, Terrance Millet, Chris Riseley, Robin Havenick, Rob Priewe, and Jane Walker – and to all my friends and colleagues at Linn Benton Community College, especially Liz Pearce and Scott McAleer who always keep me grounded. Thank you Maria Isabel Rodriguez for 25+ years of support and for being the world's fastest reader. Thank you also to Kim Pippin, Jen Nery, Amanda Gallo, Lori Major, and Shannon Parrott for reading my work. Thank you to Linda Kay Silva for your friendship and guidance. Thank you to Chris Svendsen, Schileen, and everyone at Sapphire Books for helping make my dreams come true.

Thank you to Opacity.us for preserving images of the Northampton State Hospital after which I modeled Pittock Asylum. Thank you also to the Willamette Writers. Thank you to Steve Fletcher. Thank you to the Albany Police Department's Citizen's Academy. Thank you to Robert Whitaker, author of *Mad in America: Bad Science, Bad Medicine, and the Enduring Mistreatment of the Mentally Ill* which I consulted frequently when writing Dysphoria. Thank you to the Calapooia Brewing Company where so many good ideas were hatched over a pint of Whitewater Wheat.

Also, thank you to my parents, Elin and Albert Stetz, for supporting me and supporting my love of writing since I was a little girl. You gave me everything. And finally a big thank you to my wife, Fay Stetz-Waters for believing in me for so many years. I could not do it without you.

Prologue

He lowered the woman onto the rough gravel that bedded the train track just beyond the bridge. In the blue light of the forest before sunrise, her legs were almost as pale as her white underwear, paler where the scars twisted her thigh. Carrie stirred, the oxycodone slowing her speech.

"Are you really mad at me?"

He draped one of her legs over the train track and then the other, arranging them carefully.

"No," he whispered into her hair, as he withdrew a handful of long zip-ties from the pocket of his coat. "You know I love you."

The heat wave had broken, at least temporarily. A hurricane battered the eastern coast. Even in the Berkshires, the air had cooled and grown damp with imminent rain. His fingers slipped on the plastic straps.

"I can see the stars," Carrie murmured. Her eyes were closed. She was light years away, drifting through drug-induced dreams. "I can see Jupiter."

Listening carefully, he could hear the train approaching, not just the whistle but the rumble of wheels on metal rails. He wrapped one of the stiff, plastic bands beneath the rail and around Carrie's calf then pulled, hard. She whimpered, but did not open her eyes.

He felt a surge of arousal. He would love to watch her heal, love to watch the open wounds seal and harden into knots of scar tissue. Perfect. Complete. He stopped himself. Carrie would not heal. He had to focus. He had to remember. He could not let her heal. She had to die.

He glanced down at the rails, silver in the moonlight, like a ladder crossing the low, concrete bridge and disappearing into the forest. In a way, this was everything she wanted. She'd been ready to do it when he met her, ready to sever her own legs right here on the Berkshire–Western in an attempt that would have cost her life.

"I would have given you this." He stroked his index finger across the top of her thigh. "We could have had everything."

In the distance, the light of the train flickered through the underbrush. He pulled the second tie tight.

"And this is how you repay me? You expose me? Ridicule me to your support groups?"

Carrie was unconscious now, but he could still hear her voice echoing in his head. *I want us to be a normal couple. I want to tell everyone I love you.*

Angrily, he pressed his lips to Carrie's. Then he unfolded the forest-green bed sheet he'd brought. He threw it over her like a shroud and stepped away. Standing in the shadow of the bridge, he checked his Movado. A single diamond gleamed in the face of the watch. The gold hands indicated 4:55 a.m. The train's headlight flashed through the forest.

When the train struck her, she rose for one exquisite moment. He saw her torso lift off the ground. Her back arched, her head flung back, her mouth opened so wide she ceased to be human. It was as if the roar of the train emanated from that mouth. Then she fell back to the ground. He felt the cool air on his skin.

A few drops of rain hit his forehead. He unrolled the sleeves of his poplin shirt, shrugged on the blazer he'd hung on a tree, and smiled.

Chapter One

Helen Ivers straddled the man, thrusting her hips against him until her cervix battered the tip of his cock. She had already forgotten his name. Devon or maybe Taylor. It was one of those gender-neutral names yuppie parents gave their children so they could be self-actualized. Whatever the man's name, his eyes were wide with a look of surprise. For all his vigor, young Devon had no idea what he was doing. He could not have been more than twenty-five. The girlfriend he mentioned—and then quickly forgot when Helen invited him to her hotel room—probably had sex with the lights off. Prone, in the dark, with the sheets pulled up to her waist, that was Helen's guess. Poor girl.

Helen had not bothered to turn off the television, let alone the lights. As they moved together, a 24-hour news channel played clips from the New England hurricane. Bodies floated out of a flooded Boston subway tunnel. Thugs shot a rescue worker in Jamaica Plain. *Another tragedy.* Helen leaned back, her hands on her heels, her pubic bone grinding the man's body. The heat wave in Boston was breaking, but not before a gun fight erupted over nothing in a hot bar. "We are all on edge," the bartender said. That was only blocks away from Helen's room in the Boston Hilton. The man beneath her groaned.

"That's right," Helen said. "Again." She closed

her eyes, tried to concentrate on his lean, muscular body in order to forget.

Without preamble, the news on the hurricane was interrupted. The station cut to a different reporter.

"I'm here at Pittock College, a private college in the remote southwestern corner of the Berkshires, where a body was recently discovered..."

Helen's eyes flew open, her attention riveted.

She dismounted the man just as quickly as she had mounted, separating their bodies with one swing of her leg. He let out an explosive moan. Helen turned up the television.

"Shhh!" she said.

"After police dismissed her student's claims as a prank, theater professor, Adair Wilson, investigated further. What did you find, Ms. Wilson?"

The camera cut to a woman with cropped, blonde hair. The professor glanced back and forth, as though scanning the space beyond the camera for something she could not see. When she spoke, her voice held none of the shrill self-consciousness of citizens unaccustomed to the television spotlight.

"I believed Marcus," she said quietly. "He said he saw something in the woods. I believed him."

"And what did you find when you went out?" the reporter asked.

"I found a body," the professor said. "Or... part of a body." Her eyes found the camera, and, for a moment, Helen felt like the professor looked directly at her. "I found two human legs, tied to the train tracks."

The camera returned to the reporter's lip-sticked smile.

"Police confirm Professor Adair Wilson's findings. Reports say the police found two human legs bound to the Berkshire–Western train tracks. The legs were apparently tied down with industrial-grade zip-ties. Police are saying that the legs were severed around 5:00 a.m. yesterday morning when the Berkshire–Western passed through Pittock. Crime scene investigators have been delayed by the hurricane. Police have secured the crime scene in anticipation of their arrival. Preliminary searches have not revealed the whereabouts of the rest of the body or the identity of the victim. Police are advising students and faculty at the small liberal arts college to stay out of the forest and avoid isolated parts of town and campus. If you have information about the crime…"

Another tragedy, but this one is mine.

Behind Helen, the man let out another cry of protest. "What are you doing?"

"I'm sorry, Devon."

"It's Flynn."

He looked hurt. Helen leaned across the bed and cupped his cheek in her hand. He had the shaggy, blond hair of a boy and a smattering of freckles across his nose.

"You're lovely. You really are." She meant it, not that it mattered. She drew in her breath, feeling a sadness so heavy and tangible, it might pull her to the floor. Her sister's face flashed before her eyes. *Eliza!*

Helen strode into the bathroom and wiped herself with a tissue, then pulled on the pants of her black Armani suit, tucked in her blouse, straightened the lapels of her jacket, and smoothed her auburn hair. She glanced in the mirror. The face that greeted her was as hard as the diamond solitaire at her throat.

"You'll have to get dressed," she told the young man. "I'm checking out."

"What happened?" he asked. His erection sagged. Goose bumps appeared on his arms.

Helen furrowed her brow, as though the question was too obvious to comprehend. Then she nodded toward the television where the news reporter was interviewing a student.

"I work there."

The man draped one arm over his eyes. "Do you have to go right now?"

Helen was already halfway out the door, stepping into the quiet hallway. The Boston Hilton logo, an interlaced B and H, repeated in the pattern of the carpet, receding into a calico of blue and gray. Helen turned once before closing the door behind her.

"Give my best to your girlfriend," she said, shooting the man a half smile as she closed the door.

Chapter Two

In the hotel lobby, the predawn light mixed with the light from the chandeliers. Helen rang the bell at the front desk. A minute later, a sleepy man in hotel uniform appeared.

"Checking out?" the clerk asked.

Helen nodded.

"Early flight?"

"Just an early start. Do you have the *Boston Herald*?"

The clerk handed Helen a copy. She scanned the headlines. She had not expected Pittock College to make the *Herald*, but she was still relieved to see that the front page remained preoccupied with the hurricane. She flipped through the local news section and the state news section. On an off chance that the editorial staff had a sick sense of humor, she also checked the education section. Nothing. She handed the paper back to the clerk.

Loath to encounter Flynn in the lobby, Helen waited until she found her car in the parking garage before checking her voicemail. From where she sat in the driver's seat of her Lexus, she could see across the open–air garage to the warehouse building next door. Around her, the early light made long shadows out of the vehicles. In the corner near the staircase, a figure darted behind a truck. Somewhere behind Helen, a car engine turned over and then sputtered to a halt.

She tucked her Bluetooth into her ear and checked her unlisted, personal cell phone. The first message was from her friend Terri asking about the conference.

"Let me guess," he said. "They wanted to 're-envision their values statement.' Please tell me you didn't encourage them. And by the way, congratulations." Helen had not talked to Terri since she accepted her position as president of Pittock College two months earlier. "I knew you would land on your feet. Screw Vandusen. If that school couldn't appreciate what you did for them and understand what you were going through..." Terri paused. "Anyway, good luck at Pittock. Call me."

There were no other messages on her personal phone. The first messages on her campus voicemail were innocuous announcements from her secretary, Patrick. The New Hampshire Alumni Association had scheduled a fundraising dinner. An emeritus professor died. The Women Administrators Association wanted her to speak at their annual symposium. The next message was from the theater professor. Helen's pulse quickened when she heard the voice.

"President Ivers, I think something has happened on campus. One of my students... he thought he saw a body in the forest. Please call me."

The next two messages were also from the professor. Increasingly insistent, they explained the situation in more detail. The plea was always the same: call me. In a final message the professor said, "I found the body." Her voice was bleak. "She's dead. It's horrible. Please call me before you talk to the police. There are things you need to know."

She tried to square the somber voice with what

she knew of Wilson. Helen had met the entire faculty personally, but it had been difficult to get a read on Wilson. She was one of the younger faculty members, perpetually surrounded by a flock of students, usually laughing and jostling along with them. Once, Helen had glanced out her office window to see Wilson do a handstand, much to the delight of a surrounding crowd. Still, there was a seriousness about Wilson. Everyone Helen asked said they liked her, but were certain other faculty and staff members did not.

There were no other messages, and that troubled Helen also. She dialed the provost's number.

"Helen, how are you?" Marshal Drummond, the provost of Pittock College said. Even through the static of a poor cell phone connection, his voice had the resonance of a grand piano. He was true New England aristocracy, and he hated Helen. She understood that.

"I'm as good as could be expected under the circumstances," she said.

"What can I help you with?"

"Have you seen the news?"

There was a significant pause on Drummond's end.

"I presume you have," Helen went on. "If not, you'll want to go online as soon as we are through."

"I hope you're not planning on charging back with the cavalry." He had seen the news.

"Of course I'm driving back. A woman was murdered on our campus."

"*Someone* met an unfortunate end on state land, almost a mile from Pittock College," Drummond corrected. "This is police business. Forgive my presumption, but if you cancel your engagements with the Boston alumni you'll send a very clear message:

we're afraid. You'll incite a panic."

A sparrow swooped into the garage and alighted on a van nearby. It stood motionless, a black silhouette against the growing daylight. Then it squawked, and a flock of identical black shapes swarmed in behind it, cutting the air like scythes.

"We should be afraid," Helen said. "Our students' safety is at stake. Nothing matters more."

"At least give the police a day to rule out obvious explanations. The New England alumni are our primary source of funding after enrollment. Cancel your first visits with them, and we could lose thousands by the end of the quarter. You must establish a relationship."

It was a transparent ploy. If Drummond persuaded her to stay in Boston, then, whatever the police discovered, he could paint her as an ineffectual president. "You see," he would say through layers of carefully veiled rhetoric, "this is what you get when you hire a young blood who can't maintain a work-life balance." He'd be quoting the reason she lost her last job. In Drummond's world there was only work.

She sighed.

"Of course, I trust you entirely," he said with overweening courtesy. "You probably saw things like this in Pittsburg all the time. But the alumni who hired you..." It was a dig. "They would be very disappointed if you didn't at least pay them a visit to say thank you."

Helen cut him off. "We are not going to have this conversation." She tapped her manicured nails on the steering wheel. "I am three hours away from campus, and I will be back by 10:00 a.m. at the latest."

At the other end of the garage, a door slammed. Startled, the birds rose and exited in a squall of black wings. Another shadow darted toward the staircase at the corner. Helen shivered. She could handle Drummond. She could handle the alumni, the endowment, even the bad PR from an incident on campus. It was the shadows that troubled her.

Chapter Three

Helen drove through the Pittock campus gates, once again noting the cryptic school motto emblazoned above the entrance. According to Josa Lebovetski, emeritus history professor, the first class of students had chosen the famous Latin phrase, *Et in Arcadia ego.* I too was there in Arcadia. However, Lebovetski had explained at great length, Jedidiah Pittock, the founder, a man of intense religious fervor, had demanded they change that motto because of its carnal implications. They ended up with this one: *Ego quoque angelos vidi et tremui.* I too have seen the angels and trembled.

Viewing the campus through a haze of summer heat, the students' first motto seemed the better choice. Most of the buildings were in disrepair, but from a distance, the whole campus looked like a postcard. The same lack of funds that hindered repairs on the old buildings had prevented new construction. The academic halls were 19th century originals, not the mishmash of architectural styles common on New England campuses. That was one of the things that had drawn Helen to Pittock. It was under-funded, but it was secluded and unspoiled. At least until now.

She parked in front of the administration building. Drummond emerged just as she entered. A familiar figure, he was about sixty with a full head of silver hair, a tie knotted close to his throat, and a tweed sport coat, buttoned despite the heat. She greeted him with a handshake and as much of a smile as she could manage. The picture of blue-blooded decorum, his face belied nothing.

"The police are investigating the scene," Drummond said. "The media has arrived. I presume you'll be joining me." He gestured toward the playing fields and, beyond that, the forest. Together they crossed the campus.

"Fill me in," Helen said. "What do you know?"

"Marcus Billing saw the body first. He's a freshman. Barely eighteen. From the Midwest. He's in the summer theater program and starting his first year this fall. Apparently, he was jogging with some of his friends and went off the path to urinate." Drummond frowned his disapproval. "He was shaken up when he returned, but did not say why until they went back to campus. Then he told his boyfriend." Another frown. "He thought he had seen something in the woods. The boyfriend told some upperclassmen. They told the head resident in the Ventmore dormitory. She told Adair Wilson."

"Ah." Helen shielded her eyes as they stepped out of the shaded quad onto the sunlit street that separated the academic buildings from the grassy hill leading to Barrow Creek and the playing fields. "Marcus told his boyfriend, who told some upperclassmen, who told the head resident, who told Wilson."

Helen caught a flicker of a smile on Drummond's face.

"You can see why security did not sound the five-siren alarm immediately," he said. "When Wilson dragged Marcus into the security office, he was so busy apologizing and trying not to be a bother that he practically recanted. He wasn't sure what he saw. It could have been a deer. He didn't look closely. His boyfriend agreed that Marcus was easily spooked. Mark Miller, the head of security, took a few men into the woods. They didn't find anything."

"And then?" Helen asked.

"Blame Wilson."

"Or thank her?"

"After security turned up nothing, she went back into the woods."

"To look for the body?"

"Yes."

"By herself?"

"Apparently."

Helen had to admire the nerve.

"It must have been after eight or nine when she called the newspaper," Drummond added.

"Is Wilson all right?"

"Oh, Wilson is fine. You can't touch Wilson."

Helen glanced at Drummond, trying to read his thoughts. His face was relaxed except for a slight twitch at the corner of his eye. He tucked his hands in the pockets of his slacks and shrugged.

They had just crossed the footpath that led over the Barrow Creek. To their right stood the Pittock House, Helen's new home and home to every Pittock president since Jedidiah Pittock. To their left lay the playing fields and past those a blue forest. Beyond the forest, Helen knew, stood the ruins of the old Pittock Asylum, a Kirkbride building, saved from the wrecking ball by its architectural significance. They met the path that led into the forest.

Helen paused. "She contacted the media. Did she call the police first?"

"No," Drummond said.

Helen waited for him to expound. When it was clear he would say no more she asked, "Why not?"

"Because it's Wilson."

"How are the media handling it?"

"They are capitalizing on the gory details. It is a mystery and reporters love a mystery. They are not trying to link it to any other incidents, though. Count your blessings."

Helen raised her hand to stop him. "What incidents? What link?"

Drummond didn't answer. She and the provost had rounded a bend in the narrow, woodland path and walked directly into a throng of television reporters, each one trying to lift his camera higher than the next, hoping for a glimpse of the crime scene. On the sidelines, newspaper reporters badgered the students who had been brave or morbid enough to follow the police through the woods. Beyond the crowd, a strip of yellow caution tape barred the path. Behind the tape and a screen of slender maples, Helen could make out figures moving slowly in the humid air. Police radios crackled in the distance.

As soon as the reporters caught sight of the two administrators, they rushed over.

"Can you tell us what the college is doing to protect the student body?"

Helen smoothed her hair and adjusted her collar. Her black suit felt funeral. She tried to soften her expression without actually smiling. "We are concerned, but not panicked. Pittock College has adopted additional security measures to protect our students, staff, and faculty. With increased security and awareness, I am certain...."

The small, detached voice in the back of Helen's mind said, *tomorrow, wear navy.*

"In the past three decades, Pittock College has experienced less than one violent crime per year. It is one of the safest colleges in America."

Helen felt like she was looking into a mirror that kept talking, in calm, melodic tones, about safety shuttles and lighting. Meanwhile, the real Helen stood frozen, staring at the yellow caution tape. It was still there: the pain the victim had felt. That much pain did not dissipate into nothing. It lingered like smoke. Helen felt it burning, hot and tight in her throat. She could smell it.

"You're new to Pittock College. How has this campus tragedy affected you, President Ivers? I understand you recently lost your sister," a young, female reporter asked, trying for the human angle.

"It is an honor to be able to serve the college at this time. I believe we will come to learn that this crime has no connection, beyond proximity to our campus. In the meantime, there is nowhere else I would rather be. We will weather this together, as a campus community."

Behind them, an ambulance grated its way over uneven ground. A young, African American police officer emerged from the woods and signaled for the crowd to back away. They were extracting the remains.

I can smell it. Helen knew that smell. She clasped her hands behind her back and pinched the skin on the back of her hand until the pain seared up her arm. *Focus.*

"In many ways, this is the safest place for students. Unlike an urban campus or a large state school, we know all of our students by face and name." It was a lie but a plausible one. "All students live in residences on campus. No one is isolated or unaccounted for. With our new security measures, this campus will be a safe haven for all who study, work, or live in its shelter."

The reporter thanked Helen and turned off her microphone.

For the first time, Helen noticed Wilson perched on a granite boulder, her head held in her hands. Her blonde hair glistened in the dappled sunlight. The muscles in her bare arms were visible like cords of rope. She sat like a broken marionette, her head limp, her spine crumpled. As Helen watched, Wilson looked up. Her eyes were swollen and red from crying. For a moment, their eyes met.

"I have to talk to Wilson," Helen said.

She felt more than heard, Drummond's grumble.

"If there is something worse than finding a body near campus, it's Adair Wilson finding a body near campus."

Helen did not like administrators who bad-mouthed faculty any more than she liked faculty who bad-mouthed students. If nothing else, both groups—with their quirks and foibles—were job security. At best, they were acolytes, tending a fire that fuelled human inquiry. Lose sight of that and there was no point in salvaging a little liberal arts college on the brink of financial ruin. However, as Helen considered Drummond's statement, she realized it was a joke.

She chuckled. "I guess it will be trial by fire. I have it coming, don't I?"

"No." Drummond shook his head. "You don't."

"Thank you," Helen said.

They stood in silence, watching the police step back and forth over the crime scene tape. When Helen looked back at the boulder where Wilson had been, the professor was gone.

Chapter Four

Helen was not able to find Wilson in her office, nor could she reach her on her private phone. She asked her secretary, Patrick, to keep trying. With everything else going on, she did not have time to search further. She barely had time to take a drink of metallic–tasting water from the drinking fountain in her building before the police arrived. They met in the conference room. Helen took her seat at the head of the table. Drummond sat to her right. Across from them sat three uniformed officers.

Drummond introduced Chief Robert Hornsby. He struck Helen as a blue collar version of Marshal Drummond. She had never seen Drummond out of his sport coat. One look at Hornsby told her she would never see him out of uniform. His crew cut looked as permanent as Mount Holyoke.

"He is a pillar of our community," Drummond added. "We are fortunate to be in his charge."

Helen took Hornsby's hand across the table and shook it firmly.

"These are his officers," Drummond continued. "Tyron Thompson and Darrell Giles,"

The junior officers looked like perfect opposites. Thompson, the African American officer Helen had seen at the crime scene, was lean and loose jointed with the improbable lightness of a grayhound. His colleague, Giles, had the body of a bulldog and the complexion of something that lived underground. Both of the younger men shifted anxiously in their chairs. Helen guessed it had only been a few years—or months—since they graduated from the police academy.

"What can you tell us, Mr. Hornsby?" Helen asked.

"I'll tell you what we know, but it's not a lot. We'll do our best to keep you up to date. The college is a big part of Pittock." Hornsby sat with his arms spread apart on the table, a man used to accommodating the bulky gun at his side.

"Of course," Helen said.

The chief drew a notebook from his breast pocket and flipped through the pages. "Yesterday, around 1100 hours, your chief of security dispatched a search party. At 1500 hours they returned and reported that the student's concerns were unjustified. Adair Wilson—thirty-five years old, faculty, employed by the college, no criminal record—pursued her own search starting at 1800 hours, resulting in the discovery of two human legs. She alerted the media at 1900 and the police at 1940."

"So she did call the police?" Helen looked to Drummond. His face was grim.

"She arranged for the media to arrive in time for the excitement." Drummond picked his words like a man picking over an unappetizing plate. "Had Chief Hornsby not worked quickly, the results could have been disastrous."

"We were further delayed," Hornsby added, "because our investigators were working with the Boston coroners during the hurricane cleanup. We secured the crime scene and placed a guard on duty until the team arrived this morning. And you."

"What do you know so far?" Helen asked.

"The coroner identified two human legs," Hornsby said. "Female. Caucasian. Probably between the ages of seventeen and twenty-five. Apparently, severed by the train. The coroner estimated time of injury around 5:00 a.m. because that's when the Berkshire–Western comes through. Emergency personnel took the limbs to the morgue in Holyoke."

Despite the air conditioner humming in the background, the room felt hot. Sweat ran down Helen's side. *Another tragedy.* Pittock was supposed to be her refuge, or at least her last resort.

"Chief Hornsby, do you think that it's one of our students?"

The police chief exhaled heavily. "She was between seventeen and twenty-five. I wouldn't rule it out."

"However, there is the asylum." Drummond directed this comment toward Helen. "The old Pittock Asylum closed several years ago. There were supposed to be halfway houses built, but with shortfalls in state funding, allocations had to be made selectively. Not every project received funding." He was such a politician. "A lot of the mentally ill simply got let loose. They did not have the resources to move, so they stayed here."

"It's what they know." Hornsby concurred. "She may have been a vagabond."

Hornsby returned to his notebook. "There was a thunder storm that night, a lot of rain. It washed away most of the trace evidence. We'll send samples to the lab, but I know we won't get much."

Helen's jaw tightened. A dull ache filled the back of her head.

"There was no sign of a struggle," Hornsby went on. "So the victim may have known her assailant. Of course, there were the straps. The legs were tied to the track with zip ties." He set down his notebook. "I'll call the local hardware stores to see if one recently sold zip ties. They're at most stores, used for staking trees, household stuff. Unless we get a hit on that or someone reports her missing, we don't have much."

"Are we certain this woman is dead?" Helen asked. She spoke slowly, understanding the implication. It had taken more than an hour for her sister, Eliza, to "exsanguinate" as the coroner had termed it. The bloody handprints on the cupboards were proof. Eliza had crawled around the kitchen after she could no longer stand. Helen tried to dispel the image of a young woman bleeding to death in the leaf litter on the forest floor or, worse yet, struggling to escape her assailant. Under the table, Helen pinched her hand.

"The girl is dead," Hornsby said. "Thank God. The train cut her legs above the straps so she would have bled out instantly."

Thompson cleared his throat. "The ties aren't the strangest part. The real question is: where's the rest of the body?"

Hornsby shot him a look that said he was meant to be seen and not heard, "We're going to search this afternoon. Naturally, the body will tell us a lot."

"I think we should call Great Barrington," Thompson added. "They will loan us their K-9 officer."

"K-9 officer," Hornsby snorted. "You might as well send my beagle."

"Dogs have been instrumental in solving thousands of cases. We worked with them in the Academy. Dogs can find a body in minutes whereas a human search team takes hours, and that's *if* they find the victim at all."

"With fifteen mile per hour winds and six inches of rain, I don't think so," Hornsby said.

"A dog can find a scent in water, but you're right." Thompson held up his hands for attention. "Every hour that goes by, it gets harder. Let's get out there now before we lose any more time."

"That whole forest was soaked," Hornsby said. Despite his pressed uniform and upright posture, he looked exhausted. "This whole thing makes me sick." He ran a hand over his crew cut. "Some sick bastard did that to a woman. If I thought it'd help, I'd get out there with a magnifying glass and a herd of Chihuahuas, but that's not going to change facts. That forest was drenched, and everything we want to know washed away in the storm."

Thompson opened his mouth to speak.

"I think the chief has this under control," Drummond said in a conversational tone. He dismissed Thompson, summarily, like a child. Helen made a mental note to talk to Thompson in private when she could. In the meantime, she cut the debate short.

"How can Pittock College help?" Helen folded her hands on the table and met each officer's eyes in turn. "We are ready to put all our resources at your disposal." She looked at Drummond to see if he would protest. He nodded.

"Keep your people out of my way. Let us do our job." Hornsby hooked his thumbs in his gun belt, puffing up for a moment. Then his hands dropped to his sides and he slumped in his chair. "I don't know. We've got a small department. We're borrowing men from around the area."

"Who does this?" Helen asked, not really questioning Hornsby. "What kind of a person butchers a woman like this?"

Chapter Five

He had been seven years old, almost eight, when he first experienced the need. In retrospect, it had been the end of his childhood. For years to come, his nannies would defend him to Father. "He's just a kid," they would plead as Father uncoiled his belt. But he knew what Father did not guess: his childhood ended the day he found the book on forensic medicine.

He was waiting for Father under a table in the asylum library. He had pulled the book from the shelf and was examining the pictures. It was an old book with a heavy binding. If not for the gruesome content, it would have made an attractive book for Father's parlor, one of the many rooms Father forbade him from entering.

He leafed through the gunshot wounds, the stabbings, and the process of decomposition. The last chapter was entitled, "The Forensics of War." It was short and consisted mostly of text. He was about to close the book when he caught sight of a black and white photograph of a woman seated on a pedestal. She was dark-skinned with gray hair, and, to his seven-year old eyes, very old. What caught his eye was the place where her legs should have been. Instead of limbs, her shorts exposed a mass of hardened scars like the gnarled roots of a tree. Below the picture, the caption read, "Polina Petrova: Landmine victim exhibits unusual scarring."

He stared. His groin hurt. His whole body trembled. He was afraid he had been struck by one of the strange diseases pictured in Father's books. Then he closed his eyes. He could see Polina Petrova. And he knew what to do. The orgasm frightened him but not enough to eclipse the pleasure that washed over him.

For six years, the image of Polina Petrova tormented him. Six itching years, when he knew only the need and not the solution. Then, when he was thirteen, he found Carla Braff. Carla was admitted to the asylum with paranoid delusions. Father said her diagnosis was "burdening her family." Her speech was slurred by a congenital defect that twisted her head to one side, and she was retarded. She had also suffered meningitis as a child, and the resulting septicemia had destroyed her lower legs. Both had been surgically removed at the knee.

He learned this later, when he stole her file. When he met her the first time, all he saw were the empty footrests on her wheelchair. Without knowing she was coming, he had waited his whole life for her arrival.

For a week, he lingered in the hallway outside Carla's room, watching the staff deliver medications, memorizing the rhythms of the hospital wing. Then, when he was sure all the nurses were occupied elsewhere, he stepped into her room and closed the privacy screen over the observation window.

Carla lay on a narrow bed. He lifted her blanket. Beneath it, she wore baggy pants. He cursed. The pant legs had been stitched closed. He squeezed the stumps. He had to see. He could feel the pulse pounding in his legs. Carla babbled and whimpered. He hooked his fingers under the waistband of her pants and pulled.

She was wearing diapers. He didn't care. The pleasure was so intense, nothing would ever be the same. He had stepped through the portal. He had been born.

But it could not last. One day, he walked past Carla's room and she screamed, "Go away! Go. Go. Go."

In the hallway outside her door, two doctors conferred over her charts.

"Something must have triggered a memory of past events," one of the men said, glancing at his clipboard. "There is nothing in Carla's current regime that would cause this kind of response."

He knew, however. The assaults had begun to register on Carla's softened mind. At first, she only struggled under his weight. Then she began to scream as he entered her room. She was easily silenced with a hospital-issued towel. When she started to scream at the sight of him—in the garden, and in passing—he grew worried. For a month, the fear of discovery warred with the fear of losing her. Then the doctors glanced at him. Inadvertently. Unconsciously. Wondering.

He remembered something Father had told him. Before the Kirkbride asylums had been built, there was a time when weekend tourists paid a nickel for the pleasure of watching, taunting, even beating the insane. "We have grown squeamish," Father had said once, "It is a natural inclination to seek out the aberrant, examine it and destroy it."

Then he realized he would have to kill her.

The night of Carla Braff's death, the asylum was particularly quiet. A visiting theater troupe had agreed to perform for the patients. Most were in the theater, laughing at the performers as they cavorted around the stage. He took a risk. He sat down next to Carla.

Immediately, her screams pierced the air, threatening to send the entire horde into fits. One of the nurses took her back to her room. A half hour later, he slipped out.

He had chosen his method carefully: an insulin injection into the vein in her inner elbow. He had read about the procedure in the library's medical books. Insulin coma. It was believed that the coma could clear the mind of delusions. With too much, the patient slipped over the edge. Madness. Coma. Death.

He brought five syringes in a cigar box. The first needle hit bone, but enough of the insulin entered her blood to slow her movements. Her muffled screaming subsided. He took out the next needle. It was easy to find the vein this time. He waited for the decerebrate rigidity that signaled a dangerous imbalance in insulin and blood sugar levels. Then he injected the last three syringes, remembering what Father had told him.

Father relayed his anecdote again, a few days later. One of the hospital orderlies caught him in the hall and told him that Father wanted a conference in the study. He ran, slowing only to catch his breath before walking into the office.

"Bourbon?" Father held up a decanter.

This was not what he had expected but better than he could have hoped for. He often drank out of the decanter when Father was not around. Still he shook his head. As soon as he declined, he could tell he'd made the wrong choice.

"Suit yourself," Father said, then told the story of the tourists and their nickels. "We've become so sentimental," he concluded. "Have you been following the Braff case?"

Father was the hospital administrator, and he knew almost everything that took place within its walls.

He felt his blood chill. "No," he lied.

"She died, just drifted away in her sleep." Father raised the bourbon to the window and examined the golden liquor. "It's the best result really. There was nothing we could do for her except save her family the burden, and her father was out of money even for that. What a waste. A good horse has more wit and commonsense than that girl." He chuckled. "For that matter, Peter's mule has more sense."

It was no secret that Father hated the gardener's mule, a stubborn, useless animal with a threadbare coat and one leg shorter than the rest.

Father took a sip of the bourbon and stared out the window. "Some lives are worth less than others. I know you've heard the nurses talking. Everyone is a gift from God. Everyone brings a light into the world. I would like to see their Christian charity when their sons get meningitis, and they have to care for them at home for no pay. The Carlas of this world are their living. God provides for the lilies of the field, and he provided Carla Braff so those nice Catholic girls could feed their broods. Don't you ever make that mistake." A faint smile flickered across Father's face. "Don't you forget. Carla Braff's death was a blessing."

He relaxed a little. "Maybe I will have a bourbon."

"Maybe you will," Father said. "We are defined by our appetites." Father leaned over the chair in which he sat, gripping the armrests, trapping him. "I don't object to what happened, not morally. Carla Braff was a wasted life."

He could feel Father's hot breath on his face. He smelled the bourbon.

"But I will not have my son be less than a mule."

That night as he lay in bed reading, Father flung open his bedroom door and ripped the blanket off his bed.

"It smells like the stables in here," Father said. "Like a mule."

Father grabbed him by the arm, pulled him out of bed, and marched him down to the basement. There, Father threw him in the chair. It had seemed like a huge throne when he was a child; now it fit him like a regular chair. Whistling an empty, repetitive tune, Father walked to the chest and took out the belts. One to beat. One to wrap around his arms and torso so he could not ward off the blows. The leather bit into his arms. He couldn't breathe.

"Stop," he choked.

Father would never stop. Instead, he rotated his class ring so the stone faced inward. Holding his palm up to show the stone, Father said, "There is no place for mules."

For a moment, he didn't even register the pain of Father's blow. Then Father hit him such force that the chair crashed over.

Upstairs, the doorbell rang. It would be the Lanatierres and the Vettals coming over for gin martinis. Mother would be serving in a gray silk dress with a peach-colored scarf, the silver tray balanced perfectly on her palm.

Father squatted down beside him where he lay

with his face pressed to the dirt of the unfinished floor.

"I know you won't scream. Scream and they'll throw you in prison. Or maybe they'll put you in foster care. Would you like that? To live with one of the nurses and her eighteen mewling brats? You could wash their diapers in a tub out back and get scabies like the rest of them. Do you understand what I'm saying? I am protecting you to protect this family."

He couldn't tell if it was blood or pain that made everything go red. All he knew was that time slowed, and he felt an odd clarity. He saw the picture from the forensic book: Polina Petrova's. He understood now. She could never hurt him. She could never run from him. She could never tiptoe around the cocktail guests in little silver heels while Father beat him.

A moment later, he lost consciousness. When he woke up, he could not say how long he had been out. The pain was confounding. One minute it was excruciating. He had to bite his lip not to scream. Then it became so total, his body could not make sense of it. It was like looking at the sun. Upstairs, Mother laughed. His hearing seemed more acute. Father said, "Let me show you "The Whistler." It's a small painting of which we're very proud. How about a little tour?" The guests would see the whole house—or so they thought. Mother and Father were wonderful hosts. They would even take the guests to the attic where they could see the town of Pittock like a model railway set. "Forgive the dust. You just have to see the view." No one would notice the door behind the ornamental wine barrel in the kitchen. No one could imagine the basement. A family like this had been noble since Jedidiah Pittock first set foot in Berkshire county.

Chapter Six

"I'd like security to run extra campus shuttles, especially after dark," Helen said, once the chief had left. "Let's get facilities to check all the lights and emergency phones on campus. We'll ask what they're missing. If there are security measures they've wanted that we couldn't afford—locks, bars, phones, cameras—now is the time. I'll find the money."

Drummond nodded. Helen closed the notebook she had set on the conference table. There were no answers to write down.

"Have you worked with Hornsby before?"

"Hornsby is a good man. His father was chief before him," Drummond said. "I've known him for years."

Those were two things people confused in small towns, Helen thought. Quality and longevity: they weren't synonymous.

"That's something," she hedged.

Drummond paused. "His wife is dying." He spoke quickly, as though even this small revelation bothered his sense of New England decorum or his desire to keep Helen at arm's length. "It's uterine cancer. The doctors want him to call hospice."

Drummond was also a widower. His wife had died a year or two earlier. Of what, she didn't know.

"I'm sure that's hard," she said. "My sister passed away recently. It takes a toll." She rose from the table and walked over to the window. "Eliza."

The name hung in the ether between sound and thought, reverberating like a tuning fork. *Eliza.* Helen did not want to talk about her, and yet, on some level, she wanted nothing more. She wanted to tell Drummond the whole story. To grab him by the lapels of his ubiquitous sport coat and say, "You see? My being here has nothing to do with you." Beyond that, she simply longed to be back at the Pittock House or, better yet, in an anonymous hotel room, a room designed, like Teflon, to shed all traces of its occupants. A space devoid of memories.

Through the window she could see three students, two girls and a boy, tossing a football back and forth in the slanting, yellow light. The boy was very handsome, with an angular, arrogant face. Each time, he threw the ball harder. One of the girls complained with a musical squeal.

"My son. Ricky," Drummond said, following Helen's eyes. "I have always cared about Pittock College, but now that he is here, it means even more."

Helen watched the students dart in and out of the sunlight. The days were getting shorter. Soon the rest of the students would arrive for fall term with their Pittock sweatshirts, their suitcases, and their dreams.

"You have done a lot for Pittock."

Two months at Pittock and a drive past the provost's Georgian mansion, had given her insight into his worldview. He was a man to whom birth had given everything, who simultaneously believed in a meritocracy as well as a natural progression of founding fathers. For twenty years, he had served Pittock College, waiting for the proceeding patriarchs to die or retire. Then, as he prepared to take his rightful place, the college board caved under pressure from alumni and hired Helen, a forty-five-year-old upstart. During Helen's eight year stint at Vandusen, the school rose from bankruptcy into the top fifty private liberal arts colleges. The alumni who wanted her knew this, and knew that she came cheap. In Drummond's mind, she had jumped the line. She had taken what was rightfully his.

Drummond stood and joined Helen at the window.

"I have loved this school since I was his age, *since I was a boy*." He spoke without looking at her.

He had been acting president for two years before Helen's hire.

"You kept this school together." She resisted the urge to add *barely*.

She did not mention the shrinking endowment and diminished enrollment. Drummond had been doing the job of provost, president, and countless other duties that, at another school, would be delegated to separate individuals if not whole departments. Under those circumstances he was bound to fail at some things. He had stewarded, and tended, and taken on until every one of the college's problems could be traced back to him, although he was the root cause of none. She did not have to like him to see that it was unfair.

"I trust what you say about Hornsby," she said. "But if I have reason to believe he doesn't pursue this with due diligence, I will call in other authorities. I will not rest until this is resolved."

Walking into the Pittock House that evening, Helen wondered how past presidents had stomached living there even without the taint of a murder investigation. The house was a saltbox built in 1890. In the intervening years, it had become a dumping ground for antique furnishings. An enormous painting of Jedidiah Pittock dominated the parlor. Beneath him sat three horsehair sofas and several armchairs. In the far corner, someone had parked a wicker pram complete with an antique baby doll.

Helen had decided to wait a polite six months before shipping it all to cold storage. Then she would buy the ecru, microfiber sectional from the Pottery Barn catalogue. She would buy the White Lilies giclée and bowls of the ersatz white seashells the catalogue was touting at a ridiculous $189.99 for three. It would look just like a hotel. Hell, she thought as she dropped her keys on the hallway table. She would be satisfied with a card table from IKEA if it meant she could dump the pram with its cadaverous baby doll.

She walked into the kitchen, poured herself a shot of vodka, and dropped into a chair. She downed the shot in two sips, then picked up her phone to find out if, by some miracle, her friend Terri had not learned of her situation.

"Of course I have," he replied. "Disembodied legs discovered on an isolated college campus. That is prime real estate. Too bad they didn't find some politicians philandering at the scene."

Terri was a shrewd, old-timer who claimed to loathe all young professionals except Helen. They had met at Vandusen, when Helen was a dean and Terri was lead counsel for the college. One day, the old lawyer had sidled up to her after a particularly contentious faculty union meeting.

"The rest of us are stuck, aren't we?" he had said.

Helen had shrugged. "You mean the negotiation? We'll work it out."

"No," Terri had said. "I mean us. The rest of us are who we are, but you are whoever you need to be."

The remark had hit close to home. Helen had just received a call from her father. He had visited Eliza at the University of Nebraska, where she was supposedly getting a Masters in psychology. When he arrived in Lincoln, he found Eliza's apartment knee-deep in garbage and Eliza ranting about her thesis advisor stealing her thoughts while she was sleeping.

"I'll come home," Helen had told her father. Then she had turned off her phone, smoothed her hair, and presided over the union negotiation with the poise of an orator.

"I like you," Terri had said. "You suffer gracefully."

Not gracefully enough it turned out. Helen could still hear the Vandusen board president. "We admire your commitment to your sister. Family. But in your absence, we realize the position of vice provost is, to a great degree, redundant."

"I'm not absent," Helen had pleaded. "Give me a month."

In one month, she could stabilize Eliza's medications. She would put her in a home this time. She would do whatever it took. The board president had just smiled.

Now Helen was at Pittock and Terri—her best and only friend—was a voice on the other end of the phone.

"I'm glad you called." He grew serious. "How are

you holding up?"

"I think we have the media under control, at least for now. Thank God for the hurricane. The police conducted a search this afternoon. They covered the campus, the area around the asylum. That's just a mile from here. They're going to go back out tomorrow to do a wider sweep. There's no evidence to say it's one of our students except that she's young."

"She?"

"It was a girl. Seventeen to twenty–some."

"That's sad," Terri said.

"It is sad." Helen paused for a few beats. "The city police force is slim. Drummond says the chief is a good guy because his father was. Hornsby doesn't trust his rookies. It's all very small town."

Terri interrupted. "What about you, Helen? How are *you?*"

"I'm worried about this professor." She outlined Wilson's role in the past 48 hours, including her search for the legs.

"That's brave, I guess. It's ballsy."

"I know. Marshal doesn't like her, and I can't find her."

"She's probably with a friend."

"Why wouldn't she answer her phone?"

"There are a lot of reasons why someone might want to check out after seeing something like that. She might be with friends or her family. Maybe she went out of town."

The tenderness in Terri's voice grated on her.

"She has responsibilities here."

There was a long silence on Terri's end. "You have to talk to someone about Eliza," he said finally.

"I'm not going to go to some Birkenstock–

wearing therapist so she can tell me to breathe deeply and get in touch with my anger."

Usually Terri would have laughed. This time, he was serious. "You won't talk to me. You won't talk to a therapist. How about a friend who lives in your zip code? I don't know what young career women do for fun, but I know *you* don't do any of it. How about you reach out to somebody?"

"You want me to join a bowling league? A book club?" Helen poured another shot of vodka and knocked it back in one gulp. The comment about her zip code hurt. "This campus is in financial ruin and, as of two days ago, that's the absolute least of its problems. This is a murder investigation, and I've got to handle it."

"Listen," Terri said. "This is a murder investigation, but it's not your investigation. Your job is to spin the PR, keep the students out of trouble, and raise a hell of a lot of money. And to live Helen. To live."

"Goodnight, Mr. Self Help."

Helen hit END and stared at the vodka.

Upstairs in her bedroom, she peered into a distorted antique mirror, pulling her cheeks back with her palms. She was attractive. Helen understood that like she understood her 401K. Anyone who had worked in politics—and college administration was politics no matter what people said—knew the value of a handsome face. Still, the last year had left permanent circles beneath her eyes, and her face looked puffy, the product of too many fast food meals eaten at the onset of a migraine. Helen rubbed at a smear of makeup on her cheek.

"Good enough?" she spoke to the silent house. The only answer was the creaking of the roof.

She shook three sleeping pills and swallowed them dry. Then she broached the mirror again. With the pills and the alcohol softening her vision, she looked downright pretty. She allowed herself to wonder if there might be someone in Pittock—a stranger at that moment—who would someday come to love her face.

Chapter Seven

In Helen's dream, she was on a date at a restaurant, but when she looked over her date's shoulder she saw Eliza's face pressed against the galley doors of the kitchen. "Help me, Helen," Eliza screamed. She was going to do it again. Helen ran and wrenched open the galley doors. She was met by a wall of garbage: magazines, junk mail, TV dinner cartons. From somewhere deep inside, Eliza called out. "I don't want to take the medication. It's killing me." Helen began clawing at the wall of trash. The more she pulled down, the more there was. Near her face, a threadbare stuffed toy of indistinguishable species stared with human eyes.

Helen's own eyes flew open. She lay in the four poster bed, in the Jedidiah Pittock House. A down comforter protected her from the blast of a window-mounted air conditioner. She sank back into the pillows. Then her phone buzzed again. It was the phone that had woken her. She fumbled for it, knocking a bottle of pills off the bedside table and sending them scattering under the bed.

"Helen Ivers," she answered, hoping the poor connection hid the roughness in her voice.

"It's Patrick," her secretary said.

Helen glanced at the window. The sunlight shining through the curtains barely illuminated the room. It couldn't be later than 6:00 a.m.

"What is it?"

"Well..." Patrick did not seem inclined to expand on the thought.

"Well what?"

"What are you doing right now?"

Sleeping. She wanted to pull the covers over her head and disappear. But Eliza would be waiting on the other side of her dreams. *Help me, Helen!*

"Can you come to the office right now? It's important, and once I talk to you, you'll want to be here anyway."

Helen hung up and got out of bed. The room smelled musty. There was dust on the headboard, scrapes in the hardwood floor, a black line, like an incision, where two panels of filigreed wallpaper failed to meet properly. "Pleasantly rustic," was how the board had described it to Helen in an email.

"Fucking House of Usher," Helen grumbled as she made her way to the bathroom to splash water on her face.

A few minutes later, Helen was dressed in a navy suit and pink ascot—serious but not funereal. A group of reporters met her on the steps of her office building. She paused, turning away from the sun, so she would not squint into the camera. She wanted her expression to convey confidence.

"We continue to come together in the face of this tragedy. Thank you. My office will send out regular reports as we learn more."

"But what about the search, ma'am?" one man called out. "Can you tell us about Adair Wilson?

Bloggers are saying you're using students."

"I have great confidence in the Pittock Police Department."

The reporters followed her up the stairs, nudging her with their microphones like eager dogs. They had to be the locals, up early before the *Boston Herald* arrived. What big city reporter referred to their subject as ma'am? Helen let the door close on the reporters' questions. Inside, Patrick stood behind his desk, looking worried. His computer screen was black, the overhead light dark. He had the air of a man poised for action but uncertain of what to do.

"Okay. Why are we here?" Helen did not mean to sound curt, but she was tired, and she could still hear Eliza's voice in the back of her mind.

Patrick raised an eyebrow. "You better appreciate this," he said.

"I'm appreciating. What is it?"

"Adair is my friend. We've been friends since senior year of high school. I would never have made it through English lit if it wasn't for her."

"I'm happy for you both."

"Hell, I would never have made it through college if it wasn't for her."

Helen waited.

Patrick wore a purple polo shirt. He twisted a matching purple lanyard around his hand. "Addie likes to be helpful. But past administrators haven't always appreciated her help."

"I'm getting déjà vu. What did Dr. Wilson do?"

"The Pittock police department is understaffed. They need more than three officers. I guess the Chief felt like they covered a lot of ground yesterday. He said they covered every square foot. He said he'd send a few more men today, but basically they've got no leads." Patrick pursed his lips. "Addie doesn't think it's enough."

Helen knew what was coming next.

"You can't do a search with only one person," Patrick said.

"Who went with her?"

"Where do you get twenty people with nothing to do at 5:00 a.m.?"

Students. Helen didn't have to ask.

"They're at the scene now." Patrick cleared his throat. "They're going to search the forest around the asylum."

"Did you call the police?"

"No."

"Mr. Drummond?"

Patrick shook his head.

"Well call them! Call them right now and tell them to meet me out there." Helen headed for the door. "Why didn't you call all of us immediately?"

Patrick shrugged.

Helen waited a beat. "Why?"

"I called you. I figured Addie had it under control."

"She's a theater professor. She teaches kids to enunciate their vowels and, I don't know... find their inner Hamlet. What about that says 'I can lead a murder investigation'?"

"Hmm." Patrick turned back to his desk. "Don't shoot the messenger. There's more to Adair Wilson than you'd think."

Chapter Eight

Helen had to hand it to Wilson; her search seemed as well organized as anything the police had mounted. She'd gathered her students on the path near the railroad tracks and was pairing them off when Helen arrived. Everyone, including Wilson, wore blue latex gloves. One student in each pair carried a fistful of orange marking flags. Some students had already planted flags in the ground near the path. A few more stood in the woods.

Wilson projected her voice like a drill sergeant. "I want a line from there to there." Wilson pointed.

The students giggled as they jostled into line.

"This is not a joke." Wilson pulled a whistle out of her pocket. The students fell silent. "Imagine you have a box around you, twenty feet on each side. This is how far you can be from your neighbor. Do not go in or near the asylum."

Turning to survey her crew, Wilson caught sight of Helen. Their eyes met for a second, then Wilson turned away.

"It is *not* safe to go in or near the asylum," Wilson repeated. "What did I just say?"

The students answered loudly in unison.

On the wooded path swarmed the reporters who'd earlier talked to Helen. Someone tried to maneuver a van past the search party. Boom mics bobbed among the trees like flora. Cameras flashed. Pittock's PR problems had gone from bad to worse.

Footsteps signaled the arrival of Hornsby and Drummond. They had clearly come at a run. Hornsby doubled over, panting. Drummond touched his forehead with a pristine handkerchief. He had not taken off his blazer.

"Helen, why haven't you stopped her?" Drummond asked by way of greeting. "They'll destroy the evidence."

Helen ignored him for a moment. "Why wasn't this scene taped off?" she asked Hornsby.

"We searched the area," Hornsby gasped. "We took evidence. It's done. That's how crime scenes work."

"How confident are you in yesterday's search?" Helen looked around. The students were setting off in a line. Every few yards, they planted an orange flag.

Drummond answered for Hornsby. "That search was conducted with absolute precision. If there had been a shoelace, they would have found it."

Hornsby added, "You can always search more. We did a five mile radius. We could do twenty, or forty, or a hundred. We could drive to Pennsylvania and search there. New Jersey. New York. Everyone knows, you've got 48 hours to find an abductee and you've got five miles to find a body. After that, you might as well throw darts at a map."

"Hornsby has been the Chief of Police for twenty–two years." Drummond beckoned to Helen. "Walk with me."

They took a few steps. On the side of the path, one of the students had placed a flag next to a silver gum wrapper.

"This isn't Pittsburg where people come and

go. His *father* was chief of police. Hornsby knows his business."

Helen kept walking. She did not particularly care that she'd offended their hometown pride. If she called off the search in front of the cameras, she'd be sending a clear message: the woods were not safe. In an instant, she'd populate those woods with every serial killer imaginable. If there was someone in the forest, however, she was sending students out with only a renegade professor to protect them.

"Those students are not going to find anything if Hornsby couldn't," Drummond said.

"You said they were destroying evidence."

"They are meddling where they shouldn't be. The sooner we get them out of here, the sooner the press loses interest. They. Will. Leave. Now." Each word was a sentence.

Helen took a few steps off the path into the trees. She could see the concrete abutments that carried the Berkshire-Western over a bend in the Barrow Creek. The bridge. The crime scene. Ivy tangled the ground. She shook her feet loose and kept walking. Several steps in, she stopped at another orange flag. Beside it lay a shred of fabric so dirty it was almost the color of earth.

"What's this?" she asked.

"Helen, it's trash," Drummond said.

"Mr. Hornsby," Helen yelled. She motioned for the chief to join them. When he arrived at her side she repeated the question.

"Trash," Hornsby said.

Drummond's mouth pulled into an irritated frown.

"Why isn't it evidence?" Helen asked.

"Just because some kid stuck a flag on it,"

Drummond said. "doesn't make it evidence. They don't know what they're looking for. These woods are full of the homeless. If we picked up all their trash, we'd be out here for weeks."

"Someone died out here." Helen's voice was cold.

She caught a glimpse of Wilson ducking behind a birch tree, listening. The reporters were watching too. Salivating. She couldn't worry about them now.

"I want every piece of *anything* that's not a stick or a leaf put in a plastic bag and headed to a crime lab."

"Look, lady. I don't know what you saw on CSI, but that's not real police work. We're not going to fingerprint every stick in the forest. We don't have the manpower. We don't even have the supplies."

Helen was close enough to see the shadows under Hornsby's eyes, the broken veins on his nose. He looked as tired as she felt. That had never stopped her from doing her job. Or had it? What had she neglected at Vandusen? What had she missed that was so important they eliminated her position? Redundant. It would not happen again. It could not.

"Every grocery store in America has plastic baggies," she said.

"We don't have the facilities in inventory," Hornsby interrupted. "We are doing the best we can. We will get to the bottom of this faster if you let us do our jobs and get these kids out of here."

"The chief is right," Drummond said.

Helen ignored him. She pulled her cell phone out of her pocket. "Patrick? I need a crime scene team. Get online, find out who does that, and get them out here."

"I think the police do that," Patrick said.

"They're not."

"Well if they're not, who would you call?"

Helen turned away from Hornsby and Drummond and cupped her hand around her phone. "Google it, Patrick."

He would find something. When Eliza died, she had searched for "human blood clean-up." There were more than a dozen companies that provided that service in Pittsburg. "We beat competitors prices," one advertisement read.

"This is America, Patrick. You can buy anything," she said. "Tell them cost is not an issue. I want them out here now."

Helen felt Drummond's hand on her shoulder. The touch surprised her. She thought he only shook hands.

"You don't have to do this, Helen. Hornsby will help."

Hornsby was walking back to the path. His head hung down like a chastened boy. His shoulders stooped. Helen wondered what Drummond had said to him. She had the impression she'd just won a battle. Only time would tell if she'd won the war.

"I'm going out there," Helen said. "I presume I'm going with police escorts."

Chapter Nine

"I would not send students to do anything I did not feel confident doing myself," Helen told the reporters, stopping to allow them a shot of her calm, untroubled face. She recited something about cooperation between college and town, the two Pittocks. Then she dismissed the reporters and caught up with the line of students.

Through the trees, the asylum came into sight. Bars covered the windows. Metal lattices screened sagging porches. Turrets rose from every corner of the building, and a central observation tower loomed over an interior courtyard. Sloppy graffiti marked the walls, as if the perpetrators were hurried.

In the clearing around the asylum, Wilson waited. Helen had the impression that Wilson was one of those beautiful women who tried to make herself unattractive, perhaps out of some misguided feminist sentiment, so her male colleagues would take her seriously. Her hair was cropped in a militant do. Her clothes bore an overabundance of pockets. In her ears she wore huge, cubic zirconium studs. Such earrings had been popular with the young men in Pittsburg. "Ice," they called them. Ridiculous. However, the young professor had been pretty on television. She was gorgeous in person. Beneath her tank top, she had a dancer's body, graceful from a distance but muscular as rebar up close.

"Thank you," Wilson called. "That was well done."

Wilson's stance told her she would not tolerate a brush-off. Instead, Helen stopped at the edge of the clearing where she hoped no one would notice. She beckoned for the young professor to join her, then slipped behind a massive oak. A moment later, Wilson appraised her with such intensity that Helen looked away.

"You had no right to take this on without consulting me," Helen said.

Wilson crossed her arms.

On the other side of the clearing, the students had broken into groups and were filing around the asylum buildings. The sun caught in their hair like halos. Helen gestured toward them.

"We have a duty of care to all of them. They shouldn't have to see what they might find." Helen knew. She had seen. "They're young, and they have a right to be happy."

I had a right to be happy.

"They are happy," Wilson said, "because they're alive. But they're afraid, and nothing is ever going to be this real again."

"That's horrible."

"Don't worry. They won't find her. Not out here in the open. But they have to do something, don't they? They have to feel like they tried."

"No. They don't. They have to follow college procedure. *You* have to follow college procedure."

Wilson stepped so close that Helen could see the sheen of perspiration on her neck and smell her cologne.

"There *is* no procedure for this." Wilson's voice

was choked.

A shingle broke free from a nearby roof and clattered down the slope, landing in the underbrush. Helen jumped.

Wilson nodded toward the asylum. "No one knows what goes on in there. People say there's still a whole network of passageways underneath the asylum. You can get anywhere you want if you know the way, even onto Pittock campus, *into our buildings*. But we don't know the way. Certainly the police don't. We don't know who has a map or remembers the ways, or who's figured them out. It's like a black hole. You go in there and never come out."

Helen felt rough bark against her back and Wilson's breath on her face.

"Dr. Wilson." Helen put up her hand to push Wilson away but stopped short of touching her skin. "I need you..."

She was about to tell Wilson to move. That she shouldn't need a policy manual to know that leading students into the woods to look for half a human body was not procedural. She was about to appeal to common sense. But on the other end of the search line a ghostly cry had gone up.

It took Helen a moment to realize it was a human voice. One of the students had started singing. Another voice joined the first. Then students from both ends of the line picked up the song, their voices echoing off the brick walls.

"If this comes off looking like some sort of field trip..." The song was so sad that she couldn't finish the sentence.

"They're looking for their classmate," Wilson said softly.

"You can't say that. We don't know that."

On the other side of the clearing, the reporters tromped through the brush with the students.

"I know it, and I need to talk to you about a student named Carrie Brown and a woman named Anat Al-Fulani. We don't have a lot of time, and you can't talk to Drummond. Not Drummond, not the police." Wilson held her with her stare. When Helen looked away, Wilson put her hand on the tree trunk behind Helen's head, blocking her in. "Helen, I'm going to say this quickly. You have to listen, and you need to believe me."

"If you have information, you must go to the police."

This time Helen did push Wilson away, but it was Helen who staggered as she broke free. The heat had grown oppressive. The humidity hung close to the ground. Helen's head pounded.

"Are you okay?"

Before Helen realized what was happening, Wilson's arm encircled her waist. For a moment, Helen sagged against her, feeling Wilson's body as warm and solid as the sunlit boulders that marked the forest floor. Unshakeable. A landmark. A place to rest. Then she pulled away. It was too close, too intimate.

"Sit down," Wilson said. "You're not all right. I'll call someone."

"I'm fine."

"Then we need to talk."

The young female reporter who had asked Helen if she regretted coming to Pittock stood nearby.

"No," Helen hissed. "They're listening. Watching us."

She hurried away from Wilson until she broke

the twenty-foot rule and found herself alone at the far end of the asylum. Cautiously, feeling like a trespasser, she walked up to one of the windows. Through the dirty glass, she spied a large counter, like the front desk at a hotel. Hallways extended in either direction.

A chill traveled down her spine as Helen remembered her first walking tour of campus that winter, the brief foray through the snowy woods up to Hospital Hill. "A possible site for renovation and dormitory expansion," Drummond had called it, "A remarkable tribute to the history of mental health care and American architectural innovation." To Helen, it looked like a prison.

Staring into the building, Helen noticed a stain spreading across the floor. Blood! Helen's breath came in a shallow gasp. The students were still singing. She heard their voices reverberating in the bowl of her skull. She reeled backward, caught by the fear that someone might appear in the window and try to pull her inside. Then she felt a wave of lightheadedness. The air was hot. The blood rushed to her head. For a second everything went orange.

Heart pounding, she leaned against the warm, brick wall. Slowly, she turned back to the window, cupping her hands around her eyes. Inside the building, water stains bubbled the plaster ceiling. Copper-green streaks dripped from the windowsill. Every metal fixture, right down to the nails beneath the plaster, had rusted. All that had once been white was discolored. The marks on the floor were just pools of rust, nothing more. Then a movement. Out of the corner of her eye. Something detached itself from the wall. Someone disappeared into the corridor.

Chapter Ten

He made his first amputee the year the asylum closed. He had gotten the idea—the passion—several years earlier while still in college. He made friends with a boy whose family was in the international hotel business and other "businesses" that catered to the tastes of American tourists. He began traveling, using the money Father gave him, to visit countries where girls like Polina Petrova were plentiful. The girls were poor and thin as reeds. None of their amputations compared to Carla's stumps. Most could not afford wheelchairs. Instead, their pimps and madams dressed them in long gowns that draped far below their limbs. They were cheap. He could not complain about that, but ultimately they were boring. Too pathetic, too pliable. The rush he felt when he mounted them grew less and less potent. The travel and the hassle of concealing his habits grew burdensome. The amputee prostitutes did not satisfy his need.

Then one day he was drinking beer at a café in a small village outside Battambang, Cambodia. He watched a girl walk by with a basket of palm leaves balanced on her head when, out of nowhere, a moped raced by, scattering chickens and children. The girl leapt out of the way but tripped and tumbled on the dusty ground. Her leaves scattered. She was in the process of collecting them when another, much larger motorcycle, roared into sight, clearly pursuing the first.

It was gone by the time anyone realized what had happened. The girl was screaming. Her right leg lay crushed in a widening pool of blood. A few of the café patrons looked away. Three women from a nearby hut came out and knelt over the girl to wrap a length of fabric around her thigh. One of the woman dabbed at the girl's forehead with a scarf. The other two lifted her onto a mat. By the time they disappeared back into the hut, the girl had gone into shock and stopped screaming. The pedestrians on the road had moved on, and the men at the café had resumed their conversation.

He could not go back to his warm beer. He felt the same merciless desire from the first time he saw the picture of Polina Petrova. He knew now what he needed. He did not need to find amputees; he had to make them. He was a god cutting angels out of clay.

So on his return, he went hunting. Carefully. Father had taught him an important lesson. People like Carla were disposable. No one missed them because no one wanted them. But there were still procedures he must follow, techniques, precautions. Even in the asylum, where the doctors had bound their patients, drugged them into rigor mortis-like rigidity, and electrocuted them until their eyes screamed, there were still precautions.

He made his selection judiciously. One evening, when he was out walking, a homeless woman—probably a former asylum patient—lurched out of an alleyway in downtown Pittock.

"Can you spare some change?" she asked, exposing blackened teeth. "A dollar? Can I have a dollar?" She looked like something from a Nazi concentration camp but without the victims' empty humility. "You can give me a dollar. I know you have it."

"I could give you more than that," he said.

"What do you want?" She pressed her bony chest forward. "Do you like me?"

She was clearly on or coming off drugs. Her teeth chattered, and she scratched at the sores on her arms. She was like Carla Braff. In fact, she was less than Carla. At least Carla had belonged to a family that felt some grudging responsibility. This woman had no one, and even if she did, they would have given up on her long ago.

"I do," he said. "How much?"

"Forty dollars."

He nodded. "But I don't want anyone to see us, and I'm not paying for a hotel."

"I know," she said. "We can go to the asylum. I have my own room."

"That's just what I was thinking."

The woman led him through dark halls until they arrived at a tiny room set apart from the hallway by a narrow corridor. He tried to remember what this had been. A nurse's room? A seclusion chamber? The asylum had not been long abandoned. Yet it had fallen into ruin. It didn't matter. He had picked up a length of rope left in one of the main hallways. He promised the woman an extra hundred dollars if he could tie her up. She agreed.

"Just do it fast," she said. Her face contorted with anticipation. She was already thinking about her next fix.

"I'll be fast," he said.

Once he had bound her to the metal cot, he

pulled a wad of pink insulation out of a hole in the wall and stuffed it inside her mouth. Then he left the room and the woman's muffled protests to find the proper instrument.

While he searched, the need grew stronger, suffusing his groin with warmth. By the time he found his tool, a rusty ax propped next to the boiler, his body was on fire. Father had stopped him for so long, but Father could not stop him forever.

When the woman saw him, her eyes grew wide and her body arched off the bed. He raised the ax. She screamed through the insulation. Then the ax fell. Twice. She expired with the first blow. He didn't care. He leaned over, reached into the tangle of bloody veins and muscle and touched the jagged bone. He pressed the tip of one index finger into the marrow. For a second, his vision flashed white. He felt like his body had been vaporized. The abandoned asylum disappeared. Then it was over.

Trembling from the release and a sudden fear of discovery, he returned to the foyer of the asylum, where he had seen a homeless camp set up near the door. He took an empty sleeping bag and wrapped the woman's body in it. Then he dragged it to the deepest well on the grounds, filled the sleeping bag with rocks, cinched it shut and pushed it in. The body splashed. The water crashed against stone walls, lapped, then stilled to a flat mirror reflecting the sky. A single, golden maple leaf drifted onto dark water, and the woman had never existed.

It went on like that until the day he met Carrie

Brown, the day he made Anat Al-Fulani.

It was winter. Anat Al-Fulani was an immigrant janitor who worked at Pittock. Every afternoon he passed her hurrying across campus, her burka an anachronism among the students' ski jackets and stocking caps. He had not given her a second thought until one ferocious, winter day he caught sight of her walking, bent against the gale. For a moment, the wind dislodged her headscarf, revealing black hair so glossy it shone. Quickly, she fixed the scarf. Meanwhile, he had decided.

He grew tired of the homeless women with their loose breasts and gray teeth. Anat was a mule like them. Her English was a stutter. Her burka made her an object of ridicule for some, pity for others. But she was healthy, gorgeous, full-figured under her robes, and so proud.

Making her was a joy. It was the first time he used the train. He laid her on the tracks, threw the green sheet over her body and watched the orgasmic moment when the train hit. She was barely breathing when he emerged from the shadowed woods and the darkness of the gathering snowstorm. He stared at her stumps. She was his.

He was just leaning over to touch the bone where it protruded from the muscle when a voice stopped him.

"I see you."

He whirled. A woman emerged from the nearby darkness. She stood, watching him, her hands in the pockets of her jeans. Despite the cold wind, she held her head high, looking right at him. He knew she had seen the making. She had watched him drag Anat to the tracks and secure the ties. Her eyes dropped below his belt. She saw his fly open.

Without thinking, he picked up a rock. She had seen it; she had to die.

"Wait. Don't!" she called from the edge of the clearing. "I'm not going to tell. I just want to know..." Her voice was breathless. "Can you do it to me?"

"What?"

He took a step toward her, expecting her to run. She stood still, letting him move into her orbit. She had dark blonde hair cut in a angular bob and slashes of eye shadow over her eyes. She looked about twenty-five. He thought he had seen her on campus. She put her arms around him.

"I've been watching you," she said.

He had never shared a making with anyone but those he made. He ran his hands down her jeans, transferring Anat's blood to her clothes.

"They don't understand you, do they?" she whispered. She was wearing a leather jacket and the leather creaked as she moved. "They don't understand *us*. They don't know how much we need it."

We need it. That became their mantra. In bed at the cheap hotel he rented, he tied the bands around her thighs so she could feel her cells dying. He took her in her wheelchair, a prop they bought together. She leaned back in the camel pose, her feet tucked under her thighs, so he could experience what they wanted to make real.

He barely noticed the investigation into Anat's death. When he did, it was easy to convince the police chief, Robert Hornsby, that he could serve the greater good by not stirring up a scandal. That cost him a donation to the police cruiser fund and a promise to talk to the city council about the police department's woeful benefit package. He forgot the promise as soon as it left his lips.

Then one day he went to the Cozzzy Inn where he'd met Carrie so many times. This time, he brought a bottle of champagne. Everything was settled, finally. This was to be the last time they met like children playacting. In his jacket pocket, he carried a roundtrip ticket to Bhisho, South Africa.

The procedure to remove her legs would take three hours. Then Carrie would convalesce in a beautiful villa surrounded by orange trees and armed guards. It was where "political men," as Dr. Mobuzi described them, recovered from stab wounds and venereal disease.

"It is the safest place in South Africa," the doctor had assured him.

"How long before I can have her?" he had asked. He needed her. He needed to feel her stumps, hot and meaty, yet helpless.

"One fortnight to fornicate without the possibility of hemorrhage, but a month would be more appropriate for courtly relations." Mobuzi spoke good English. He had learned from a Catholic textbook. "Of course, for this procedure of great magnitude it will be of significant expense." He bowed.

"Money is not an issue."

"Then everything is established and will be completed to meet your desire."

But it wasn't.

He had walked in expecting to find Carrie naked in the wheelchair. Instead, she'd sat cross-legged on the bed, wearing a turquoise sundress instead of her usual black. She was fiddling with something in her lap.

"What are you doing?" he had asked, although he could see she was knitting, an idiotic hobby that all the girls at the college had taken up that summer.

"It's a cap." Carrie smiled. Her skin looked radiant. She was putting on weight. She hung her head, but her voice was cheerful. She was excited about something. "Oh, honey, I've changed my mind. I can't go."

"It's all settled." He spoke gently. "Carrie, you want this. Don't be scared. You've always wanted this."

Carrie squeezed her knitting. "Do you know what Body Integrity Identity Disorder is? BIID?"

He didn't.

"It's a disease, and I have it." She sat up like an eager student reciting her lesson. "BIID. It's when the map in the brain doesn't match the body, like the men who want to be women. The map inside their brain is for a woman's body, but they're born a man. It's called a dysphoria. It's a body dysphoria. I was born into a body with two legs, but my mind-map is an amputee. It doesn't have lower legs. That's why I hate them so much." She stroked the familiar place on her thigh, the nexus of all her violent attentions. "Here. This is where the mind-map ends."

He was getting angry. He wanted her in the wheelchair, and then he wanted her on the plane. The need was growing.

"You don't understand what this means," Carrie went on. Her eyes were bright beneath dark eye shadow. "It means I'm not a freak. I'm sick, and there are treatments, psychologists, even drugs. There might even be a cure. I don't know. But I don't have to cut off my legs."

"What?" He clenched his fists. Rage swelled in his groin. He had made women, but he had never gotten to keep them. Not for more than a few minutes. Carrie was supposed to be his. He would own her forever. "I risked *everything* to get the money for this trip. I put my career on the line for you."

"Don't you understand how wonderful this is? If there's a cure for me, there might be a cure for you. We could have a *real* life, a *real* relationship."

He didn't want a real relationship. He wanted Carrie secluded in a rental apartment far from campus but close enough to serve his need. His mind raced as Carrie kept talking.

"I know we're not what people expect, but fuck them. I want to *walk* hand in hand. I want to run in the surf. I want to chase after my kids. We could do that. We could get married."

"No one can know about us. Not with you at the college."

"I know, so I've transferred to UMass."

"You are getting on that plane."

"I love you." She gazed up at him. "We deserve more than this. There are other people like us, who feel the way I do and the way you do. And they're normal people. I've been going to a web forum."

"Who did you tell? No one can know about us! If you told..."

His hands were on her throat before he realized what he was doing. Carrie struggled out of his grip. He often forgot that she had lived a few years on the street. She was tougher than the others, and now she was angry.

"I didn't tell anyone. But I will. I'm not ashamed anymore. I want a real life. I wanted it with you, but if you won't get help, I want it on my own. And there's something else."

"What is it?" He swallowed his rage for a moment, folding his hands in front of him and squeezing them together. "Darling."

"I'm pregnant."

The look on her face was so pathetically cheerful, like the smiling women on the pro-life billboards that lined the highway. *A baby! How precious.* This was a woman who had planned the amputation of her own legs a thousand times. She knew the serrated edge of a bone saw by heart. She had memorized the stages of atrophy like a catechism.

"A baby," he said. "Well that changes everything."

He spoke gently after that. He agreed. He apologized. He asked her the name of her web forum, the details of her so-called disease. He talked, and he held her, and he remembered what he had always known: Carrie Brown had to die.

Now, in the distance, he could hear the search party, and he cursed her. She was supposed to be in South Africa with Dr. Mobuzi. Barring that, she should have been deep in the asylum well, weighted down by a bag of cement. He was usually so careful. He was not like the criminals in books who played intellectual games with the police. He did not want to be caught. He did not want to leave a judicious smattering of clues. He wanted a woman he could make and keep. He had thought it was Carrie.

It was her fault it had gone wrong. After her

confession in the room at the Cozzzy Inn, he had offered her an oxycodone. She had downed several. Once the drug began to relax her limbs, he had tipped the bottle back into her throat. She spit up several of the pills. Most went down. Then he walked her out to the parking lot while she could still stand.

Finally, he carried her to the tracks. She was heavy. Mumbling idiotic nonsense. He couldn't carry her far enough. That was why he made her near the bridge over Barrow Creek instead of farther down the tracks, where he could have hidden her in the forest. By the time they got to the bridge, he was stumbling. She made him weak. He was glad she had gone back on her promise, glad he'd decided to end it as he had with the others.

He bound her to the tracks and watched the train make her his. When he went to free the body, he realized he'd left the wire cutters in his glove box, half a mile away. The zip-ties only pulled in one direction. They could not be loosened in reverse. The moon was setting. Dawn turned the sky yellow. He was about to go back for the cutters when he heard them: students out for a morning jog.

He tried to loosen the legs by hand, but he had pulled the zip ties so tightly they cut into Carrie's muscle. One of the bones had shattered. His hands were slippery. The ties would not yield. He was covered in blood. The students were coming. Closer. A whole choir of them. Then one voice broke off from the rest.

"I have to take a leak." The boy began tromping through the underbrush.

Back on the path, the boy's friends yelled, "We can't see you. You don't have to go that far."

He wanted to kill the boy. He glanced around for

a weapon. But if he missed, if he struck the boy and he screamed, his friends would hear. There were too many of them. They would come looking.

"I'm shy," the boy yelled back in a high voice, like a Midwestern girl. "I can't go with you watching me."

The boy was almost to the railroad tracks.

He could not free Carrie's legs. He needed the wire clippers. The boy would see him. He grabbed the torso, wrapped it in the green sheet, and ran.

Panicked, he threw the bundle in one of the asylum wells. He didn't even unwrap her and put stones in her pockets. He just pushed her in and hoped she sank. Her leather jacket was heavy. That was the only thing holding her down. Then he washed himself in the creek and drove the back roads for hours until his clothes dried.

Now he leaned down and ran his fingertips along the metal rail that had been Carrie's executioner. He touched the ground that had absorbed her blood. He felt the need rekindled. In the distance, the search party moved through the forest. He caught a glimpse of the new president: Ivers. She picked her way through the tall grass, her face serious. She was pretty, although her long legs repulsed him. So spindly. So quick.

The thought struck him suddenly: Carrie had been a mule. She was not much better than the whores in Battambang. He had wanted to keep her, but why? He was no longer the weak boy Father had tied to a chair and beaten, not any more. He deserved someone better, a woman of quality, like Mother. He deserved a woman like Helen Ivers.

Chapter Eleven

A lady in the woods?" Helen leaned against the stone wall of the asylum, frozen. For a moment, she thought she hallucinated. A figure emerged from around the corner. It looked like an animal wearing a bowtie and coat. Then she realized it was a tiny man, so wizened he looked smoked, his shoulders barely reaching her waist.

In one hand he grasped an aluminum cane, which he waved when he saw Helen. It was Dr. Lebovetski, the emeritus history professor.

"Do not be afraid," the shrunken professor said. He had a slight Polish accent. "I was just exploring the grounds when I discovered I was not the only one who took an interest in the asylum today." He blinked at the bright sunshine, then extended his hand. "I have frightened you, as well you should be frightened. Have you done your homework?"

He was teasing. Helen tried to smile.

"Ms. President, our fearless leader. Did you know I have walked these grounds every day since 1965?" He took his cane in two hands and rocked back on his heels. "I met my wife while walking this path. Even in the winter of 1980, every day, I walked this path, out of the history building over the Barrow Creek and to the asylum."

Since 1965, Lebovetski had perfected his

delivery. Now his story flowed like water down a hill, one sentence pouring into the next.

"That year the snow was up to my waist," Lebovetski continued, still rocking on his heels. "The students thought I was mad to go out." He chuckled. "You know these asylums were closed communities for many years. They farmed their own food, wove their own clothing. When the patients died, they were cremated and buried right here on the grounds. Some asylums even had bowling alleys and playing fields. Not unlike the college, except your husband can't throw you in college for believing in spiritualism."

He paused for effect, not long enough for Helen to interject.

"What I'm interested in now are those burial practices. We don't examine the burials of the unclaimed." He pointed one finger in the air, clearly warming to a favorite topic. "Buried Practices: The Unclaimed Dead of Kirkbride Asylums from 1855 to 1955." That's what I am working on. You know, there is a mausoleum just over there, covered in ivy. It is invisible like their deaths, but I know where it is, and now you do too."

Helen regained her composure and jumped in to end the lecture. "The asylum is not safe, Dr. Lebovetski, especially now."

"Ah, the legs. An administrative issue for you to untangle in your first months. How intriguing."

"It was a crime, Dr. Lebovetski."

"Dr. Ivers is right."

Helen turned at the familiar voice. Drummond had appeared, as if out of nowhere.

"Dr. Lebovetski, it is so good to see you, but I must ask you to retire to your office."

"Am I in danger?" A smile cracked his leathery face. "Is there a mad man loose in the woods? It would not be the first time, although it's hard to say whether the madmen wore white coats or straitjackets." He had made that joke before; Helen was certain. "Where have you looked? Perhaps I can help you."

"We have a team of students and the police at work," Drummond said, putting a hand on Lebovetski's shoulder and gracefully turning him toward campus. "You must leave, Dr. Lebovetski. For your safety."

"All right, I go. I leave the asylum to the students." He began to hobble away. "I suspect my beautiful Addie is at the forefront of that army. If this doesn't have her name all over it, I am lost in the woods." He waved a gnarled hand toward the students. "They will remember this search for the rest of their lives. How alive they are today! There is nothing like a little *memento mori* to give our lives significance."

When Lebovetski was several paces away, Drummond said, "You're looking a little peaked. May I drive you back to campus?"

She hesitated.

"You've made your impression," he added with a bit less gallantry. "You and Wilson."

Helen did not have the energy to protest. She let Drummond lead her back to the clearing, where his gray Bentley was parked on the grass. She was grateful for the car's air conditioning and relieved to evade the reporters. Still, she scanned the side-view mirror, staring long after the asylum was obscured by trees. It was only after she decompressed in her office that she realized who she'd been looking for: beautiful Adair Wilson. *They won't find her. Not out here in the open.* How could she be so certain?

About half an hour later, Patrick appeared with two cups of coffee and a sheaf of papers.

"Bet you hoped the murders would wait until you'd had time to balance the budget. Coffee?" Patrick held a cup out to Helen.

"Thanks."

Helen's phone rang for the third time since she'd returned. She set down her coffee and silenced the ringer.

"We've got a little problem." Patrick shuffled the papers. "Eight students have already withdrawn, six incoming and two returning. I've had calls from about forty panicked parents."

"They're calling me too."

Helen pulled her Blackberry out of her pocket and scrolled through the messages. "I got a hundred and forty emails this morning."

"Well," Patrick said. "I asked Media Services to put an update banner on the website. That will at least field a few questions." He hesitated. "Mr. Drummond went out again. And your car registration renewal got sent here by accident. I filled out the papers and mailed them back to the DMV." He looked pleased with himself.

"Anything else?"

Helen motioned to one of the gold wingback chairs that dominated her office. The furniture was too Louis XIV. "Come in for two minutes, drink your coffee with me?"

"I thought you'd never ask." Patrick plopped down in one of the chairs. "So the shit hit the fan, didn't it?"

"Yep." Helen liked Patrick. A good secretary should not be cowed by the people he worked for, and Patrick exuded self-confident efficiency.

"Can I help?" he asked. "I mean more than I have already." He grinned over his coffee cup.

"Tell me about Adair Wilson."

"She's crazy," Patrick said.

Helen swallowed too quickly, coughed, then set her mug on an ornate end table.

"I'm kidding," he added. "She's my best friend, but she's *that* friend. You know what I mean."

Helen did not.

"You know. You've got all your friends from high school, college and work, but there's always one that's larger than life."

"All your friends," Helen repeated. Eliza had not left time for *all those friends.* "How long have you known her?"

"Senior year in high school. I got a scholarship to the Aster Campbell Institute in New Hampshire. It's a private prep school. Worst thing that ever happened to me. Those kids were so rich. They owned horses. They drove Miatas. You could buy anything. A test. A professor. A woman. Forget cocaine; they did it at lunch in front of the library. And there I was, this blue collar kid from Manchester on scholarship." Patrick folded his arms over his chest. "Those kids were so mean. Adair was as rich as any of them, but she wasn't mean like that. It wasn't in her bones.

"When she got into Smith, I didn't know what to do. She was the only friend I had who was going to college, and she picked a girls' school, so I applied to UMass because it was down the road. She was smarter than I was, or better at it, or maybe she bought her grades. I don't know. It almost didn't matter for rich people. They 'got' how to be smart, like it was a game. If they bought the answers to a test it was just because they didn't feel like they wanted to learn them." He smiled. "God, she was insufferable. She wouldn't hang out with me unless I had done my homework. Can you believe that?"

He took a swig of coffee.

"I think she understood that I needed that degree in a way she didn't, but if you had told me that back then, I would have said she was just an asshole." He shrugged, apologizing for the swear and dismissing it all in one gesture. "It was hard to take her seriously."

Helen raised an eyebrow. "Really?"

"Oh, she wasn't always Mr. Butch Dyke. I guess she had her own stuff to work out too. When I met her, she was one of those girls who carried a purse that probably cost more than my car and no pen. She had long blonde hair and weighed about eighteen pounds."

Helen tried to square Patrick's story with the woman who'd cornered her in the woods. "And now?"

"I was here first." Patrick pointed his finger in the air. "I want you to know that. *She* followed *me* to Pittock."

"What's she like to work with?"

"Hmm." Patrick shrugged again. "She's my best friend."

"And if she wasn't?"

"I'd say she was… demanding, stubborn, moody. She doesn't take no for an answer. She won't do paper work. She doesn't go to meetings."

"She thinks she's better than her job?"

"She *is* better than her job, but that's not it. She

loves her students. She's passionate about the theater. She's just… Adair. She's different."

Different. That was one way to describe a woman who searched the woods at twilight, alone, for a body. A woman who claimed to know the outcome of a search before it was over. A woman who knew secrets she couldn't tell the police. *I need to talk to you about a student named Carrie Brown and a woman named Anat Al-Fulani.*

She's crazy, Helen thought. It was Eliza all over again: the delusions, the paranoia, the conviction that only Helen could be trusted. And yet, Patrick in his purple polo, purple lanyard, and matching purple Bluetooth headset, seemed the most stable person on campus. If she could rely on anyone, it was Patrick.

"I have to talk to her," Helen said. "I have to see her again."

Chapter Twelve

An irrational fear seized Helen as she stood at the door to the Ventmore Theater. Patrick had informed her that Wilson was back, and she had set off across campus in the late afternoon light. Situated on the edge of campus, the Ventmore was one of the few "modern" buildings at Pittock. The architect had designed it to look like an Elizabethan theater, though it was built in 1970. Since then, years of neglect had grayed the plaster and left the painted beams flaking.

There was something menacing about the building, like a drawing in a Grimm's fairytale, the old version where the witch boils the children alive. It reminded Helen of a low-budget amusement park they'd visited when she and Eliza were children. Her mother had commented on what a wonderful trip it was, her voice growing shrill in the family's silence. All Helen remembered were Eliza's bizarre rantings, as if the strange surroundings had aligned with Eliza's inner world, and she was relieved to see her visions manifest.

Helen shook her head and pressed her fingers to her temples. This was the kind of fantasy Eliza had entertained. She walked resolutely up to the side door and pulled it open with such force it swung back and hit the wall, adding to a sizable hole in the plaster.

Inside, Helen's eyes adjusted to the dark. Up front, on the stage, Wilson sat in a large, red armchair surrounded by students. Floor lamps cast a warm glow on the ensemble. However, the theater's acoustics carried their voices, and Helen could hear their anxiety buzzing like high tension wires.

"Is she really missing?" A girl's whisper.

"Do you think it was Carrie? I mean, could you tell?"

"Who's going to play her part if she doesn't come back?"

"Shut up." Two students said in unison, then, "The show must go on?" It was a question.

Wilson leaned forward, her elbows on her knees, her head bent as if in prayer. "Has anyone heard from Carrie?" she pleaded.

There was silence. Helen waited for someone to notice her, but the darkness shrouded her, and she felt like an interloper. The girl sitting nearest Wilson scooted closer and rested her head on Wilson's knee. Wilson stroked her hair absently. Though the touch was maternal, Helen briefly wondered if she was sleeping with the girl. The professor was young enough to be attractive to her students, but her pulling power would be waning. She was thirty-some to their twenty-some. She was no longer "one of them." She would miss that perhaps.

"Dr. Wilson?" The girl at Wilson's feet looked up at her. "Are you okay?"

The students fixed their attention on Wilson. Helen felt the high wire crackle.

"I don't know," Wilson said. "I don't know."

Helen cleared her throat. "Excuse me," she called out.

The students started, as though they had heard a gunshot. Wilson just raised her eyes, finding Helen immediately.

"Go on," Wilson said to her students. "Get out of here, get something to eat, and go together. Don't go out there alone."

Like a choreographed dance, the students rolled, ran, and leapt off the stage into the wings. In a second, they were gone. Wilson sat alone in her crimson armchair, like a Shakespearian king. Helen thought of elegant, ineffectual Richard II. Then Wilson rose and Helen thought, no. She was one of the warring kings. "*Then will he strip his sleeve and show his scars...*"

The theater had an eerie, after–hours feel, as though a calamity had emptied the space. As indeed it had. She joined Wilson on the stage, and Wilson shook Helen's hand, holding it a second too long, like a telepath reading her subject's mind.

"Patrick said you didn't find anything," Helen said, extricating her hand.

"No." Wilson looked defeated. "I knew we wouldn't."

"How did you know?"

Wilson's eyes were an unnatural pale blue, the color of a winter sky just above the horizon where the atmosphere thins.

"Come up to my office." Wilson gestured toward the back of the stage, where a spiral staircase led to a trapdoor in the ceiling. The staircase was painted black and nearly disappeared into the black wall behind it. Helen climbed the stairs, feeling every vibration. Ahead of her, Wilson pushed open the trapdoor and leapt from the top step into the room above.

The office, lit by several Tiffany lamps, appeared to be a retrofitted attic. It ran the length of the theater, with dormer windows every few feet. The furniture was not the usual assortment of Pittock antiques. It even smelled rich, as if mahogany had a scent. But it was not the roll-top desk or the sumptuous leather furniture that caught her attention.

On the wall, hung a family portrait in a gilt frame. Four men, ranging in age from octogenarian to twenty-something, stood around a white settee on which posed two exquisite women, a mother and a young daughter, both in black evening gowns. It took Helen a moment to recognize the child, her swan-like neck accentuated by an elaborate twist of blonde hair. Wilson. On the opposite wall, hung two enormous nudes.

"That's you," Helen said staring at the flawless oil-on-canvas.

Wilson cocked her head so her pose matched one of the nudes. "It's art."

On another woman, the gesture would have been coquettish, but in the portrait, as in life, Wilson's shoulders rippled like the muscular back of a panther and her face was stern.

Helen sat without invitation. "What the hell are you doing?"

There was something liberating about the dim light and the giant nudes. There was no need to be politic.

"I'm glad you came." Wilson stood with her back to the darkened window. "We need you. I need you. No one stands up to Drummond. No one questions him, and we have to." She shivered. "We can't trust him. Listen..."

"Sit down." Helen pointed to the chair across from her. "This has got to stop. If you have information, you need to tell the police. You can't drag your students into a murder investigation. We went forward with the search today because you had already started. I couldn't call those students back. The whole town was watching."

Was it only PR? Had she only let them go because of the reporters? It was not the whole story.

"I have complete faith in Mr. Drummond and the police." She seized the arms of her chair to lend force to the lie. "I want to make that clear."

"Nothing is clear." Wilson slid into the chair across from Helen and folded her legs underneath her.

"You cannot terrorize your students like this. You cannot tell them stories. You cannot make them wonder. We don't have any information. We *don't* know."

"I'm not telling them anything. I'm asking."

Helen felt the first pulse of a migraine behind her left eye. "Your questions are going to tell them everything they know."

"I'm asking about Carrie Brown," Wilson said, as though Helen had not spoken. "I'm asking where she is. I'm asking who's seen her. I'm asking what happened to her. We are standing on the edge of a precipice."

Wilson sat cross-legged between the two paintings. Helen felt like she had stumbled onto the set of an avant garde performance. *Death and the Two Nudes.* Despite Wilson's rhetoric, her voice was earnest and she chewed on her lower lip, then ran her hand repeatedly through her short hair.

"I'm worried," she said. "Please. Listen to me. I'm worried about Carrie. She hasn't been to rehearsal for two days."

"Have you told the police?"

"I have."

Wilson must have sensed Helen's doubt. "I told them. I keep telling them. But it's summer. Half the students who are supposed to be here are at the Cape. They're all missing. The whole campus is missing."

"Students do skip classes," Helen ventured. "They drop out. They go home."

Wilson rose and paced the sitting area, then leaned into a dormer window, her back to Helen, her shoulders tense. "Theater was her life. It was all that kept her going. The play is in weeks. She wouldn't leave." Wilson turned. "It's not just a school play. It meant more to her. It's *Voices from Within,* a collection of stories from patients who spent time at the Pittock Asylum. Carrie did some of the interviews. She knew those people and she… had problems." Wilson's voice grew quiet. "Real problems. It was her story too. There is no way she would skip rehearsal."

"You think it's her body?"

Wilson nodded.

"And you told the police that?"

Wilson crossed the room and knelt beside Helen's chair, one hand on the arm rest, almost touching her hand. "Hornsby said he'd follow up, but he's going to find a reason not to pursue this. He *won't* look. How do you think the police missed the body the first time? It was by the train bridge. It was *right there.* They said they searched and found nothing."

Wilson's voice sent shivers down Helen's spine. Suddenly, she wanted out of the grandiose office with its trapdoor and garret isolation. Out from under the nudes and the gaze of the delicate child Wilson had once been. Away from Wilson's aggressive beauty and her bare shoulders and the bedroom light of the Tiffany lamps.

"I have to go."

Her head pounded. An aura formed around the lights and Wilson's blonde hair.

"Hornsby's not going to find who did this. There's more. I have to tell you..."

Helen hurried out of the office, her footsteps echoing in the silent theater.

Chapter Thirteen

It was late when Helen climbed the stairs to her bedroom in the Pittock House. How could she have handled Wilson so poorly? She knew professors like Wilson: big personalities in small departments, used to working on their own, watched only by the adoring eyes of their students. Egos. There was practically a script. She should have reprimanded her firmly and specifically, the first step in progressive discipline. The meeting should have been followed up with an email, copied to HR and Wilson's dean.

Hell, she should have comforted her. The woman had begged the police for help, been dismissed, and then found the remains of a body in the woods. There were no words for what Wilson had seen, no way for the mind to hold that picture and go on as though a chasm had not opened up under the feet of everyday life. Helen knew. Of course Wilson was on edge; she was in shock. In Wilson's office, her paranoia had seemed sinister. Now that Helen thought about it, calm reserve would have been stranger. Carrying on as though nothing had happened would have been worse. *Wilson loves her students.* Naturally, she was upset. The least Helen could have done was listen to her story. Instead she had fled, haunted by the image of Wilson quadrupled: the sumptuous nudes, the delicate girl, and the woman, sitting in front of her, who was both of those and neither.

Was it attraction? Helen had sometimes wondered what her sex life would have been like without Eliza. Her sister's care had consumed every spare minute and more. Worry had eaten away at her personal life. Even in death, Eliza haunted her dreams. Her childhood and adolescence were no better. If it were not for Eliza, would she have had those seminal experiences people talked about at intimate dinner parties? The woman I met in Paris. My first coach. That night at sea. Would she simply walk up to Wilson and say, "I was wondering if you'd like to have dinner?"

Helen pulled the gold hoops out of her ears, dropped them on the bedside table, and sat on the edge of the bed. It was too late to know now. *You weren't going to do this again.* She went to the bathroom, brushed her teeth, then stood at the mirror combing her hair for several moments. *Never again.* She took off her makeup with a damp tissue, carefully removing every trace of mascara.

Then she reapplied it. She dropped the tissue in the sink, retrieved her purse, and walked back down the creaking staircase.

A half an hour later, Helen sat in a hotel bar. She'd driven past several dive bars, including one attached to a seedy motel called the Cozzzy Inn. Finally, she'd opted for the Best Western off the freeway. The voice in the back of her mind had been replaced by Terri's. *I don't know what you young career women do.* Helen scanned the room. He was right. He did not know.

It was midnight, and there was only one reason to linger in the drab sports bar. A dark-haired man leaned on the bar, fiddling with his cell phone. He wore the uniform of middle management: blue shirt, pressed khakis, bright red tie. She smiled at him when he looked up.

"You see this?" he asked.

The television behind the bar was replaying Helen's interview from earlier in the week. The man didn't seem to recognize her. Like Wilson, Helen felt she'd been split in three: the picture on the television, the woman leering at the middle manager, and someone who scanned the rearview mirror for beautiful Adair Wilson.

"That's some crazy shit," he said. "Come here often?" He winked. "Doesn't that sound like a line? But I do come here often. I travel for work. You look like you travel."

The man sidled over and stuck out his hand. "Charles."

Helen examined the pinpricks of beard dotting his cheeks.

"I've just come for a drink," Helen said.

"Yeah. Me too. Couldn't sleep."

The man leaned over her table, blocking her view of the television. "What's your name?"

"Susan."

"That's a pretty name. I always liked 'Susan.'"

"Really?" Helen purred. "What a coincidence."

I'm not going to do this again. But she already was. Her martini glass sweated against her hand. She could smell the man as he whispered in her ear, a blend of nervous perspiration and aftershave.

"You're real pretty."

He had to be fifteen years her junior, but neither of them was there for a lasting relationship. She felt Charles's eyes travel the length of her body, finally arriving at the diamond solitaire above her breasts. Helen's ring finger was bare, and she drew her hand across her throat.

She leaned toward him, so her lips almost touched his. “I’m a woman who’s interested in a good time.” She kept her eye on the television where her own image replayed again without sound. At the bottom of the screen, the ticker announced other tragedies. “I want to do something with you. All this talk. Are you going to buy me another drink or should we just go upstairs?”

As soon as they entered the hotel room, she produced a condom from her purse. She pulled Charles’s pants down and slid the rubber over his penis. Then, throwing herself on the hotel coverlet, she urged Charles into her, spreading her dry labia to make way for his penis.

“Don’t you want to wait for…?”

Charles’s question died as she contracted her muscles several times in quick succession, her hips urging him on until there was nothing left but the anonymous weight of their bodies pulsing together. When his legs began to tremble, Helen pulled away from him, her hips retreating into the pillow-top bed. The small tease was too much for him. He fell on top of her, his face pressed into the coverlet. His legs shivered. His hands convulsed, as though shaking off unseen stickiness.

“I’m gonna…gonna…oh God! Yes!”

Helen lay still. Her eyes drifted across the ceiling as Charles’s breathing returned to normal. She listened to the hum of the air conditioning, trying not to think of anything, because as soon as she let her mind open up she was back in Eliza’s house. Whole rooms filled with garbage salvaged from the streets of Pittsburg, and on the kitchen floor… so much blood she couldn’t make sense of what she saw.

Finally, Charles let out a musical whistle. "Whew! That was good. Hello, Susan! That was amazing! Did you…?"

"Yes," Helen said, her voice slow and deliberate. "And now you have to leave."

Chapter Fourteen

The following morning, Helen drove straight from the Best Western to her office. Drummond, Hornsby, and the two junior officers were already seated in conference, the table covered with topographical maps, presumably of Pittock forest. Some areas had been shaded pink, others blue and yellow.

"There you are," Drummond said.

Helen checked her watch. Exactly 8:00 a.m. She straightened her jacket and took her seat at the head of the table. "Let's get this over with."

After Charles had left, she'd watched television until the images blurred. It was Eliza hawking jewelry on the shopping channel, and she could not tell if she was awake or asleep. Now her eyes were raw and her mouth pasty.

Drummond and Hornsby exchanged a glance, which Helen noticed but ignored.

"You see here, we have a map of the Pittock area," Hornsby began.

He explained the maps and their markings. They were, as Helen had guessed, a representation of the search and its findings, which he went over in detail. She wondered if he mocked her. Here they found a shoe lace. Here they found a Pepsi bottle.

Beside Hornsby, Thompson and Giles looked as impatient as Helen felt. Thompson leaned forward, his long fingers curled into two fists. Giles slouched in his chair, scanning the room. Neither said anything.

Finally, Helen interrupted. "What does this all mean, Mr. Hornsby? What should we tell our students?"

"It means your students picked up a whole bunch of trash out there in the woods. It's possible one piece of trash is the clue that brings this together. In the meantime, we're waiting for the crime lab to get back to us, the medical examiner. There's a backlog, especially with the hurricane."

The storm had dissipated and she'd almost forgotten it.

"The chief is saying that it's difficult," Drummond said. "It's hard to solve cases when no one is reported missing and there are no identifying marks on the body."

Helen jumped at this. "What about Carrie Brown?"

"Carrie Brown?" Drummond's face registered apologetic confusion.

He's putting me on. Helen said, "Wilson thinks she's gone missing. She said she told Mr. Hornsby."

"Oh, that woman." Drummond chuckled. "That's Wilson for you."

"What?"

"Then you've got nothing to worry about, ma'am," Thompson interjected. "Your registrar gave us a list of all the students on campus. Everyone who is supposed to be here is here." He pulled a notebook out of his pocket. "See?"

It was a list of student names with checkmarks next to some of them. Thompson scanned his finger down the list.

"Brown, Carrie. Transfer."

"She's at UMass," Drummond added. "I checked too. I even called their registrar." Their eyes met and his face softened. "I do care," he said, then resumed his usual patriarchal glower.

Helen excused herself and hurried back to her office, where she dialed the Ventmore Theater.

"Carrie transferred," Helen said when Wilson picked up. "She's at UMass."

"I know," Wilson replied. "That's what the records say."

"When did you find out?"

"I know the registrar says she transferred, but I don't believe it."

"Dr. Wilson, please." Helen felt a wave of frustration and sympathy. "You need to believe this, for your own health, for your sanity. I know…" Helen reconsidered. "I don't want to go into details, but I've been through something like what you saw when you found the body. Let me help you. I can get her transcript. I can get the registrar at UMass to call you."

Helen was about to continue when Wilson interrupted.

"Wait there," she said. "I'm coming to see you."

The line went dead.

It seemed like only a minute had passed when Helen heard the door to the administration building open and Patrick protest.

"Adair. Wait. Let me call her and tell her you're here."

Footsteps stomped past his desk.

"At least let me pretend to do my job," Patrick

called after her.

Wilson opened Helen's door without knocking. She wore army-green and heavy silver bracelets on each wrist like manacles, a combination of beauty and militant dress.

"Generally, one knocks," Helen said.

Wilson closed the door. "I'm sorry." She seemed genuinely abashed, but also agitated, her body rigid. "And I'm sorry you have to go through this, Helen."

It's Dr. Ivers.

"I know how this sounds, but you have to listen. That was Carrie Brown I saw in the woods."

"She transferred to UMass."

"No. She didn't. There's more to this." Wilson dropped her voice to a whisper and glanced at the closed door. "Carrie Brown was Ricky Drummond's girlfriend. Did you know that?"

"Ricky Drummond?"

"Marshal Drummond's son."

Helen stepped from behind her desk so Wilson could not corner her. She sat in one of the two ornate chairs and pressed her fingertips to her forehead.

"Let's pretend, for a second, that I'm going to entertain this. What are you implying, Dr. Wilson?"

Wilson balled her fists in her pockets. "I'm saying towns like Pittock have their own laws, and one is that families like the Drummonds protect their own. They're old money. They're old power. They've been here forever, and they don't let boys like Ricky Drummond go down for anything. I come from a family like that. It was sad," Wilson continued. "Carrie was troubled, and she liked Ricky. I think she saw him as an adult. His mother had died. His father was the provost. He understood the college in a way the other students didn't. She hung around him, and he used her in one way or another. She's attractive, but not the kind of girl he would ever take home to Marshal Drummond."

Again, Wilson knelt next to Helen's chair, so close that Helen could smell her cologne, much sweeter and richer than Charles's cheap, manly aftershave. Still, Helen leaned away.

"He sounds like an asshole," she said wearily.

"The police are just going to overlook the evidence because it's Ricky."

"He sounds like an asshole," Helen repeated. "But that doesn't make him a murderer. Nor does that mean he forged the registrar's records to make it look like Carrie transferred."

Helen wanted to tell Wilson that every time there was an incident on campus, faculty suspected the administration. If an asteroid hit the library, at least one professor would allege wrongdoing on the part of the administration. If Carrie Brown dated a hundred men, including a dozen serial killers and a drug lord, the faculty would still suspect the provost's rugby–playing son. It was not even Wilson's fault; it was a law of nature.

"Why are you so sure it's her, Dr. Wilson?"

"Did they tell you about the marks on the legs?"

"They didn't find any marks."

"Because they didn't want to. That's why I had to find the legs. That's why I called the press first. That's why we need you. You're not a part of this place yet. People disappear here. I saw the ties and the place where the bones were crushed like meat. I could see the marrow, and I don't understand."

Helen remembered the president of Vandusen,

a gray haired lady with the body of a teddy bear. She hugged faculty at retirements and promotions and sometimes in the hallway just because she had not seen so-and-so from biology for weeks. If Helen had ever hugged a colleague—let alone a subordinate—she might have done it again at that moment. Despite the trouble she'd caused, Wilson looked so frightened, Helen felt an urge to hold her and warn her. *Stop. I have gone down that path.*

From one of the pockets in her cargo pants, Wilson withdrew a newspaper clipping marked with a post-it note. "See the girl in the front?"

It was a grainy photograph taken from the student newspaper. "*Angels in America* cast takes a bow," the caption read. The woman at the front of the stage looked radiant.

"That's Carrie Brown. She's a senior, an older student. Twenty-four or twenty-five. Those were her legs I saw in the woods." Wilson's voice trembled. "I knew the scars I saw. There was something wrong with Carrie Brown."

Wilson cupped the clipping in her hand like a relic. "Her legs were all cut up, scars from childhood and fresh cuts. I referred her to Student Health Services, but she wouldn't go. She was tough. She didn't trust anyone to help her or understand. She told me she went, but she didn't.

"I've seen girls who cut themselves. Overachievers. Victims of sexual abuse. It's ritualistic. It's clean. They *want* to show you. But Carrie hid it. When I did find out, it was because she fainted on stage. She'd carved a chunk out of her thigh." Wilson held up her clenched fist. "She had taken out this much flesh. It was like she was trying to get to the bone."

"And you told the police?"

"It doesn't matter. They will lie unless you do something. They won't investigate. Not in Pittock. It's too close. There are rules."

Wilson reached into another pocket and pulled out her cell phone. She pushed it into Helen's hand. "Look!"

The photo on the screen was overexposed, taken at night with a flash, but it was clear from context that Wilson was showing her the legs. The feet were swollen, and there were dark marks across the thighs, as though the legs had been slashed. When Helen looked again, she saw they weren't slashes at all. Black, plastic straps cinched the thighs.

Helen looked up and saw Eliza's face stuck onto Wilson's head, like a mask with black holes where the eyes had been. *No! Focus.*

"Look, here and here. Those scars didn't happen that night. Do you understand what I'm saying?" Eliza's mouth moved with Wilson's words.

Helen's heart seized, as though someone grabbed it in a closed fist. The pain in her chest was excruciating. She blinked, but couldn't clear the fog. In the distance she heard Wilson's voice.

"Do you care?"

"Of course I care."

"You have to help me."

Suddenly Helen was back in her sister's kitchen. She was vaguely aware of dropping from her chair. Her knees hit the hardwood floor. Then she was leaning over Eliza, pressing a dishtowel to her face. Eliza was swimming in blood, the linoleum slick and dark. Once again, Helen's cell phone was slipping out of her grasp. Once again, she was frantic, feeling for the phone in the sea of blood. It was too late to get help. She couldn't breathe.

"Somebody help me!" The sound of her own voice jarred Helen back to reality. For a moment, she felt herself swimming up through the memories, images of Eliza slipping past her. Then she saw Wilson's face.

"Look at me," Wilson was saying.

She heard Drummond's voice in the distance. "Dr. Wilson, let go of her."

Helen blinked convulsively. She was crouched on the floor. Wilson was clasping one of her hands, her other hand pressed to the back of Helen's head, her fingertips digging into her skull.

"Look at me, Helen. Look at me."

Without preamble, Drummond swooped down on Helen, lifting her to her chair as though she weighed no more than a child.

"What did you do to her?"

"Helen, are you okay?" Wilson tried to maneuver around Drummond.

"It wasn't her fault," Helen mumbled as she rubbed her eyes. "Asthma. I'm fine. She didn't do anything."

Drummond kept a hand on her shoulder and an eye on Wilson.

"She was just in a meeting." His voice was both sonorous and comically at wit's end. "She was fine a minute ago."

"Really," Helen said, trying to smile. "I must have fainted. That's all. I just need a drink of water." She found Wilson's eyes. "We're done here."

Chapter Fifteen

He glared at Hornsby. He wanted to reach across the desk and strangle him. Perhaps the last seconds of asphyxia would spark a fire in Hornsby's eyes. He had seen that in some of the Cambodian whores. They had no zeal, no fight, but something in the hindbrain still roared against death and made their last seconds their most passionate.

"I just don't know." Hornsby spoke as though no one was in the room. He massaged his crew cut temples. "I'm too old for this. I can't believe…here in Pittock…and with Alisha so sick. I don't have time for this."

Hornsby was a mule; that had never been clearer. And if Hornsby was the only man on the force, he would have botched the investigation on his own. There was a chance—just a chance—however, that one of the rookies would stumble on evidence. The rookies. Or Wilson. Or beautiful Helen Ivers. He could not take that risk.

"I came to talk about the investigation," he said.

"You and everyone else."

"I'm not here to criticize." He sat in front of Hornsby's desk. It was covered with gutted folders, their papers splayed across the desk and neighboring chairs.

"What's your take on this situation, Chief Hornsby?"

"Like you said, some lunatic from the asylum, homeless probably. I don't even know. I can't stomach this stuff anymore. They can." He gestured to the rookies' empty desks. "Not me."

"Is there a real danger to the town?"

"Maybe. Maybe not. We got some forensic psychologist working on a psych profile. What can they know?"

"As much as you're willing to pay for," he said, with a sympathetic grimace.

"And we can't afford any of it," Hornsby agreed.

He wondered if Hornsby was skimming the police budget; he hoped so. "You've been working hard," he said, keeping his voice amicable.

Hornsby waved his hands over the paperwork on his desk. "I haven't been home in two days. I haven't seen Alisha…"

"How is your lovely wife?"

It was so pathetic. Hornsby's whole body deflated at the mention of that musty-smelling woman.

"It's bad," Hornsby said. His grief was as obvious as a billboard, though he tried to hold it in. "The doctors called hospice. The insurance plan says she's maxed out her benefit, something about life expectancy to benefit ratio. They're saying her life isn't worth preserving. It's not worth the money. How can you put a value on life?"

On some lives, not on all of them. "How long does she have?"

"Weeks. Maybe months."

Now was the time. He pressed the tips of his steepled fingers to his lips. "Have you looked into the Le Farge trials?"

The chief shook his head. "What's that?"

"Doctors here don't have access to the trials, so they wouldn't talk about them. It's an experimental treatment they're testing in Switzerland. Nothing has been released yet, but the hospital says it's a miracle cure."

"For uterine cancer?"

"For all cancers."

"How do you know about it?"

"You know my father managed the asylum before it closed." He withdrew a paper from his pocket, unfolded it and pushed it across the desk towards Hornsby.

"Is that the price?" Hornsby asked.

"Minus expenses. Insurance won't pay, of course. Even if she still has benefits."

Hornsby looked like he was going to cry. "I could never afford that. If I mortgaged my house… if I sold my house, my car, everything, I could never get that kind of money."

"I can help."

Hornsby looked up from the paper, apprehension crossing his face. The fool! It had taken him this long to realize what they were discussing. *Quid pro quo.*

"I…" Hornsby could not even finish.

In the front office, the phone rang and Margie, the dispatcher, answered like a cheerful hacksaw. Hornsby froze. They could hear her through the wall. If she listened, she could hear them too. Hornsby began to sweat.

"You and I both know the whole 'Pittock legs' case won't amount to anything. A crazy, homeless women and reporters with nothing better to do. Just hype."

Hornsby nodded slowly. "You want to help

Alisha?"

The only help for Alisha Hornsby was to shoot her on bare dirt where the blood would not leave a stain. For a second, he entertained the idea of making her, but Alisha Hornsby was a mule, and he was done with mules.

"I *can* help Alisha, then I want you to help me."

"I don't know." Hornsby's lip trembled. "What... what are you asking?"

If he were as weak as Hornsby, he would end it with a leap off the Sunderland Bridge. Hornsby still wore the same haircut as the cadets. He cared about being a cop. Alisha Hornsby and being a cop: the two compartments in Robert Hornsby's brain. He had to move carefully.

"I want to help Alisha, and I want this case to disappear... so we can all go back to living. So we can enjoy our normal lives. So we can enjoy Pittock."

Chapter Sixteen

Patrick was on the phone, eating a Twinkie, when Helen arrived the next morning. He pushed half the Twinkie into his mouth. With one finger he drew circles around his temple.

"Crazy," he mouthed, through the crumbs.

Whoever was on the line, Patrick couldn't get a word in edgewise. He wasn't writing anything down either. Helen shot him a sympathetic smile on her way past. Back in her office, Helen too had a vast influx of email and voicemails. She had just compiled a priority list when Patrick knocked on her door. He held a sheet of paper.

"You want the long or short version?" Patrick asked.

"Let me guess. Somebody's mom from middle America just heard about the legs and wants to know what we're doing about it."

"Nope."

"The whole freshman class has withdrawn?"

"Luckily not."

"Okay. Give me the short version. Who have we got?"

"I'll give you the short version, although that's *not* what I got. I've been on the phone for thirty minutes with some guy named Blake. Wouldn't give me his last name. Apparently he is president and webmaster for the Devotees of Boston, and he *must* talk to you."

Helen spread her hands in the air. "Why?"

"Funny you should ask." Patrick read off a sheet he had printed from the Internet. "'Devotees of Boston is a social support group for devotees, wannabes and amputees. We welcome all who appreciate the beauty, sexuality, and unique potential of those differently bodied and celebrate those who identify as disabled, disembodied, or uniquely abled.' From what I gather, Mr. Blake is not just the president, he's a client, if you know what I mean."

"I have no idea."

"It's for people who pretend to be amputees." Patrick grimaced. "Plus, there are a few amputee fetishists in the mix. Blake calls it a social group." Patrick wiggled two fingers to show he was placing "Blake" and "social group" in quotation marks. "They meet every second Tuesday in Boston."

Helen had worked with too many different groups to be hugely surprised. Even at conservative Vandusen, the gay and lesbian group included bisexuals, transsexuals, and one young man who called himself intersexed because he possessed two thirds of an ovary. From a college president's perspective, it was best to lump them under the heading of "diversity" and leave it at that.

"Let me guess. They want to talk about the Pittock legs."

"Yep," Patrick said. "Mr. Blake got your email address and sent you fifty-some pages of smut from some creep who's been posting to their website, and he wonders why you haven't read it, because he sent it last night at 10:00 p.m."

"Did he send it to the police?"

"Of course. He probably sent it to the mayor."

"Does he have any real reason to think this has something to do with the college?"

"Actually, yes." Patrick's voice suddenly lost its affected lisp as he explained that the webmaster had traced the threatening posts to an IP address in Pittock.

"The town of Pittock?" Helen asked.

Patrick shook his head. "The college."

Helen had just clicked on the email Patrick forwarded when Drummond knocked on the wall outside her open door. He stood at stiff attention as always, his blazer buttoned over a dark tie. Still, there was something tentative about his posture.

"Come to my office for a coffee?" he asked.

Helen was about to refuse. His hesitation stopped her. It was the first time Drummond had invited her into his office. For the most part, his door had remained closed, whether he was in or not. The message had been clear: you're not welcome. Now Helen rose.

Drummond's office was as modern as hers was full of antiques. She paused in front of a glass-fronted cupboard and admired a bronze sculpture of a naked man sitting astride a horse. The man's muscles rippled with effort and his hands were lost in the horse's mane.

"A Jean-Luc Broussard replica," Drummond said as he tinkered with an espresso maker on a shelf.

Helen smiled. She would not have guessed that he made his own coffee.

"It's called 'Le Chevalier de la Nouvelle Monde.' It represents man's ability to control, not only nature, but his own destiny. The man's legs hold the horse and the rock beneath it, symbolizing Broussard's belief that everything can be controlled by the mind of a man who doesn't compromise his desires."

The espresso maker sizzled, filling the room with the smell of fresh roast.

"I suppose I've taken that motto too seriously."

Helen looked up, searching his face.

"It has been a long time since I had a colleague who did not report to me. I was curt to you on the day of Wilson's search. You made an excellent decision in a tight situation."

"Thank you," Helen said, waiting for criticism to follow.

"It was great press: the college and the town coming together in difficult times." He handed her a demitasse.

"Yes," Helen raised her cup in a small salute. "It was."

Drummond pulled a set of car keys out of his pocket. "Would you like to go out to breakfast? Off campus? There is a bed and breakfast in Sheffield." He stumbled, perhaps embarrassed by the connotations of "bed." "They do a nice English tea on the patio."

In the parking lot, Drummond directed Helen to a yellow Jeep.

"That is quite a vehicle," Helen said, taking in the blinding yellow exterior and black vinyl upholstery.

"I walked to campus this morning. We live about a mile away, Ricky and I. My wife passed away a few years ago."

"I heard. I'm sorry."

Drummond nodded to acknowledge her

sympathy and cut it short at the same time. "This monstrosity belongs to Ricky. He had it on campus, and since he belongs in class, he has no good excuse for not letting us borrow it. It's in remarkably bad taste, isn't it?" Drummond opened the door for Helen. "I bought it for him. That's the worst of it."

Had she heard a touch of tenderness in his voice? Helen caught a glimpse of the father behind the façade of New England reserve.

On the drive, they discussed the email from the Devotees. Patrick had already forwarded it to Drummond, and Drummond declared it smut.

"One more desperate person trying to find some meaning in this," he declared, and they were silent until they took their seats on the white porch of the Carriage House in Sheffield.

Then Helen said, "What would we be talking about if there hadn't been the legs? I want to give this situation its full due, but there are going to be times when we can't do anything about the case. I want make sure I serve the college in every way possible."

A warm breeze blew under the umbrellas shading the porch. Geraniums, petunias, and sweet Alberts grew in urns along the railing, their red, white and blue a leftover from the Fourth of July weekend.

Drummond spoke thoughtfully. "Do you know who Adrian Meyerbridge is?" He sipped his coffee.

"I've read the alumni prospectus," Helen said. "Meyerbridge made his fortune in the tech boom and invested wisely when it went bust. We estimate his net worth at three billion. He's an influential donor."

"Full marks. He also has ALS. Did you know that?"

"No. That's too bad," Helen said.

"It is too bad."

These conversations were always delicate.

"Adrian recently finalized a significant estate gift to Pittock," he said. "Upon his passing, the college will receive a considerable sum as well as a portfolio of holdings that, if we manage them properly, will be a meaningful asset to the college. Meyerbridge Hall was recently renamed in Adrian's honor."

Helen knew it was not that simple. The naming and renaming of campus buildings was as romantic as the sale of beef. The price was negotiated, the term established by contract. Modern colleges did not name buildings in honor of great men; they named them for the highest bidder.

"Here's what's on my mind," Drummond said. "Adrian has heard about the legs. I won't lie to you. I know Adrian personally, and I wanted to keep this from him. I studied at Pittock, you know. Adrian and I both did. We were best friends." Drummond fingered the purple stone on his Pittock class ring. "ALS is an awful disease. Adrian can't move or speak. But he could make a donation that would make Pittock his progeny. I invited him to convocation this fall, and I want to keep him as far away from this business as possible." Drummond was quiet for a moment. "I'm worried that he's going to withdraw his gift."

"We'll figure something out," Helen said. For the first time in days, she was on solid ground. She knew how to handle this kind of the crisis.

Drummond raised his coffee mug to hers. "To the difficult beginning and the bright future."

"The bright future," Helen repeated.

"The college really is lucky to have you." Drummond toyed with his fork, staring at his white china plate. "We need someone who can talk to the students and handle people like Adair Wilson. I didn't see that when the board made their decision." He looked up. "Friends?"

The waiter appeared to place a three-tiered tray of tea sandwiches in front of them. They both started as if a tiny UFO had landed on their table. Helen laughed, and a smile pulled at Drummond's mouth, making him look almost boyish. He cast his eyes upward as if to say, what a strange world we live in.

"Friends," Helen said. She chose her next words carefully. "I was eavesdropping in the quad. You know you should never do that."

They both chuckled.

"I heard the students saying your son used to date Carrie Brown, the one who transferred to UMass."

She could not bring herself to place Wilson in Drummond's crosshairs, but there had to be something to discredit her accusations or ground them in reality—however misperceived.

Drummond's smile disappeared, as though a cloud passed over the sun.

"I'm sorry," Helen said quickly. "That's student gossip, and it's none of my business." For a moment she thought Drummond was going to concur: it was not any of her business. She knew better. Students lied.

He closed his eyes and said, "No. You should know. Ricky and Carrie Brown did have an understanding. They were intimate. I did not approve. Carrie wanted a relationship. Perhaps she wanted to marry. I don't know." Drummond moved his plate to the center of the paper placemat, then exchanged the dinner and desert forks so the smaller implement was on the outer edge of the place setting. "I would never sanction him using a woman like that," he went on. "I also felt it was not my place to meddle, especially since the relationship was consensual. Carrie was twenty-five. She was not a child.

"I think that's why she transferred. She's starting a new life without Ricky. I'm not proud of how my son treated her. But there is one thing I know: Ricky was home with me that night." He did not need to say which night.

"That's not what I was asking," Helen said.

Was it? She felt a sudden chill despite the warm breeze.

"Hornsby even checked my computer. Ricky was logged onto an online video game. He talked to his friends on the computer all night."

An IP address in Pittock.

"Now that my wife has passed on," Drummond said, "Ricky is my pride, my life. He's my world. He would never hurt anyone."

Chapter Seventeen

Every student at Pittock was someone's pride and joy, Helen thought, as she settled back at her desk. They certainly were hers. Sometimes she thought it was her great failing: the people she cared for the most were kids she watched from a distance. Boys like Labrador puppies tearing up the grass with their cleats. Girls like preening swans, adorning the steps of the library. She knew only a dozen by name, but she loved them all in a distant, distracted way.

She opened the file from the Devotees of Boston. The email began with the words WE ARE NORMAL typed in all caps by Blake, the president and webmaster of the Devotees of Boston. In the email, he had pasted long threads from the web forum. Some were dated. Most included multiple voices.

The first threads that Helen read struck her as a cross between a disability rights forum and a fetish website. A participant named GothGrrl33 wrote, "How hard is it to install a fucking wheelchair ramp? We are talking about people's human rights here." In response, Gimpy_Hal wrote, "I love your casts. Last time, I couldn't take my eyes off them. Atrophy sets in after only a week. Thank God!" Helen was about to delete the message, when she came to a post Blake had flagged with the words, READ THIS ONE. The post, by someone named Cutter_01240, read, "You will always be alone, because you are a mule."

Helen's phone rang. The caller ID listed "V-Theater Costume." Adair's office. She ignored it and read on.

Scanning the email, Helen found the next post by Cutter_01240: "Your fetish is inherently a lie. You pretend. Even your most devout followers are "wannabes." You mules. You mules. I will cut the tendon from the bone."

Another read, "You took her away from me. You liars. You say you want and yet you hide behind your diseases and your excuses. But you don't know my need, and how I made her right. Can you feel the saw?"

Helen called the Devotees of Boston.

"I'm surprised." The man on the other end of the phone sounded petulant. "Most people don't care. We're not sick, you know. We have a right to be treated like human beings."

"Right," Helen said. "Can you tell me a little more about your group?"

"We're a social group for amputees, devotees, and wannabes. We want to be amputees or be with amputees. But everyone treats us like freaks. Just because I get off on being in my wheelchair, doesn't mean I deserve to be stalked by this fucking psycho. So I feel safe when I'm in my chair. So I like to get my dick sucked when I'm on wheels. Does that make me a pervert?"

Yes. That was as good a definition of "pervert" as Helen could imagine. She said only, "You don't need to share the intimate details with me. I'm calling to find out what you know about the Pittock legs and what you think I can do for you."

"Get this guy. Bust him. You have to do something. The police don't give a shit about some 'perverts' in Boston. But this guy is writing from *your* town. His screen name is Cutter_01240. That's *your* zip code."

"That's the zip code for all of Berkshire County. Mr....?"

"I'm not giving you my last name."

"*You* contacted me. I don't know how much I can do for you, but the first thing I need is your real name."

There was a long silence. Blake cleared his throat.

"What do you want?" he asked. "What do you really want? How do I even know who you are?"

"I don't want to play games, Blake. We are getting hundreds of calls about this. If you have something to tell me, do it now."

"You don't get it! Everybody looks down on us. Do you know what would happen if my work found out about me? That I use a wheelchair when I'm not at work? The guys at the mill would fucking beat the crap out of me. If I talk to you, you have to swear none of this is going into the papers. Do you know what would happen if this guy Cutter finds out I've been talking to the police? I don't know what he'd do. Shit, maybe he's someone in our group. Maybe I know him already. I won't talk to you unless you swear no one is going to find out."

"I'll do my best, but if you have information that leads to the killer, I'll have to tell the police."

The next thing Helen heard was the dial tone. When she called back the phone rang, but neither Blake nor his voicemail picked up.

She leaned back in her chair and wrapped her arms around her chest. A glass of water on her desk threw a long shadow. Autumn had arrived. Convocation was approaching. Fall term students were already arriving on campus, lugging suitcases and greeting each other with squeals. Their parents, hugging them goodbye, trusted that Pittock College would keep their children safe. Up until a week ago, Helen had been certain the college would do that. Now she wasn't sure.

Chapter Eighteen

He slammed his hand on the desk. He was at home watching Internet pornography, irritated by banners that flashed at the top of the screen. "Live hot girls want to talk to you! More Asian action! Trans-Girls!" He did not want to talk, and he did not want to read the inane comments posted by other viewers.

On the screen, a girl with a below-the-knee amputation touched herself. How could she lose a foot and not amputate above the knee? It wasn't finished. It was too long. He wanted to crack the knee joint. He wanted her prone. He wanted to strip away the banners and the comments—"Big tits! She's hot!"—and have her alone in a gray room.

He clicked through the website, looking for another video. They were all so inadequate, brightly lit and overly coiffed, all the girls trying to look like supermodels. Even the midget amputees—those mules!—wore lipstick and black lace panties. Watching them was like trying to lick water from a sponge. The need was so strong, and everything on the Internet was a sham. He wanted something real. He needed Helen Ivers.

Angry, he stomped from the house. He wasn't sure where he was going. Then he saw her.

She stood in the space between the art building and Pittock's small art museum, examining the sculpture in the center of the courtyard. The sun illuminated the bronze. It was a Rodin, a muscular male torso without arms, legs or head. He had walked by the sculpture a thousand times. Certainly she had too. For a moment, they both paused and looked at it as if for the first time. She smiled at him.

"Amazing work," she said.

"I do a little sculpting myself." It was thrilling to come so close to the truth, right there in the open. "Nothing as dramatic as this, of course," he added.

Who would take the arms? Who would take the head? That was just butchery.

"I'd love to see your work sometime," she said.

She stepped closer. Did she know? She looked like Mother, and Mother always knew everything without speaking. It was the way of women of quality. Carrie and the whores in Battambang screamed, "Do it, do it, do it" as he took them.

Ivers just blinked slowly, and said, "Well, I guess I should get back to work."

Did she know? Could she already feel the phantom pain where her legs had been?

"Me too," he said.

Oh, he had work to do! He'd been distracted, but everything was clear now.

❧❧❧

The night was hot. He could smell the warm earth and dry foliage as walked to the asylum. When he arrived, he found the deepest asylum well and lifted the trapdoor, hoping that Carrie remained submerged, held down by her leather jacket. Still, he knew enough about death and physics not to hope too fervently. Shining his flashlight into the depths, he saw her floating face down, her clothes bubbling around her bloated body. The smell of putrefaction rose from the water. He could not believe he had been so careless. Luckily, he'd arrived in time. No one had been here.

Earlier that day, on a casual walk around the asylum, he had seen the equipment he needed: a pile of heavy chain, the links as thick as a girl's wrist. He flicked his flashlight off until he neared the spot where the chain lay, then turned it on to find the rusted metal in the underbrush. The asylum was a remarkable place. It took everything, and yielded everything. He pulled a pair of pristine work gloves out of his pocket, and began lugging the chain toward the well.

Fortunately, it was not a solid length. The section he grabbed was a manageable ten or twelve feet. If he needed more, he could go back. Once he returned to the well, he opened the trapdoor again. He flashed his light down on the water, memorized the location of Carrie's body, set the flashlight down, and cast the heavy chain into the well.

The splash echoed in the dark woods. No one was nearby. When he turned his light on the water again, Carrie had disappeared except for one corner of her shirt, which floated stubbornly on the surface like a fallen leaf. Panting from the exertion, he returned to the pile of rusted chain, pulled another section to the well, and dropped it in. This time, Carrie disappeared entirely.

"Good bye," he whispered. He turned back toward the road, whistling as he walked. The Pittock woods were beautiful at night, and he felt almost giddy. The need was bubbling up inside him. Unlike Carrie's body, the need would always rise again. He had work to do.

He hoped his next kill would lessen the need, at least make it tolerable for a few days while he waited for Helen Ivers. Careful not to let his footsteps crackle in the underbrush, he moved through the moonlit trees. The homeless camp was located three miles from the asylum, near an abandoned shoe factory. He needed to get there before the moon set below the trees.

Everyone in Pittock knew about the homeless camp. The Pittock Gazette reported on the deplorable conditions about once a month. Men living in filth. Women raped and prostituting themselves. Drugs. Alcohol. There had once been an outbreak of tuberculosis. It shocked all the liberal do-gooders but, except for the occasional reporter, no one came out there. Certainly no one of quality. Certainly not at night.

He could smell the homeless before he saw them: urine, body odor, cigarettes. Mules. The smell rose from the very ground. Cigarette tips glowed in the darkness. He pulled the hood of his sweatshirt over his head. He did not have to disguise himself well. These people were so drunk and insane they wouldn't recognize their own mothers. They would certainly not know who he was. Still, they might offer a description, enough to alert Hornsby that an outsider had trespassed.

A few men sat by a campfire, one of them eating out of a can. In the darkness, he heard a woman's voice, shrill and self-important.

"Don't look at me. I'm pissing," she yelled, as though she had any right to privacy while she lived in filth.

He moved toward the voice. In the dark, it was hard to determine the woman's age, but she had long hair like a girl. She wore a pink halter top, and had long, slender legs, which were folded up around her as she hunkered, bare-assed over the ground. She would do.

As he approached, he could see the shadow between her buttocks or perhaps it was excrement smeared up her crack. *Filthy mule.* The woman was talking to herself, at least no one else was visible. She hadn't noticed him.

"Why are you always looking at me? I'm fucking Princess Diana," she yelled. "In that big, white limousine, but you think you can fuck me? Don't look at me while I'm pissing."

She continued to rant, still squatting.

He took a towel from the poncho pocket on the front of his sweatshirt. He had one chance. He lunged and clasped the towel to the woman's nose and mouth. At the same moment, he slammed his knee into her back. Her face hit the ground, and he fell on top of her, his hand still pressed to her lips. He had planned on suffocating her. He was patient. She would thrash. He just had to wait. Three minutes. Maybe less. Then she would go limp.

Now she was writhing. He had not counted on her madness. She was half-naked and snaking out from under him, like an animal worming out of the slaughterhouse chute. She must not get away. He brought one knee up and dropped it onto the back of her neck. Her face hit the ground again. This time, he released the towel to keep his hand from being smashed between her face and the ground. She gasped. Before she could draw in breath to scream, he pulled the back of her head up by the hair. Some essential piece of cartilage snapped. He felt the grind of bone on bone. She went limp.

Making Carrie on the railroad tracks had been half seduction. Even though he had been furious with her, she was still his, and she had wanted it in the end. In the last ecstatic moment, when the train crossed her legs and her scream arched into the sky, Carrie had said yes. The homeless woman just cracked and went limp. It was like pulling the wing off a chicken. He waited for the rush of pleasure, and felt nothing.

He stood and kicked her ribs. Then he bent back down, and shoved a handful of zip-ties in the pocket of her bra. Recoiling at the touch of her flaccid body, he lifted her to his shoulder and began walking. She would do. The amputation was gory and joyless, performed in the asylum in a cell in one of the men's wards. He tried to focus on the anatomy of the woman's legs, to remember the crisscross of tendons over the knee, the exact pressure needed to saw the bone. He was training for the ultimate surgery, for Helen's surgery. Somehow it did nothing to make the process appealing. Beneath his saw, the woman was just meat. He was done with corpses. He was done with mules.

Chapter Nineteen

Helen was in a hotel in upstate New York when Drummond called with news about the torso. She had spent all day with a group of wealthy alumni, touring their homesteads and complimenting their charitable works. All things considered, they were a congenial bunch, but Helen found their self–congratulatory conversation both dull and depressing. These men and women had everything, and yet their lives seemed to pass in a drab mirage of country club socials and ballet recitals.

She had been glad to return to her hotel and the small pleasures of room service and television. She was just opening a bottle of vodka from the mini bar, when the phone interrupted. It was almost 10:00 p.m. If it was business, it was an emergency. Helen picked up.

"They found the body," Drummond said.

Helen fumbled for the remote and switched off the television. The hotel air conditioning was fierce, and she felt an additional chill. "Where? Do they know who?"

"It was a woman from the homeless camps, like Hornsby expected. Apparently, she was drunk and high. Hornsby thinks it was a suicide. She tied herself to the tracks and then passed out. While she was unconscious the train came and her torso… you don't want to hear details, do you?"

"Just tell me what I need to know."

"The body was... transported. When the train stopped to unload in Pennsylvania, one of the workers smelled something coming from the car. It's not that unusual for the trains to collect... debris from the tracks. When they found her, local police contacted Hornsby. It was not difficult to identify the connection. The medical examiner in Holyoke will look at the remains, but I think it's clear what happened."

Clear? A woman ties herself to the train tracks, binds herself so tightly the plastic straps rip her thigh apart. *Nothing is clear.* Helen wrapped the phone cord around her fingers and watched the tips of them turn gray.

"What a violent death," she said.

"They think she was mentally ill." Drummond chose his words carefully, as if the proper vocabulary could mitigate unpleasant images. "They found the same kind of ties in her undergarments."

Helen exhaled deeply. She felt like the breath came all the way out of her soul. She should have been relieved. If there was no foul play, then there was no danger to the students on campus. If there was no danger to the students, their PR problems were disappearing. She would go back to the capital campaign for which she had been hired. She could rebuild her life like Terri recommended. A bowling league. A book group.

"I don't want to minimize this," Drummond said. "But I'm glad. A young woman has died because she was mentally ill or addicted to drugs or both. That is a tragedy, but it is an isolated tragedy."

Helen ran a hand through her hair. *It could have been Eliza.* "Hornsby agrees? He thinks it was a suicide?"

"He's certain of it."

Helen was silent, staring at a painting of lilies on the wall.

"Helen?" Drummond's voice was kind. "I'm sorry this was your first experience at Pittock, but I am glad to be working with you. We could not have gotten through this without you. *I* could not have gotten through this without you. I've missed you."

Helen hung up the phone. The hotel room felt empty. On the street below, a siren announced another tragedy. *Another tragedy and another.* Her mind filled with voices. *He's certain of it. A suicide. I could not have gotten through this without you. They don't let boys like Ricky Drummond go down for anything.*

Helen lay on the bed, but as soon as she closed her eyes, visions of Eliza filled her mind. Visiting Eliza. Fielding her panicked phone calls. Cajoling her to bathe, to take her medication, to stay in the house. Then driving the streets of Pittsburg, searching for Eliza's familiar form: a mountainous woman lumbering down the sidewalk, speaking out loud to no one, occasionally rifling through debris in the gutter.

Helen rose and pulled on a silk sweater to ward off the air conditioning. It was nearly closing time at the hotel bar. There were only a few patrons loitering under the neon Budweiser signs. Helen caught the eye of a man playing Keno.

"Winning?" she asked.

"Born to lose," he said.

"Maybe I could change your luck."

Upstairs in his room, Helen slipped out of her clothes.

"I got to turn on the TV," the man said, apologetically. "I'm on a business trip. I probably shouldn't be doing this."

Helen lay down on top of the covers. She spread her legs. In the back of her mind she saw Eliza sitting on the doctor's examining table. The familiar conversation: why hadn't Eliza taken her medication?

"It hurts in my bones," Eliza mumbled.

Helen tried to focus on the man taking off his trousers. Now he was leaning over to kiss her.

"It hurts my bones." Eliza's voice got louder, although her face remained incongruously expressionless.

Helen had replayed the scene a thousand times.

Again she was asking the doctor "Is there anything stronger?" She was thinking about Vandusen. She was thinking about the president. *In your absence we realized the position of vice provost was redundant.* Again the doctor was saying, "I could give her an injection of haloperidol. It's an older drug. The medications she's on target individual sites in the brain. Haloperidol has a wider effect."

"Do it." Helen spoke out loud.

"You sure you're ready?" The man from the Keno machine asked. He seemed uncomfortable with his good luck. He wanted her, but was waiting for Helen to change her mind. The TV clamored in the background.

"Go," she said.

She closed her eyes. Behind her eyelids, she saw Eliza's doctor, a handsome man in his late thirties. Laugh lines at the corners of his mouth hinted at a sense of humor, politely tucked away. His ring finger was bare. *This is my whole life. Every moment is created by Eliza. Every moment is ruined by Eliza.*

"Give her something. I don't care."

"It has more pronounced side effects," the doctor said. "You don't have to decide now."

"Do it."

"Haloperidol has helped thousands of patients, but many have reported side effects. I can give you some literature, and you can talk this over with Eliza. Give it some thought."

"Do it."

The man shoved into Helen.

"Can you feel that?"

Helen's eyes followed a crack in the ceiling. The man thrust his pelvis against hers.

"Harder," Helen commanded. She had to get out of her memories.

She was in the examining room.

"No. No. No." Eliza was standing up, shaking her head violently. "I don't want it. They use it to torture the prisoners. They shoot them full of neuroleptics because they don't believe in the system."

"Who, Eliza? What system?"

"The Soviets. Tell them I believe in the system. It will make my face close up. And it hurts to sit down. It hurts to stand up." Her voice got louder and louder. "It rips me up inside. It takes my soul away."

Helen rolled up Eliza's sleeve to reveal her bloated arm. "You will take it."

The nurse swabbed Eliza's skin. Suddenly, Eliza leapt from the examination table, stumbling into a cart, sending syringes and tongue depressors scattering to the floor. Looking around frantically, Eliza grabbed the biohazard disposal box from the wall. Its plastic mooring shattered, scattering red plastic fragments like drops of blood. Eliza pushed the box into the nurse's chest.

"I'll give you AIDS!" she bellowed. "I'll stick you in the eye!"

The nurse dropped the vial and needle, and tried to grab Eliza's wrists. Eliza was neither strong nor agile, but her bulk gave her an advantage, and she swung the plastic disposal box, knocking the nurse onto the table. Eliza raised the box to smash it over the nurse's head. Helen threw her arms around her sister's back, pinning her in an embrace.

"Hold on, little sister," she whispered. She kept repeating the words. "Hold on."

Slowly, she felt Eliza's body relax.

"It's me. It's Helen."

For a moment, Eliza was motionless. Then the plastic box dropped to the floor. Eliza turned to face Helen and slumped in her arms.

"I would never hurt you, Lizzie. I would never let anyone hurt you."

Out of the corner of her eye, she saw the nurse exit the room and return, a minute later, with the doctor and two orderlies.

"I love you, Eliza. Take the shot."

On top of Helen, the man grunted and thrust. He had forgotten his inhibitions. His hips pumped faster and faster. The TV roared. A commercial for dish detergent, then for antiseptic hand wash. The weather outside was seventy-five degrees and clear. Helen couldn't feel the man inside her, only his weight crushing her chest. She could not breathe. *Help me, Helen.*

She pushed the man off her and staggered to the window, fumbling for latches she hoped would be there. She needed fresh air, but the windows did not open. She turned, her back pressed to the glass. The man too was standing. The condom sagged like a sheath of dead skin.

“Get out.”

“I’m sorry. What happened? I didn’t hurt you. I didn’t.”

“I don’t want this,” Helen gasped. “It won’t help.”

Chapter Twenty

He sat with Hornsby in a corner of Washington Park, a quarter acre of grass circling a plastic play structure. The day was hot. The shade of an oak tree only changed the color of the heat. Hornsby was sweating. He feared it was not just the heat that turned the police chief's face into an oily, red pool. Hornsby sat on the edge of the park bench, clasping and unclasping his hands.

"This isn't right. I can't do this." Hornsby drew a deep breath. "The medical examiner's report came in today. The legs don't belong to the same woman. It's the wrong blood type. The injuries don't match. The legs belonged to a young woman. The body they found is probably thirty-five, forty. This makes things worse, not better. Now we have two dead women and no explanation."

He wanted to shake comprehension into Hornsby's skull. He wanted to grab Hornsby by the neck, to press his thumbs into Hornsby's arteries, to feel the pulse panic in his throat. Hornsby still thought he could own both lives, the one in which he was a good man and the one in which Alisha lived. Instead, he sighed, as though the deaths weighed as heavily on him as they did on Hornsby.

He let the silence speak, then said, "I was talking to Dr. Le Farge today. He said the first test group returned for their annual check-up. One hundred percent remission. In most cases, there was no sign that cancer had ever been present. They're starting the next round of tests in October."

He let the words hang in the air.

"That's amazing," Hornsby said. "If I could have Alisha whole, healthy..."

"I can count on your cooperation?"

Hornsby's bloodshot eyes darted back and forth like those of a frightened animal. "What do you mean?"

"I told you. I want the legs to match."

Hornsby slumped. "You know I can't. If we don't investigate this, more women might be killed." Hornsby was pleading with his own conscience. "We thought it was just an isolated instance. We can't ignore the new evidence. You can't be asking for that?"

He had to be clear. "I've already bought Alisha's way into the trial, and I'm prepared to pay your expenses and hers. But I could pull her. I could tell Dr. Le Farge she died. I could tell him you had second thoughts."

"You wouldn't." Hornsby's voice cracked.

On the other side of the park, a woman appeared pushing a stroller. Beside her, a child of about four jogged along the sidewalk.

Very quietly, he said, "I am offering a guarantee for Alisha. She gets a place in Tier 1 of the study. She gets the full treatment. She gets to *live*. But her life is worth a great deal. You said you would make this go away."

"That was before the second body." Hornsby looked frightened. "Why do you care so much?"

"I care about Pittock and how we look to the rest of the world."

"You know who did it." Realization swept across Hornsby's face like a curtain opening on a stage. The police chief stood up. “I will not cover up a crime. You have to tell me who did it.”

Across the park, the woman with the baby stroller put a protective hand on her child’s head, though she wasn’t really worried. She trusted the police. They protected her sleepy town. Or so she thought and would always think. The world was full of mules.

“Don’t be ridiculous,” he said. “If I knew who did this, I would tell you. Case closed. That’s what I want. I just want this out of the media, and the fastest way to do that is solve the crime. It helps you. It helps Pittock.”

He waved to the mother. She waved back.

“Plus, you already said yes.” He stood, putting a hand on Hornsby’s shoulder. The muscles in Hornsby’s back twitched. “I’ve already bought Alisha’s place in the trial. If the city council finds out, you’ll never work again. Not here. Not as a cop. Not anywhere. You can’t afford the COBRA on that insurance plan and the Mass plan won’t cover additional treatment for Alisha. In six months, you won’t be able to afford a morphine drip while she dies in the one-room trailer you’ve moved her into. She’ll die in agony because you wouldn’t help her.”

He moved his arm around Hornsby. An embrace. From a distance, the gesture would look friendly, a kind companion offering comfort before leaving his friend to private grief. He leaned down and whispered, “Before she dies, wherever you go, I’ll find her, and I will tell her. You could have saved her life, spared her suffering, but you didn’t, because you were proud.”

“People will ask…”

“There is only one question that matters. How much pain can Alisha bear?”

Chapter Twenty-one

To Helen's frustration, Hornsby had summoned a crowd of reporters to the small cinderblock building that housed the Pittock Police department. By the time she arrived—also at Hornsby's behest—they'd formed a wall in front of the door, and she had to muscle her way through. Once inside, Hornsby brushed off her request for a conference.

"I wish you had contacted me earlier," she said.

"Come outside," he said. "I'm only going to say this once."

Before Helen could stop him, he was out the door.

"Sorry," Margie the dispatcher called from her seat behind the counter. "He's in a mood."

The only thing left was to stand at Hornsby's side and hear his news. It was the same story Drummond had told her, only delivered with more vehemence.

"We are certain of our findings," Hornsby spat, as though doubt and uncertainty had been the fault of the gathered reporters. "This concludes the case. We are grieved by this tragic accident."

He sounded angry, not sad, and Helen briefly wondered if he'd wanted a bigger win. Had he wanted to arrest a serial killer? Did he secretly hope this was the last in a rash of unsolved killings across the country? Had he seen his name in lights? It was hard to imagine, given his bloodshot eyes and stooped shoulders, but maybe he had ambitions.

Helen tried to look both serious and pleased, and when it came time to shake Hornsby's hand for the cameras, she placed her other hand on his shoulder. *See?* She smiled at the assemblage. *We're great friends.*

But they weren't. Later, she sat in her office, the phone tucked under her ear, with Terri on the other end.

"There have got to be *real* answers." She'd just finished telling him about the discovery of the body. She sighed. "I'm not satisfied."

"Why not?"

Helen gazed out her window. The sidewalks that crossed the quad were packed with students toting bags and wheeling micro-fridges. She thought she saw a keg go by. They were so unruly and so charming. She wanted to gather them up in the cafeteria, bar the door and stand guard until she knew they were safe.

"There was that guy from the devotees group…"

"You think he has something to do with this?"

"Patrick confirmed it. The posts in the devotees' forum came from campus."

"Do you have records of who uses the school computers and when?"

"We tried, but they were made under a public user name. The school's got an account for community members and students who forget their password. They whole town knows it. Username: Pittock. Password: College. Anyone can log onto those computers."

"You know," Terri said. "the Internet is like other people's sex lives. Poke around long enough, and you'll find something hideous. Any day. Anywhere."

"Thanks for that uplifting insight."

"You could just leave this to the police."

"Isn't it my job to keep the college safe?"

"Yes, but it's the police department's job to solve crimes."

"What if they're not?" Helen spoke quietly. "What if they're not looking into this? They're saying it's a suicide. They're saying she tied herself to the railroad tracks and just waited for the train to run over her. I can't imagine someone doing that."

There was a long pause filled with Los Angeles traffic on Terri's end of the line. "Helen, of course you can imagine that," his voice was gentle. "That's what Eliza did."

It wasn't exactly what Eliza did, though it was close enough.

"You went through a lot with Eliza," Terri went on. "It's bound to color your perceptions."

"You think I'm going crazy, like she did."

"I think you want a rational explanation, even if it's an awful one. I think it's easier for you to accept an act of violence than to figure out why a young woman would kill herself. Why Eliza killed herself. Why no one could save her. Not even you."

There was a rational explanation for Eliza's suicide. Terri had given it to her a year and a half earlier. He hadn't meant to. He'd just been talking, trying to shed some positive light on Eliza's madness in his own academic way.

"She's not altogether crazy," Terri had said. "The Soviets *did* use neuroleptics to torture people, haloperidol, in fact. There was a big senate investigation in the 70's." Terri had an encyclopedic memory. "Turns out, the Soviets were giving large doses to political prisoners. The only problem was that the US was doing almost the same thing to their mentally ill."

If he had known what was coming, he would not have spoken so casually.

Now Terri's voice startled Helen out of her thoughts. "You should drop this, Helen. Let the police handle it. Get on with your life. Do something else. What else is going on? There has got to be something."

The only thing Helen could think of was Wilson, her muscular body, her ozone-blue eyes. Helen rested her head in her hands after she hung up the phone. *Adair Wilson.* The police were lackadaisical, and Drummond was too mired in hometown loyalty to see it. Terri thought she should drop the whole thing. Even the press was losing interest in the Pittock legs. But Wilson still cared. She could not possibly believe the story about a mad woman's suicide. Wilson had to be puzzling over the same disquieting facts. She was walking the same campus paths. She was seeing the same students blithely amble across campus, fearing for them and guarding them with the same watchful gaze.

Chapter Twenty-two

By three o'clock that afternoon, Helen had been sitting at her desk for hours, staring at a stack of budget requests and thinking about her conversation with Terri. Thinking about Wilson. Thinking about the legs. This brought her no closer to an answer. She wasn't even sure what the question was. It was like the night after Eliza died. Helen had sat in her kitchen, her head in her hands. *Why? Why?* But the question was bigger than why. It was how? How do I live in a world where this happens? How can the world bear so much suffering and not buckle and crack?

Helen stood up. She had to go back to the woods. She had to see the train tracks, the stones around them, and the earth that had absorbed a young woman's blood. To know how it was possible nothing had changed. A woman was butchered in the woods and the world simply went on living. The biology department wanted test tubes; the soccer field still needed re–sodding. The media would move on to the next sensation. The story would fade from the public eye. The students would go back to drinking and dating and occasionally studying for midterms. Quite possibly, the identities of the victim and killer would remain a mystery. She headed down the hall. There had to be something there, some clue to what happened and to whom.

"Where you going?" Patrick asked, as Helen hurried past his desk.

"It's a gorgeous day. I'm taking a walk."

Her face must have given away her intentions.

"Whoa!" Patrick stood up. He was a husky man, and he took up all the space between his desk and the wall. Several file folders scattered to the floor. "Not in the woods. It's not safe out there."

Helen turned. "You typed the press release. 'No fear for our students' safety.'"

"'Provided they take reasonable precautions,'" Patrick quoted.

Helen raised the back of her hand as she continued out the door. They were all lies. What reasonable precautions could they take? Living in a town of three thousand in the Berkshires should be precaution enough. She heard Wilson's voice: *There is no procedure for this.*

Helen crossed Barrow Creek, pausing at the top of the foot bridge that led from the campus to the athletic fields. She rested her hands on the wooden railing. Before her, Arcadia pond spread out in a smooth mirror, right up to the dam. Then the pond tumbled down the corrugated concrete onto the rocks below. Helen could see the Ventmore theater and the windows in Wilson's office. A figure appeared in one of the dormers, barely visible behind the reflection of sky on glass. She thought she saw a hand raised in greeting. Helen waved back and continued on her way. There was another bridge she needed to see: Carrie's bridge, as the students had begun calling the railroad bridge in the forest beyond campus.

It took her several minutes to find the footpath

between the groomed trail and the crime scene. When she emerged in the clearing by the bridge, a shiver ran down her spine. The surface of the tracks shone like the edge of an ax. Helen felt a sharp pain in her legs as she imagined the girl's last moments, the weight of the train like the end of the world.

Every hair on her body lifted as she walked up the gravel mound where the tracks ran. She forced herself to scan the ground. She even walked onto the bridge, tiptoeing across the ties, and stopping every few feet to look down at the creek bed. There was nothing there. Only ghosts. Finally, she gave up and headed toward the asylum.

As Helen expected, the police had removed the orange flags planted by the student search team. To her satisfaction, they had collected the scraps of trash—or evidence—that the students had marked. Now the area looked like any other patch of forest, only without the litter. She could have been in a calendar: New England Seasons. This would have been July, although in fact it was already August. But the printers would have saved August, September, and October for pictures of fall colors. Helen walked through the leaf litter, distracted by thoughts that veered like swallows.

The path she followed led past the main asylum, to a cluster of outbuildings, no larger than park bathrooms. Most had lost their roofs. Two were covered in ivy. She was about to turn around, when something stopped her. A movement in the bushes behind one of the buildings. Just a flicker. A footstep.

"Hello?" Helen called out.

No one answered.

Helen took a few steps forward. Every hair on her body raised a fraction of an inch higher. She saw nothing but a few remnants of asylum equipment so rusted and overgrown it was hard to imagine what function they'd served. Suddenly, the bushes before her exploded with movement. Helen screamed.

Blood pounded in her ears like a drum. She turned to run. Then she looked up and caught her breath: ducks. Four ducks, of a mottled black and white, had flown from the ivy, startled by her approach. They took off like passenger jets on a short runway to land a few meters away, then waddled back in her direction.

"I don't have anything for you." Helen's voice trembled. "You should be in the pond."

She took a step forward. *The pond.* The word hung in the air. She heard wood cracking, then the sound of a door hitting a wall. For one sickening instant she thought she had tripped. Then she was falling, helplessly falling.

Helen's mind did not have time to conceptualize what happened. Only her body knew that she hit ice-cold water and went under. She had been drawing in a breath as she fell. Under water, her chest convulsed, trying to expel the water, but each cough brought in more. She flailed, pulling herself upward. Something held her down. Her feet were trapped, her ankle wrapped in a death grip. There was no air. There was no air.

Help me, Helen. Help me. It was Eliza, and Helen was back in the kitchen. The memory rushed into her mind like the water rushed into her lungs. She tried to push it away. Part of her knew she had only a minute, maybe two, to break the surface or she would drown.

But the memory held her down. She was staring at the floor, the blood. *Eliza!* Helen dropped her phone. Her phone! She had to call the hospital. *Help me!* Except she couldn't scream. The pain in her chest was excruciating. She kicked frantically. Her leg was still trapped.

Her head expanded and she grew dizzy. She opened her eyes. The water was ultra clear. It didn't hurt anymore. She watched a trail of bubbles dance past her eyes.

I'm dying.

Then the bubbles rushed down in a great column. A figure shot past her like an arrow. Poseidon with his trident. She felt her ankle released. Then she was at the water's surface, coughing. The pain in her lungs returned along with the panic. She vomited mouthful after mouthful of water, until her whole body was wracked from exertion. At least she was breathing.

Finally, her coughing subsided and her gasps became regular breaths. She was not swimming. Someone was holding her, treading water behind her. They were in a stone chamber, perhaps ten feet by ten. The chamber was entirely filled with water. Helen could not touch the bottom.

Above them a trapdoor hung open, letting in a shaft of blue sky. It was only four or five feet away, but there was no ladder, no ledge. The walls of the chamber were rough without footholds. There was no way to leap from the water to the sunlight. She had to get out. She began to struggle. Strong arms held her close.

"Relax," her rescuer said. "I've got you."

I've got you. An arm, like an iron band, encircled her waist. Her rescuer's legs pumped rhythmically, keeping them both afloat. The water around them felt warmer. The skin pressed against hers was hot.

"Who are you?" Helen turned her head.

It was Wilson, her short, blonde hair plastered to her scalp.

"I heard you scream. I came running."

"We can't get out," Helen said. She felt the room closing in around her. Something was touching her under the water. Something was brushing past her leg. She kicked violently. "Get it off me."

"It's just reeds," Wilson said. She tucked her cheek against Helen's, holding Helen's head still. Helen could feel Wilson breathe. "It's just an old spring well. Just plants and clean water. There's nothing here except you and me. Look." Wilson kept one arm wrapped tight around Helen's waist. With the other hand, she cupped a bit of water and let it splash back into the pool. "It's beautiful." Her voice was calm.

"We can't get out," Helen whispered. She tried to scream, "Help." There was still water in her lungs, and she began coughing again.

Wilson held her. "You're okay. You're okay." Finally Wilson said, "Can you swim on your own for minute?"

Slowly, Wilson released her.

"Kick off your shoes and take off your jacket. It'll be easier."

Helen followed Wilson's instructions. It was hard treading water. She was out of breath almost immediately. Wilson kept a hand on Helen's waist. In the back of her mind, Helen marveled at Wilson's lung capacity. She was hardly exerting herself.

"Some of these chambers connect together under water. If they do, we can swim to another room. There may be a ladder."

"There's more than one of these... rooms?"

"They're supposed to be secured. They were *supposed* to be drained and filled, but, yes, there's a network of chambers."

A moment later, Wilson disappeared under the surface. She was gone for so long, Helen feared she'd been trapped in the reeds. Then she emerged, shaking her head. She tried several times, but each time she said no. There was nothing but the sides of the stone wall.

"Can you touch the bottom?" Helen asked.

"At the edges, yes. In the middle it goes deeper."

Helen thought she saw a shadow of fear cross Wilson's face. "Are we trapped?"

"Never."

Wilson moved Helen to the side of the chamber, then shot up into the air, arms raised, her head thrown back. She caught the ledge of the trapdoor with her fingertips. In the sunlight of the opening, Helen could see every muscle on Wilson's arms strain as she pulled herself up. *There is no way.* Then she saw Wilson's body lift a fraction of an inch. And another. As gracefully as a gymnast on the high bar, Wilson pulled herself through the opening and disappeared.

Gone. Like a vision. The water around Helen was as still as a mirror.

"Help," Helen called out. "Come back."

Wilson reappeared. "Give me your hands."

"I can't reach you."

"You're going to have to jump and grab my hands."

Helen tried. "I can't do it."

She had a vision of waiting while Wilson got help. Could she tread water that long? Could she bear the dark water beneath her? *What if she doesn't come back?*

"You can, Helen. Jump."

This time, Helen felt her hands touch Wilson's. Wilson's hands closed around her wrists with vise-like grips. The assent was awkward. Helen's pant leg ripped on the side of the trapdoor. Her blouse was plastered to her body. She had lost her shoes.

"Are you okay?" Wilson asked, once they were seated on firm ground.

Helen could not speak. She buried her face in Wilson's shoulder, squeezing her, afraid the ground would part and the dark water swallow her again. Uncaring of impropriety, she clutched Wilson's body, needing to feel her skin, her hair, her heat. She had to know she was alive.

Wilson held her, firmly and easily, as though they'd been embracing all their lives.

"It's okay. I'll take care of you." Wilson spoke softly into her hair. "Students used to go swimming in those wells. Lebovetski told me that. Even when the asylum was operating, the students would throw down a rope ladder and rafts. They'd take a few beers in plastic coolers." Her voice was calm and cheerful. "Some of the wells have ledges or shoals, so you can sit and watch your friends. That was before the asylum closed and they boarded up the wells."

"Why are they here?" Helen whispered, still clinging to Wilson.

"The wells? I don't know," Wilson murmured. "We'll have to ask Dr. Lebovetski. You know he would *love* to tell us."

"I could have died." The reality of her near miss washed over Helen like more dark water.

"I know," Wilson said.

Before Helen realized what was happening, Wilson's lips were on hers. Their teeth collided. Their lips parted. Their tongues touched, and Helen felt an electric charge run down her spine, not dispelling the cold but moving through it like a shooting star.

A second later, she pulled away.

Wilson said, "I know. I'm sorry. I shouldn't have," and Helen said, "I'm your boss. I am the president of this college." But in the moment before she recoiled, Helen had felt the shooting star drop deep into her womb, leaving her body limp and light, as though she'd swallowed a night full of stars. *I want you.*

Wilson's short-sleeved shirt clung to her like a bathing suit. Water glistened on her skin.

"I'm sorry," Wilson said again.

"I don't know what I would have done if you hadn't come." Helen was shaking uncontrollably, and didn't know if she could walk.

"That trapdoor should never have been open," Wilson said, her expression darkening. "The asylum is falling apart and things are supposed to be secured. The historical society and a DOT maintenance crew come through here every couple of months to make sure everything is boarded up."

They sat in silence for a few minutes. Then Wilson said, "My bike is over there."

She helped Helen to her feet, keeping a protective arm around her waist.

Wilson's bike turned out to be an Indian Chief Roadmaster. Every inch of chrome on the exposed engine gleamed in the sun. The leather seat was as smooth and warm as skin. Even drenched and shaken (and not particularly fond of motorcycles under the best conditions) Helen had to admire the artisanship.

"Here." Wilson took a helmet off the back and laid it on the seat. Then she stroked Helen's hair out of her face, and placed the helmet on her head. Inside the helmet, Helen smelled Wilson's cologne, not the candy scent of women's perfume, nor the tang of men's aftershave. Something rare and expensive.

Wilson mounted the bike in one graceful motion. Helen struggled into place behind her. Her body sank into the leather seat and into Wilson's back. Wilson drove carefully. In a few minutes, Helen was back at the Pittock House.

"Do you want me to come in?" Wilson asked.

"I'll be fine. Thank you."

Helen intended to shower and get back to work, but as soon as the door closed, she was overwhelmed with exhaustion. Climbing the stairs felt like a dream. Every step was a monument. Every second stretched into eternity. When she lay down in bed, sleep took her like a sudden, blessed end.

Chapter Twenty-three

It had been afternoon when Helen left Meyerbridge Hall. When she woke, it was after dawn the next day. She had slept so well that it took her a moment to remember her ordeal had been real. It felt like a dream, half remembered and harmless.

When she came to her senses, she called Hornsby to make sure the wells had been properly searched. She also told him to call the emergency DOT contact, to make sure they were securely covered.

"Don't worry," Hornsby grumbled. "Adair Wilson called me yesterday. We've got it under control."

Wilson must have been discreet in her explanation because Hornsby did not seem to know anything about Helen's fall. Helen also omitted that detail. A dramatic event like that could define the first year of a president's office. In a small town like Pittock, it could define a life. Helen could imagine twenty-plus years of store clerks calling out, "Now you stay away from the wells."

When she went into the office that afternoon, she asked Patrick to send Wilson a bouquet of flowers.

"Roses?" he asked.

"God, no. Something polite. Carnations."

"Those are funeral flowers."

"Is Dr. Wilson going to know that?"

Patrick folded his arms over his barrel chest. "Don't let Addie fool you. I bet she knows all the flowers and all the anniversaries from paper to platinum."

"This is all too complicated." Helen put a hand to her head in mock despair. "Get her a seasonal assortment."

"And the card? What do you want it to say?" he asked.

Helen didn't know. She could not tell him to send the flowers without a card. That was too mysterious.

"Thank you for your continued efforts to support Pittock College?" Patrick suggested. It took Helen a moment to realize he was teasing her. "Don't worry," he added quietly. "She told me what happened. I'm not going to talk about it."

"Ah."

"How about just 'thank you,'" Helen instructed.

"Here you go," Patrick said, looking at the florist's website. "You can choose a poem. Guaranteed to fit on the inscription card. How about this one?" Patrick chuckled as he read. "Life is full of ups and downs but every day the world goes round, I thank the Heavens that I found, a friend as true and kind as you."

Helen remembered the water burning in her lungs, the thrust of Wilson's legs beneath her, their kiss, the trance-like sleep she fell into after she returned to the Pittock House. There was nothing she could say in an FTD card.

"I'm going for a walk."

"Be careful," Patrick said. "Watch out for the wells."

"To the coffee shop, Patrick. I'm going to the

coffee shop."

After her coffee, Helen headed back to the office, but coming around the corner of Boston Hall, she ran into Professor Lebovetski. It seemed he was everywhere, his only goal in life: to intersect busy people, who lived in this century, and delay them with interesting, but useless, details from the past. Helen could not turn and go the other direction. It was too late.

"I heard you had a little adventure in the asylum springs, lovely lady," Lebovetski said in his accented English.

Helen sighed. Apparently, Wilson's discretion only went so far.

"Don't be mad at Addie, she couldn't help it. She knows how fascinated I am by the happenings on Hospital Hill. I won't tell anyone. It is inconvenient for a woman of your stature to suffer such an indignity. You're not the first, though." He raised a boney finger to the sky. The lecture was beginning.

"Dr. Lebovetski, I apologize. I am on my way to a meeting."

Lebovetski spoke, as though he had not heard her. "You have just received a groundbreaking mental health treatment, circa 1820." He chuckled. "Unfortunately, you received the most authentic application of this practice possible."

"What do you mean?"

"You see it all started in 1788 with King George III."

We're never going to get back to the 21st century. Helen said, "Walk with me, professor."

Lebovetski fell into stride beside her, walking surprisingly fast for an old man with a cane.

"You see, King George fell ill, mad, delusional. An ambitious doctor, Francis Willis, cured him with miracle science. Only, by modern standards we would call it torture. He beat the king, bled him, tied him to a chair, and poisoned his food. He raised blisters on the king's legs so painful, the king screamed to God to kill him. Then, one day, the king was cured."

Helen raised an eyebrow.

"Ah, you are skeptical, and so you should be. We would call the king's condition porphyria. Toxins in the blood build up and cause symptoms including delusions. Then the attack subsides, and the patient is fine. But Francis Willis took full credit. He had cured the king. After that, doctors all over England invented their own miracle cures, and one was the dunk. They believed fear produced new thought patterns."

"New thought patterns?"

"Terror. Tie a madman up. Blindfold him. Then walk him across a trapdoor and drop him in ice-cold water. It would scare the madness right out of him. Funny thing is...occasionally it worked. How about your thought patterns, Dr. Ivers? Did you experience the critical shift?"

Helen thought of Wilson leaping from the water like Poseidon rising from the sea.

"They were more humane in the asylum," Lebovetski went on. "They would help their patients climb down into those wells. Bathing tanks, they called them. And then submerge the whole body—except the head—in canvas slings. Most facilities used indoor bathtubs, but there is a network of fresh water springs around the asylum, and the founding doctor believed in fresh water. Fresh water, fresh air, and the knowledge that beneath the patient's feet the well went down to the heart of the earth. That, he said, was the miracle of the Pittock Asylum. No other facility could provide such a blessing."

Helen shivered as she thought about the dark water reaching down and down.

"And of course, if it doesn't work, there's always the green bower."

"That's all very interesting."

"The mausoleum in ivy. It's so romantic really. Wilson had to tell me. You can't blame her. The asylum is fascinating. Did you know that in 1942…"

They had arrived at the administration building, soon to be renamed Meyerbridge Hall. It looked like Lebovetski was going to follow her in.

"I must get to my meeting," Helen said. She put a hand on the old man's shoulder. This happened to professors. Their whole life they were obliged to speak. Then they retired, and no one wanted to listen. It wasn't fair, but she still had work to do. "Thank you. We'll talk again."

"Dr. Ivers, there is something I was hoping you could help me with."

"Yes?"

"I have borrowed some documents from the rare book room, and someone is asking for their return. Insisting. I was promised a quarter to review those materials at my leisure. Could you use your presidential powers to persuade the library to give me my time? I am an old man. I might die before I got those books again." He spoke with a smile, as though letting Helen in on a joke only she would understand. "I can assure you, there is no one whose need is greater than mine."

Chapter Twenty-four

It was easy to keep track of Ivers when she was in Pittock. She was often in her office, bent over her paperwork or talking on the phone. Or she was at the Craven where she ate dinner when she bothered to eat at all. Or she was at the Pittock house, where she drank alone at the kitchen table, sitting in the glow of the stove light, never bothering to turn on the overhead light.

Tonight she was working. From his bench in an arbor near Meyerbridge Hall, he could see her at her desk, her fingers pressed to her brow. Finally she rose, disappeared, and, a moment later, reappeared in the doorway of the office.

He stood to follow her. There were always a few professors hurrying back and forth from their offices, always a couple of townies cutting across campus. It was easy to bow his head, carry a brief case, and pause at the campus map as he contemplated Ivers's next move. He was just another figure in the crowd.

Each time he followed her, he drew closer. Closer. Closer. Until tonight he could smell her scent drifting in the air behind her, a hint of freesias and fresh dry cleaning. He followed her all the way to the Pittock House, then slipped behind the neighboring building to wait.

At the Pittock House that night, Helen showered and changed into jeans. She took a shot from the nearly empty bottle on top of the fridge. Then she stepped out into the humid night. There were more people out than usual, mostly returning students, a few townies. In the entrance to one of the alleyways, an old woman held a hand-lettered sign. "Fortunes, $10."

She waved it at Helen.

"Do you want to know?" the woman called after her. "Is there love in your future? Will you live a long time?"

Helen put up her hand to signal disinterest and kept walking. The woman staggered to her feet and started to follow. Helen turned. "I'm not interested."

The woman's clothing smelled of cigarettes and sweat. She was missing most of her teeth. "You would be interested if you knew what I know." The woman was at Helen's elbow. "I can see things in your future. Just ten dollars. I see a man who loves you. He's watching you even now."

Helen stopped. She had a twenty-dollar bill in her pocket. "Here. Take this."

"I don't want your charity." The woman spat on the sidewalk. Helen followed the trajectory of the spittle and thought she saw blood in the phlegm. "I'm not begging."

"Fine." Helen pocketed the bill. "Good night."

She walked quickly away, the sound of the woman's muttering stuck in her mind like voices from a locked room. *Your charity. Ten dollars. He's watching you.*

Then—in a voice so clear, Helen thought the woman must have called after her—she heard, *I know who killed Carrie Brown. I saw her face in the water.*

Helen turned, but the woman was gone.

She was still glancing over her shoulder, certain the fortuneteller would reappear, when she arrived at the Craven Bar and Grill. Helen descended, pausing to let her eyes adjust to the dimness. Booths lined the subterranean bar, and a few locals and college students huddled in their vinyl embrace. Helen caught snatches of their conversation. The Pittock legs were on everyone's mind, but so too was the start of school and the promise of another rainstorm.

"Helen. Over here."

The friendly greeting surprised Helen. Drummond was seated in a booth on the other side of the bar. He gestured to her. When she slid in across from him, he said, "I thought you might be here tonight."

"I'm here every night." Helen forced a smile.

"You look worried."

"A woman tried to read my fortune on my way over here. She said someone killed Carrie Brown."

"That's Crazy Sully. A local character. Every Pittock student gets their fortune read by her once. Sends most of them straight back to the campus ministries. Don't go to her if you want a rosy future. Did she enlighten you?"

"What?"

"Did she tell you who did it?" Drummond watched her intently. Helen guessed he was gauging how seriously she took the fortuneteller and thereby how gullible she was.

"Of course not," Helen said.

She signaled the waitress and ordered the fish and chips without consulting the menu.

"I guess I'm not the only one who missed dinner at home," Drummond said.

"Were you working late too?"

"I was visiting Adrian Meyerbridge in Boston. You remember, Adrian, our key donor. Everything is set for his convocation visit. He is excited. I asked him to say a few words. He can speak using an eye-tracking computer, although he'll probably record his speech ahead of time. We don't want him to feel like the only thing he has to give is money. I hope you don't mind."

The convocation line-up was the last thing on Helen's mind. In fact, Drummond's announcement reminded her that she too should craft her speech for convocation.

"Now if we can just keep Wilson from feeding some lurid story to the press," Drummond said, "we might be able to keep Adrian from rethinking his gift to the college."

An hour later, Helen and Drummond were headed back to their respective homes. The street lamps had come on, and the sky was a dark periwinkle. Drummond touched a brick on one of the buildings as he walked.

"The flood of 1996. The Barrow Creek flooded all the way to here. Washed away the damn on Arcadia Pond. Destroyed the downtown, but we recover. Don't we?"

"Sometimes," Helen said.

They had started up the hill that led to Pittock, when Helen spoke again. Her mind was full of questions, but one bothered her more than the rest.

"Why," she said slowly. "Why don't you trust Adair Wilson? I know she is young and fiery. Is there something else?"

"That fiasco in the woods wasn't enough?"

Helen thought about it. "Not really. No."

The search had been irresponsible, but Wilson had a point. Hornsby's search seemed perfunctory. Helen shared this with Drummond, and before he could protest, added, "I'm not saying Hornsby's search *was* perfunctory. I'm just saying that an outsider, who doesn't know Hornsby, or understand police procedure, might be concerned. You disliked Wilson before that, however. I saw that the first time I saw you two together."

"Am I that transparent?" Drummond did not seem upset. "I guess I am. It's not a secret. I don't like Adair Wilson. She's demanding, pushy, unrealistic, and a very talented performer. I have seen her woo the college board. They swoon over her, just like her students do. If that doesn't work, she'll do whatever she has to in order to get what she wants. She will not lose. It's dangerous. You know how she got her first teaching job?"

Helen shook her head.

"She was sleeping with her married thesis advisor. Somewhere along the line, Wilson came to believe this woman was going to leave her husband. When the advisor didn't, Wilson blackmailed her." Drummond shrugged. "Wilson told her advisor that if she didn't get a teaching post, Wilson would sue for sexual harassment. The woman had her whole career to lose. She was married to a dean at her school. She didn't see a way out, so she agreed, and got Wilson a job at Duke. Two years later, Wilson is here."

Helen thought of Wilson's arms wrapped around her, Wilson's legs thrusting beneath the water, keeping them afloat. *If it wasn't for her, I'd be dead.* Helen brushed her hand along the top of a boxwood hedge. In the distance, thunder rumbled, promising to break the heat.

"And that's not the only time Wilson has threatened someone's career. She did it here." Drummond hesitated. "She did it to me."

"To you?"

"Wilson had fallen for a woman who worked in the physical plant, an Egyptian immigrant, named Anat. I guess Anat was very beautiful; I never met her. She was also illiterate and barely spoke English. She was a devout Muslim, and would have been horrified if she knew Wilson's intentions. She was naïve, and thought Wilson was just a friendly face on campus. Since Anat preferred not to interact with men, they became friends. Of a sort.

"Long story short, I made some unpopular budget decisions that affected the theater. Shortly after the budget went through, Wilson took Anat to the police with a story about *me*. I had never even seen Anat, but Wilson said Anat came to her in tears after I chased her down in the woods and tried to sexually assault her."

Helen felt Drummond's eyes on her face as she passed beneath a street light.

"She really did that?" Wilson was reactionary. Could she be that malicious?

"I can guess what you're thinking," Drummond went on. "People cover up sexual indiscretions all the time, but I would never do something like that. Hornsby did a thorough investigation. He said there was so little evidence, the college should fire Wilson for making false accusations and wasting police resources. Unfortunately, she'd just got tenure, and the faculty association fought for her position. We've had an uneasy truce ever since."

Together they passed through the Pittock gates. *I too have seen the angels and trembled.* Helen had a momentary urge to slip her arm through Drummond's. Instead, she said, "I trust you." She did. Despite what Wilson believed, the man with Helen was no predator.

A few minutes later, they arrived at the Pittock House. Helen was about to say good night, when Drummond cleared his throat.

"I want to get something off my chest," he said.

"About Dr. Wilson?"

"About you. I have not been entirely frank with you, Helen." Drummond lowered himself onto the bottom step of the Pittock House porch. He picked up a holly twig and twirled it between his fingers. "I knew your V.P. at Vandusen."

Helen had never talked to her V. P., Josh Price, about her personal life, but information traveled from secretary to secretary, colleague to colleague. It was impossible to keep one's personal life entirely secreted. And Josh had been there when the restructure was announced. *We are sorry to say that Vandusen will be losing its vice provost.*

"Please sit." Drummond dusted the step beside him. Helen sat, eyeing him warily.

"I don't mean to intrude, but I know a little bit about your commitments in Pittsburg, your sister and her death."

"I am fully prepared to take on my duties at Pittock." Helen's voice was sharper than she intended.

“I’m not worried about that. Josh says you will be the consummate professional now that she is… dead. I just know that you chose us because you needed an escape. I want Pittock to be the refuge you hoped for.” Drummond spoke without looking at her, as though to give her privacy.

“What do you know about my sister’s death?” Helen asked.

“I know it was a suicide. Is there something else?”

Part of Helen wanted to lean her head on Drummond’s shoulder. She wanted to tell him everything about the kitchen covered in blood and the black holes where Eliza’s eye should have been.

“I found her,” was all she said.

“Do you want to talk about it?”

Helen shook her head. Drummond allowed a long silence. He held the holly twig in his hands, gently, like a bird or a delicate sculpture. Helen had the urge to touch his face. She had slept with older men. Their patience was dull, but the power she wielded over them was intoxicating. She was fifteen, maybe twenty, years Drummond’s junior. He would be so grateful and it would refute everything he was now, his dead wife, his son, his honor. She would rip it from him, and he would bless her.

Helen stood up and tucked her hands in her pockets. She was far too smart to sleep with her own provost. Still, she liked Drummond. If she could not lose herself in his bed, perhaps she could find herself in his friendship.

“It was a real pleasure, Marshal,” she said. “Our evening together. Will you be okay crossing campus? We mandated a buddy system, and you’re walking without a buddy.”

She held out her hand to help him up, and he took it, smiling at her teasing.

"Don't worry about me. I'm a tough old soldier."

He looked like a soldier in his gray suit. His clothes spoke of dignified economy, of purpose. The only flash of ostentation was the class ring he wore in honor of Pittock. Helen stood at the door and watched him amble across the quad. Just as he was about to disappear behind a building, he turned and waved, the light from a streetlamp catching in the stone and sending a flash of violet through the darkness.

Helen turned back toward the house. Tucked on the top step was a rock the size and color of a skull. Underneath it rested a sheet of notepaper. "Call me if you need anything," the message read. "I'm thinking of you. Adair."

Chapter Twenty-five

On the day of convocation, every building on campus sported banners bearing the school colors—purple and orange—and the school's motto. Helen was glad the banners were in Latin. Given recent events, she would have liked to retire "I too have seen the angels and trembled" in favor of something more cheerful. Perhaps, something like Smith College's "In virtue one gains knowledge" or Harvard's simple "*Veritas.*"

If nothing else, Helen was glad to see workers installing the new sign for Meyerbridge Hall. The sun hitting the reflective metal letters was almost blinding. She smiled. The wheel of college donation turned. Buildings were bought. Names were expunged. New donors appeared. That, at least, was a constant.

Drummond stood on the top step of the newly-renamed hall, surveying the work. He waved when he saw Helen.

"It's official," he smiled. "Let me introduce you to Adrian."

Looking at Adrian Meyerbridge, it was hard to see him as the same man in the portraits taken for Westin, Meyerbridge, and Gray Investments. He looked like a science fiction creature, seated in a heavy motorized wheelchair. His hands were splinted. A clear plastic tube attached to a plug in his throat. His head rested between two headrests, and he stared motionlessly at the screen attached to his wheelchair. Occasionally, his caretaker, a young man with an orthodox beard, would swab a bit of saliva from Meyerbridge's lips.

"Hello" the computer screen spoke. Meyerbridge moved his eyes across the screen, blinking when he reached the key he wanted to activate. The computer spoke a prerecorded greeting.

"We are very glad you came," Helen said. "Your words will be an inspiration to the students."

"Ha." Meyerbridge blinked the sound, and the computer spoke. He added, "They just want to get drunk."

Helen suppressed a smile.

"Laugh," Meyerbridge said. "I joke."

Together Helen, Meyerbridge, and his caretaker went to the theater to make sure Meyerbridge would be able to move around the stage. There, Helen found Patrick, who had been missing from his usual post. He was lying on the ground, with his head and shoulders under a makeshift ramp. Helen knelt down and tapped his foot. Patrick maneuvered himself out from beneath the ramp. He had a cordless drill in one hand and his purple Bluetooth in one ear.

"What are you doing, Patrick?"

"You told me to make sure everything was ready for our guest of honor."

Helen pointed at the pile of scrap wood by his side. "And that?"

Patrick shrugged. "The Ventmore isn't accessible."

"So you're building a ramp."

Patrick was a wonderful secretary.

"It's not up to code, and this is *not* in my job description," he said. "But I know what you're thinking.

I *am* the perfect secretary."

Helen was just about to introduce Meyerbridge when a noise stopped her: footsteps descending the metal staircase at the back of the theater. She turned to see Wilson gliding down the steps.

Perhaps Wilson had dressed for the evening's convocation. Or perhaps, Helen thought, there was no reason—besides broad-spectrum eccentricity—why, today, Wilson had traded her military garb for this outfit. Half punk rocker, half rising heiress. She wore flowing, black pants and a corset-like top, emblazoned with a red dragon. A slash of red lipstick cut her lips in half, and her hair was spiked. She had replaced the cubic zirconium studs with a cascade of crimson jewels that brushed her bare shoulders.

"Dr. Ivers," Wilson called. "I didn't know you were coming over."

Helen stared, transfixed. Wilson looked like a high-fashion model, aggressively beautiful in an outfit no real woman would ever wear.

"How are you?"

The costume was ridiculous, but she could not look away.

"Dr. Ivers?"

Helen pinched the back of her hand.

Arriving at her side, Wilson added, quietly, "I'm sorry about the other day, at the well." She looked down with an embarrassed shrug. "I was just so relieved that you were okay."

Helen glanced at Patrick, who was punctuating his conversation with a buzz of the cordless drill. She opened her mouth to speak, but she had lost her train of thought.

"Dr. Ivers?" Wilson said again.

"You saved my life," Helen said. "I'm just not supposed to..." She waved her hand vaguely in the air. There was nothing she could say out loud in the busy theater, and what would she say anyway? I'm not supposed to kiss the faculty? I didn't want that? Her arms had tightened around Wilson's back and she had held her as fiercely on land as when she had thought she was drowning.

"Can I talk to you?" Wilson asked. "About something totally different. Will you come up to my office?"

Don't go. Even as her rational brain repeated the details of Drummond's story, her body remembered Wilson holding her in the water. Her eyes traveled the length of Wilson's neck. The back of her hand stung where her nails had pinched the skin. *She saved my life.*

Inside the office, Wilson had been grading papers. On one side of the desk, a few papers bore a profusion of comments. Helen could read "Good job" in large letters, and then a long note in slanting handwriting that ran all the way off the page. On a chair sat thirty or more papers, waiting for their notes, and a pair of reading glasses. It did not look like Wilson had made much progress. Helen was struck by an inexplicable tenderness, something about the glasses and the intractable stack of papers.

"How are you?" Wilson asked. "I was worried about you after your fall. I didn't see you on campus."

"I was busy," Helen said.

"Of course. Thank you for the flowers. And I'm sorry about the trouble with the stage. I've been trying to get the college to address it for years."

"I'll ask Marshal to look into it."

"Mr. Drummond is not a fan of the theater program, although this isn't about the theater; this is about equal access and the law."

I made some unpopular budget decisions that affected the theater. Helen searched Wilson's face. She was serious, not vengeful. *Then again, she's an actor.*

"The money is always there in the spring when they do the budget," Wilson mused. "Then, in the fall, it's gone. We can barely afford costumes."

"I'll have Patrick schedule a meeting with your department."

"It doesn't matter." Wilson leaned forward. "That's not what I want to talk about. I saw the news about the body. They think it's solved. Done. Over."

"Yes."

"What do you think?" Wilson asked.

You should drop this, Helen. She heard Terri. *Get on with your life.*

"I think we should focus on our jobs and let the police do theirs."

"Do you really trust Hornsby?"

"Of course," Helen said. Her eyes met Wilson's. She knew it was a lie.

That evening, Helen sat on the Ventmore stage waiting for the convocation ceremony to begin. The students filled the theater, whooping, as if they had no cares in the world. Behind Helen, the professors sat in their regalia, including Wilson in a voluminous black gown, adorned by burgundy chevrons. When it came time for Meyerbridge's speech, his caretaker wheeled him to the front of the stage. The speech was prerecorded on his Tobii computer, so he simply sat in front of the microphone while the computer read his words.

When he finished, Helen stepped into the bright light, surveyed the crowd, and delivered her speech. With convocation over, Helen joined Drummond, Meyerbridge, and many of the faculty for Champaign and hors d'oeuvres in the faculty club. Wilson was not there. Helen stayed with Adrian until he had been introduced to Professor Lebovetski, who was happy to expound on the history of disability rights and the Pittock Asylum. Meyerbridge's questions suggested he was genuinely interested, so Helen left the two together.

As the gathering thinned, around 9:00 p.m., Helen returned to Meyerbridge's side.

"This was a wonderful night," he said.

Helen thought she could read wistfulness in the computer voice. She could tell he had prerecorded the next part because the computer spoke fluidly.

"Mr. Drummond may have told you I have been debating whether to give my estate gift to the ALS foundation or to Pittock. This night has been wonderful, but I have decided to give my gift to the ALS foundation. No one should have to give their convocation speech from a wheelchair or hear it from one. The students of Pittock deserve the world, and the world starts in the body. I want to speak with my own voice. I am so sorry."

Tears ran down Meyerbridge's motionless cheeks. Helen knelt down and put her hand over his. His hand was cool and unnaturally smooth.

"It's okay," Helen said.

From across the room, Drummond caught her gaze. It was a question. She shook her head. No. Adrian Meyerbridge would not be the financial deus ex machina that saved Pittock College.

Chapter Twenty-six

He looked down the hall that led to the faculty club ballroom. Near the entrance to the building Meyerbridge sat in a pool of light, waiting for his attendant, who had just stepped out the door.

It was so easy. It hardly even counted. He did not make Adrian Meyerbridge. He did not even kill him. He just reached behind Meyerbridge's neck and unsnapped the collar that secured the breathing tube. Then he removed the tube from the plastic housing inserted in the tracheotomy. It made a moist pop as he pulled it out. A little sigh escaped the tracheotomy and then nothing. The ventilator kept breathing, but no oxygen reached Meyerbridge. His eyes rolled back and forth, growing wider and wider, until the pupils were like dimes. Nothing else moved.

He stayed close, kneeling beside Meyerbridge, one hand resting gently on the back of the wheelchair. A little fluid bubbled at the site of the tracheotomy, and he touched it, warm and moist. It was always fascinating to see the inside come out, even though there was no thrill in this killing. It was just a technicality. He needed plane tickets for Alisha and Robert Hornsby. He needed a few other things for Ivers. And Meyerbridge had so much money he was not using.

When Meyerbridge's eyes stopped moving, he put two fingers to his throat. Nothing. He reattached the tracheotomy tube. Then he slipped into a side corridor. Just in time. The door to the hall opened, and Ivers walked in, wearing a silky, gray dress, her blood-red hair spilling over her shoulders. A vision. So pale. So beautiful. So breakable.

Helen looked up from Meyerbridge's face. The hall was lit with smoky chandeliers, their dewdrops reflecting a scattering of light on the highly polished floor. She looked back at Meyerbridge. He was fine, she told herself.

"Mr. Meyerbridge?" she asked.

She noticed a trickle of saliva at the corner of his mouth. There was a box of tissues in the mesh bag on the back of his wheelchair. She took a tissue and touched the fluid. A noise startled her. She had not heard the ballroom doors open, but Drummond was striding down the hall.

"Adrian," Drummond called out as he strode forward. "Adrian, it has been a pleasure having you with us."

Helen looked down at Meyerbridge. His eyes were open. She thought he was reading his screen, preparing to deliver a message. She thought he was about to speak. Then she was very certain he was dead.

"Adrian!" She shook his shoulder. "Mr. Meyerbridge!"

She took his hand out of the splint and felt for a pulse. His hand felt warm. He had to be alive. She squeezed his wrist, as though squeezing it would bring him back. Nothing.

"Marshal, he's dead." She could hear the panic in her own voice. "Call the police."

She stared down at Meyerbridge. A slight movement caught her eye. A trickle of pinkish blood oozed from beneath the ventilator tube and dripped down Meyerbridge's neck. Suddenly, Helen was back in Eliza's kitchen, on her knees, the smell of bleach burning her eyes. Scrubbing and scrubbing, but the blood would never come out.

Even after the biohazard team had cleaned, she had found blood in the seams of the linoleum floor. The supervisor had run a toothpick along the crack then dipped it in a vial of clear liquid to prove that the house had been thoroughly sterilized. But Helen saw it. She smelled it. Blood in the vent at the bottom of the refrigerator. Blood in the heating duct, just out of sight. *Eliza!*

She wasn't sure if she'd spoken aloud. The hall came back into focus. She was aware of Drummond's arms around her, her face pressed into his shoulder. She let herself sag against his chest.

"This isn't a tragedy," Drummond said quietly. He released Helen. "Adrian was dying. We gave him one last evening that mattered. You gave him a little bit of his life back."

Drummond took the tissue from Helen's hand and tucked it away. He drew his hand over Meyerbridge's eyes, then pressed his lips to the man's forehead. He remained in that posture for seconds, then rose.

"Goodbye, old friend."

❧❧❧

The busyness of death took the place of its emptiness. Young Officer Giles arrived with a notebook in hand. He looked embarrassed as he asked

Drummond to recount the night's events.

"I'm sorry, sir. It's procedure," he explained.

Drummond put a hand on his shoulder. "Of course, son, and we appreciate you doing your job. We just came out here, Helen and I, and found him."

"I left him here while I brought the van around," Meyerbridge's assistant added. "I should have stayed with him."

"He had ALS," Drummond said, more to the assistant than to Giles. "He died because… people die."

After Giles was finished, Meyerbridge's assistant conferred with Drummond about a mortician. Thirty minutes later, an old man in a white lab coat arrived. He brought with him a quiet youth, whom he introduced as his grandson. The boy wheeled a gurney down the foyer, bent over as though already his grandfather's age. The mortician stroked Meyerbridge's hair with a large hand.

"A gentle death." He spoke softly, as though he was concerned about waking Meyerbridge. "A quiet death is a gift, although I'm sure he has done his suffering on this earth."

As though lifting a sleeping child, the mortician slipped his hands under Meyerbridge's shoulders and knees and raised the corpse in his arms. The mortician laid Meyerbridge on the gurney, and was about to wrap a white sheet around him, when his grandson stopped him.

"What's this?" The boy touched Meyerbridge's neck with a gloved finger.

"A little blood," the mortician said. "From the tracheotomy. Just a little blood at the very end."

Chapter Twenty-seven

It was after midnight when Helen headed for home. As she approached the Pittock house, weary and uneasy, she stopped. A dark shape moved in the bushes near the front door.

Helen froze. Her heart raced. Her body told her to flee, but she'd be hard pressed to outrun an attacker in her slim dress and silver heels. And where would she go? There was a security phone mounted outside the alumni building and more of them back on campus. Even if she could evade whoever watched her, she'd have only a few seconds lead time. There'd be no time to call for help. She kicked off her shoes. Her breath sounded as loud as the ocean in her ears.

As she watched, the shape straightened, then separated from the bushes. It was not quite human. Like some mythic beast, it possessed a head and shoulders, but the legs blended into a hulking lump. It lurched along the path, coming closer to Helen.

The sound of squeaky wheels and the rattle of a shopping cart brought Helen back to her senses. Sully, the local fortuneteller, came into view beneath a street light. Helen picked up her shoes, gave the woman a quick nod and then started walking. A few seconds later their paths crossed and Helen heard the woman call out.

"I know you, Miss Twenty Dollar Bill. You don't want to know your fortune, because you don't believe.

You just want to give me your big charity. Your big twenty."

Helen quickened her pace, nearing the Pittock House. Sully had left her shopping cart and was stumbling back toward her.

"No. I don't believe," Helen said.

"Are you the boss?" Sully asked. The whites of her eyes were yellow, and the finger she pointed at Helen was black with dirt. "Boss lady? But you don't want to know, do you? You're too scared to see the future."

"Goodnight," Helen said coolly.

"You need to see your future," Sully said in a sing-song voice.

Helen turned, then Sully was at her side.

"Crystal Leigh Evans? Do you know what happened to Crystal Leigh Evans?"

"I don't know who you're talking about." Helen walked faster. Sully followed.

"Crystal Leigh. The one they found in the train without any legs. Do you know what happened to her?"

Helen stopped. "Is this something from the news?"

"I don't need any fancy newspaper-radio-TV-man to tell me the truth. I see it." Sully made a circle with her fingers and pressed it to her forehead. "I have the third eye."

Helen wanted to snap at her. If she really had a third eye, she did not have to ask these questions. Something stopped her.

"What about Crystal Leigh Evans?"

"They found her in a train."

"Did you read that name in the paper?"

"That's her name, but it's not in any paper. She doesn't even get a name. She don't count. All of us, out at the camp, knew Crystal Leigh. They said it was a suicide. Said she was drunk. I believe it. She was always drunk. But she wasn't on the tracks *that* night. No. I talked to her as clear as I'm talking to you. We was sitting around, and we was talking about those legs. I remember because Crystal broke a cigarette in half, and we said that was what a train did to a body. Snap you right in half like a butt. That's when I saw her floating in the well."

"Who did you see?"

The woman lunged at Helen, holding out her third eye. For a second, Helen thought she saw a purple orb glowing in the space encircled by Sully's black fingers.

"I saw you."

"Get away from me!" Helen ran toward the Pittock House, the asphalt biting her bare feet.

Behind her, Sully ranted. "I saw you floating in Carrie's well. The girl who watched him do it on the train tracks. I saw her floating in the well. The well in my mind." Sully raised the third eye back to her forehead. "I see you. I see how he looks at you. I see how she loves you. I see you go down inside and die. In the dark. In the cave. Underground, where he cuts you. I see you. I see you!"

Helen's heart pounded as she fled into the Pittock House and slammed the door behind her. She checked the lock twice, then hurried to the kitchen and pulled all the curtains, as though shutting out Sully's face could shut out her fears. *She's crazy.* Helen paced around the kitchen. *She's crazy.*

Around her, the house creaked. It was after midnight. She stared at her phone. Who could she call? Hornsby? Helen knew what happened to administrators who meddled in police business. Get in the way too many times, and the channels of communication would be closed. She could call Terri, but he was a thousand miles away, working for a college where the biggest question was did Dean What-The-Hell-Were-You-Thinking sleep with the head of the cheerleading squad? He was in-house counsel, not a detective. As for Drummond, he'd just seen the mortician carry away the body of his childhood friend. Helen tried to remember the number of Charles, the young middle manager from the bar. She had long since discarded the card he gave her.

Helen slipped on a pair of flats and a sweater, picked up her purse, and stepped back outside. There was never anyone she could go to. Only a world full of strangers and the cold hum of an anonymous hotel room. She scanned the area for Sully's shadow and, seeing nothing but the still, lamp-lit campus, she ran to her car.

Chapter Twenty-eight

Helen found a bar on an empty stretch of road that was little more than a shack, attached to a sagging motel. A reviewer on Yelp had written, "Here is where alcoholics go to die." The drinks were strong, the prices cheap, and the bathrooms best avoided.

She parked in the gravel lot that Lucky Tom's Tavern shared with the Cozzzy Inn. Inside the smoky, dim-lit bar, conversation was shouted across the tables. As Helen entered, the bartender yelled to one of the pool players.

"That's dirty pool," the man called back. "Fuckin' scratch on the eight loses. I don't give a shit what the house rules are."

On opposite sides of the bar, two old men argued about the game on television. A crowd of younger men in No Fear t–shirts sat at a table covered with pitchers. One of them caught Helen's eye as she slid onto a bar stool and ordered a martini.

"I don't know if I know how to make one of them." The bartender was mocking her. Helen still wore the dress for convocation.

"It's cold vodka in a glass." She wasn't in the mood for teasing.

"I like this one," the bartender announced to the crowd. To Helen he added, "You must have had a day like mine."

That would be hard to imagine. Helen nodded.

"Bet I did."

***

She had finished her first martini and started on a second when the man who'd first eyed her sat on the stool next to hers.

"You been here before?" He was beginning to slur his speech, the smell of cigarette smoke thick around him.

"No," Helen said. "I'm visiting my mother in Great Barrington. Just couldn't take it, if you know what I mean. Had to get out. Talk to some real people for a change."

He grinned. "You wanna come sit with me and my boys?"

She was just about to say yes, when she felt a hand on her wrist. A younger man had taken the bar stool on her other side. He wore a baseball cap over long hair. Dark brown eyes stared at her from beneath shaggy bangs.

"I'm gonna buy you a drink." The chewing tobacco tucked in his lower lip made his voice thick.

"I'm fine." Helen extricated her wrist.

"Gotta talk to you," the young man said. To the other man he said, "Mind if I borrow her for a sec? I'll give her back."

The other man shrugged and stumbled off his stool. He was drunker than Helen had thought. "Suit yourself. Come on over when you're done, pretty."

The young man took a Coke can from between his legs and spat in it. He spoke quietly. Helen had to strain to hear.

"Those guys are no good. Don't mess with them.

Last weekend they called a stripper out to the Cozzzy Inn. Then two of the guys tried to fuck her. The girl ran down to the lobby to call the police. Manager locked the lobby door on her, didn't want to break up a fight. They were about to beat her up bad when the cops came."

"And you didn't break it up?" Helen asked. She wasn't sure she liked his tone. He was too young to be warning her with such authority.

"I'm not stupid," the man said.

Helen tried to glimpse his face beneath the hair and baseball cap. There was something vaguely familiar in the shape of his jaw.

"What's your name?" Helen asked.

The man glanced up at the bottles behind the bar. "Jack."

"You live around here, Jack?" Helen asked.

"Pittock." He pronounced it Pidick. "You?"

"New Jersey. I'm just visiting my mom in Great Barrington."

"Is that so?" The man ran his thumbnail along the back of Helen's arm. "Cause I'm thinkin' you came here for the same thing I did."

Helen watched him caress her arm. His nails were clean and his hands unworn. He was very young.

"You got a room next door?" Helen asked.

Helen followed the man into the Cozzzy Inn. He opened his second floor door and ushered her inside, placing his hand over hers before she could turn on the light.

"You don't want to see this place in the light."

He put his hands on Helen's waist and kissed her. His kiss was stilted by the tobacco still tucked in his lower lip. His breath was unexpectedly fresh. He moved his hands to her cheeks, cupping her face so lightly she could barely feel his touch. "Do you know me?"

She stared at his dark brown eyes. She hardly knew herself, but in a room like this everyone was the same. She nodded. When she tried to put her arms around him, he grabbed her wrists and pinned them behind her. He pressed his lips to her neck, then whispered,

"I want to make you feel good, but first I need to know: you want to go slow or you want to get fucked?"

Helen wondered at his confidence. "How old are you?"

"Thirty–five." He pressed his face against her neck. His skin felt as soft and hairless as a girl's cheek. His breath quickened

When Helen spoke, she realized hers had too. "I don't believe that."

Still holding her hands, he pressed his hips against hers. She felt his erection, already hard in his jeans, and gasped.

The man chuckled. "Tell me what you want."

Helen closed her eyes. "I want to forget."

The man had the courtesy to pull down the bedspread. Helen reached her arms around him. Beneath his shirt, strapped to his lean ribcage, she felt the outline of a gun. He pushed her hands down.

I've gone too far. Helen had always known she would eventually make a mistake. Like Russian roulette, one chamber was always loaded. Maybe it would be rape. Maybe an attack. Maybe AIDS. But that was the thrill. That was the reason. One chamber was loaded, and when the bullet clicked into place, she could forget Eliza and everything she had done.

The man had stripped her clothing in seconds. He spun her around and pushed her face down on the bed. She heard his zipper release, then felt his hand slide under her body. His fingers grazed the sides of her clit, deliberately teasing. When he removed his fingers, Helen groaned.

"Do you want me?" He leaned over her shoulder. She felt the seams of his jeans biting into her buttocks, the weight of his body pressing her public bone to the bed, the gun against her ribs.

"Yes."

He licked her shoulder and bit the skin at the base of her neck, sending a shiver through her body.

"How do I know you want me?"

"I'm wet."

He slid his fingers inside her, then pulled them out. She heard him lick his fingers, heard him unwrap a condom. Without fully removing his jeans, he thrust into her. She gasped, and he froze for second. Then he lowered his weight onto her and massaged her clitoris directly, keeping time with the pulse of his hips. Her whole body existed between the pressure inside and out. The exquisite pressure made her bladder feel ready to burst. Spirals of orange appeared behind her closed eyes

He pumped faster and faster. Helen felt her body tense in opposition, certain he would climax first and leave her to sit miserably on the toilet, unable to rub out an orgasm or pee.

"Don't stop," she said hopelessly.

"Not until you tell me to." His voice was high with pleasure, high and familiar. Helen had no time to think about that.

"Make me forget," she heard herself say, as if from a great distance. The orgasm exploded in her clitoris and raced like electricity down her thighs, into the palms of her hands, her eyelids. For a second, the world went black.

The man was in the bathroom. She could hear the toilet flush, the sink running. He was probably washing the scent of her off his hands before returning to his girlfriend, or wife, the teen mother of his unintended children. She remembered the skin on his cheek. Perfectly smooth, like a boy's. Of course he carried a gun. He was too young to own that kind of confidence himself.

Helen felt sick to her stomach. She was getting careless. This boy... Was he eighteen? He'd been so forceful, but he had a girl's hands. His voice barely deeper than hers. She searched her memory for some detail that made him older than a teenager. The only recollection she had was of a dean at Vandusen, who'd been disgraced after it was discovered he'd had sex with a seventeen-year-old girl. The girl had told him she was twenty-one. She held a job, rented her own apartment. He broke it off when he learned the truth. It was too late for his career. What would Helen have without her career? She didn't even have her own apartment.

She switched on the light. The room was bleak:

cigarette burns in the curtains, a faded print of a cowboy roping a steer on the wall. The man's wallet lay on a table by the door. She grabbed it and pulled out the contents, not worrying whether he would suspect her of pilfering his money. There were a dozen shoppers' cards, one credit card, and some cash. Then she found his license and saw the photo on the card. Her jaw dropped. She read the print as if it mattered: Massachusetts address, age thirty-five, organ donor, no corrective lenses. Her gaze flew from the name to the photo. She knew those pale, blue eyes.

Chapter Twenty-nine

When the bathroom door opened, the light shone in Wilson's hair like a rumpled halo. She had removed the wig and baseball cap. She carried the jean jacket wadded under one arm and emerged with a summery smile.

Helen looked at the ID again, terrified that what she saw was not real and terrified that it was. She clutched the card. It still read: Wilson, Adair Merrill.

"You always go through girls' wallets?" Wilson asked. Cheerful. Cocky.

Helen crossed the room in one swift motion and slapped Wilson across the face. It was not a hard slap. By the time her hand rose, the better part of her brain was already anticipating her perfunctory hearing before the college board ended her presidency. What could justify hitting a professor? By the time her hand connected, the slap was just symbolic. It was almost a caress.

Still, Wilson drew back. "Why did you do that?"

"Why?" Helen repeated. "What the hell did you do to me?"

"I made you come." Wilson held out her arms, as though she thought Helen might embrace her. "You can slap me if you want, but give me a safe word first."

She was flirting.

"I don't want you," Helen said. "I don't know you. This is a mistake. You had no right." She could barely breathe through her indignation.

Wilson dropped into a chair. "Shit." She ran one hand through her hair. Then she slipped a finger into her mouth and dislodged the roll of cotton that stood in for chewing tobacco. She tossed the cotton into the trashcan. She licked her fingers and flicked the dark contact lenses out of her eyes. She tossed them on the floor, not bothering with the trash.

"Did you follow me here?" Panic rose in Helen's chest. It was over: her career, her livelihood, the respect of her colleagues. In a flash, like an end-of-life vision, she saw herself alone. Who would she turn to when Wilson exposed her? Who would understand this wretched hotel room, the anonymous encounters that, until this night, had not even yielded sexual pleasure? She felt a warm trickle of cum run down her thigh as her body betrayed her.

"Did you come here because I wouldn't listen to your crazy stories? So you could slander me like Marshal Drummond? Is that why? To get something on me?"

Wilson set her jacket on an end table and the dildo rolled out. Her eyes were wide and worried. "I thought you knew. You *looked* at me. I asked you if you knew who I was, and you said yes."

Had she known? Her body had known.

Helen stumbled in her rush to dress. "I would *never*..." She couldn't even finish her sentence.

"But you would with Jack."

Helen froze. Wilson did not have to say anything else. Helen would sleep with Jack. Jack the child. Jack the stranger. Jack the man with chew in his mouth, who didn't take off his boots. But she would not take Wilson in her arms and say, "You saved my life, kiss me again." When Helen looked up, there was a fissure of sadness in Wilson's face.

"Everyone comes here eventually," Adair said.

"You're dressed like a man." Helen fumbled with her bra. A familiar dizziness washed over her. If she panicked now, she'd have visions of Eliza and be cast back into her madness. She pinched the back of her hand, hoping the pain would keep her focused.

"Consider it professional development," Wilson said ruefully. She stood up, and without the aid of hair, wig, or contacts, she was a boy again. Her shoulders slouched. Her bottom lip jutted out. Her whole persona changed. "Watch out for those guys in the corner. They're bad men," she said. Then she dropped back into the chair and was herself again.

"Was that all a lie?" Helen took a breath to steady herself.

With shaking hands, she tried to zip up her dress. Wilson strode over and did it for her, without touching Helen's skin.

"Did you plan the whole thing? Do you come here to... attack women?" Helen went on, uncertain whether her outrage was real or just required.

"I didn't plan anything," Wilson said. "I'm not stupid. Massachusetts may have legalized gay marriage, but out here that doesn't mean anything. There are guys in that bar that would beat the crap out of any dyke who messed with their women. Hell, they'd beat the crap out of their women just because it was Tuesday. But I don't know anything specific about the men in the corner."

Wilson picked up the flesh-colored dildo. "You can keep it if you like." The flirtation in Wilson's tone was a question. *Are you really angry?*

Helen's whole body had given in to pleasure the moment she realized the young man was not going to come until she was ready. Helen felt herself blush. Of course he wasn't.

Wilson tossed the dildo onto the bed. Helen flinched.

"Whatever. I'm sorry." A sad smile creased the corners of Wilson's eyes. "I shouldn't have brought you here."

Brought you here. That was a polite euphemism.

"I saw you at the bar, and I *knew* I shouldn't. I told myself, don't do it. But you're so beautiful, and I fall for powerful women." Wilson shrugged, as though that explained everything. "It's my weakness." She was still flirting, but there was something bitter about it now. "And I thought you recognized me. I thought we were playing a game."

"Why are you carrying a gun?" Helen asked.

Wilson stood and pulled her t-shirt over her head, revealing a tight undershirt. The leather holster rested on the white fabric. She removed the gun and held it out to Helen. "It's a Glock. It's not loaded."

"Why do you have it?"

"I'm from New Hampshire."

"That's not an explanation." The whole scene was absurd.

"My brothers are gun nuts. Anyway, I told you those guys would beat up any dyke that walked into their bar. Here. Look. It's empty."

"I don't want to touch it."

"I have a permit."

"I don't care if you have a permit. You don't bring it on campus, do you?" Helen scanned her memory for Pittock's weapons policy. Then she felt her stomach drop, as though she had stepped off a curb to find herself in freefall. How much longer would she get to play the responsible administrator? She could punish Wilson for bringing a gun on campus. In turn, Wilson could ruin her.

Helen pictured Adrian Meyerbridge sitting in the hallway, watched over by paintings of Pittock presidents. She saw the saliva on his lips. She saw her own hand moving toward the tissue box. Then she saw the blood oozing from his tracheotomy. She saw Eliza. Helen pinched the skin on the back of her hand again.

"Helen? Are you okay?" Wilson returned the gun to its holster. Her abdominal muscles rippled beneath her undershirt.

"Get out," Helen said.

Wilson took a step toward Helen and reached out to touch her hair. Helen struck her hand away. She wanted to plead with Wilson, beg her not to say anything. Even if Wilson intended no malice, she would tell a friend like Patrick. She would swear him to secrecy, and he would swear the next friend until, by word of mouth, the story traveled up the college hierarchy and reached Drummond or the board president. Then there would be negotiations, a contract buy–out, a privacy agreement. On the face of it, Helen would make out well, but when she left campus, in her heart, she would have nothing.

"Don't touch me. Just go."

"Can we talk, Helen?"

"We have nothing to talk about."

Helen moved toward the door, but Wilson stepped in front of her, the gun bulging at her side. *No one knows where I am. No one could guess.* Helen had only Wilson's word that the gun wasn't loaded.

"Please, Helen."

Helen backed away slowly and sat back on the bed.

"I shouldn't have taken you to this shitbag motel without telling you who I was. I thought you knew. You looked at me, and I just...thought you knew." Wilson looked down. "Whatever you came for, I think it was the same thing I did, but you didn't want to do it with me. I fucked that up. I always fuck it up with women I like.

"Don't look surprised. I like you Helen. I know from past experience, I'll mess things up so monumentally you'll never speak to me again." This time, her sadness was naked and raw. "I'm horrible with women. I'm horrible at love. But I am a good teacher." Wilson's lips tightened. "I know Carrie Brown. I know she would not disappear right before a performance, no matter how much she wanted to transfer."

It took Helen a minute to reorient. "You want to talk about Carrie Brown?"

"I don't believe the story about the homeless woman found in the train, and you don't either."

"I checked Banner," Helen whispered. "All the paperwork is in order. Carrie transferred to UMass."

"I checked Banner, too, but have you talked to her? She's not there. And there's something else."

"What?"

Wilson sat on the bed next to Helen. "The trains that run the Berkshire–Western track start in Holyoke and go all the way to Chicago. A few go to the West Coast. You can track them online. The train that came through Pittock the night the legs were amputated... *that* train was in Idaho the day the torso was found. But the legs were found under a train in Pennsylvania. See?

It's not the same train. I think there are two different bodies."

Helen took Wilson's hand and squeezed it. She felt the heat rising from Wilson's bare shoulders. She smelled sex and beer and cologne on Wilson's skin. *This is the end of my career. No matter what happens with the legs, this is the end.*

"Tell me about Anat Al-Fulani."

Wilson put an arm around her shoulder. Despite everything and against all rational thought, Helen relaxed at the touch.

"Anat worked at Pittock as a janitor. She was a wonderful woman. Smart. Resourceful. Hard-working. She had come through so much to get to this country. She was from Egypt and had once been very wealthy. In Pittock, she lived in a trailer behind the asylum. Anat emptied my trashcan and took out recycling for the theater. She got off work at 10:00 p.m. and walked home every evening along Asylum Road. One day, she was cutting across the grounds and was attacked by Marshal Drummond." Wilson didn't hesitate as she made the accusation. "She said he was like an animal. He appeared out of nowhere. His hands were shaking. He was babbling, saying she owed him sex and that he would rip her apart if she didn't shut up and take it. When she ran, he came after her. Luckily, a car passed by. It was one of my students, and he brought her to me."

"Did you go to the police?"

"I did, and they conducted an investigation. It wasn't just Hornsby and his Boy Scouts then. There was another cop, Roger Albon, who took it very seriously. But when it came down to it, Michael Warren, the president at the time, swore Drummond showed up at the Pittock House around 9:30 p.m. Michael was already sick. I think Drummond just told him the story and somehow convinced him. Anat swore it was Drummond. She didn't speak a lot of English, but she wasn't confused. And she was no liar."

"What happened?" Helen asked, her mind racing. Could it have been Ricky? Although he resembled his father, no one would mistake one for the other. Plus, he would have been younger then. Too young.

"About a month later, INS came in the middle of the night, and Anat was deported. The student who picked her up lost his scholarship and went back to Texas. After that, Michael died, and Drummond said there was no budget to hire a replacement."

"And you think all this was a cover up for... what?"

"Someone attacked Anat, and then had her deported. I think that person had something to do with the legs. And the legs are Carrie Brown's." Wilson stood and paced the small room. "The story about the homeless woman is a sham. Whoever is responsible is powerful. They won't get caught if the police aren't looking. Hornsby has turned a blind eye, and Tyron and Darrell can't do anything without his permission. I know Drummond attacked Anat. I thought Ricky..." Wilson ran her hands through her hair. "It just doesn't feel right. It doesn't *smell* right."

It was a relief to hear her own anxiety in another person's voice. Helen felt a wave of tenderness toward Wilson. Still, there were so many layers, so many variables. Terri had told Helen she wasn't thinking clearly. Perhaps Wilson wasn't either. She saw Drummond's gray eyes, his ubiquitous sport coat, his noble bearing. He loved his son, and he loved Pittock.

"I haven't known Drummond long," Helen said cautiously. "But I find it hard to imagine he'd attack a woman. I don't know the depths of the human heart, but Marshal Drummond doesn't raise any red flags. I'm speaking honestly, not as the college president, and not for PR. I'm not scared of Marshal."

"What about Ricky?" Wilson said, her voice bleak.

"I don't know." Fear pulled Helen down like quicksand.

"What if he killed Carrie?" Wilson wrapped around her arms around body like a humble, frightened child. "What if he killed another woman to cover it up? He's still out there. What about my students?"

The same questions were beating against Helen's skull. *I remember because Crystal broke a cigarette in half, and we said that was what a train did to a body. Snap you right in half like a butt.*

Helen stood and held out a hand to Wilson. "I promise I'll do something. Look at me. I care as much as you do. Now go home." *Please, don't tell anyone about tonight. Wait until I figure something out.*

Wilson shrugged on her shirt and jacket. Helen watched as she left, then peered through the window while Wilson descended the stairs and crossed the parking lot. A second later, she disappeared behind the Cozzzy Inn. In the parking lot, mayflies danced like snowflakes under the single streetlight. Wilson was gone as if she never existed, like a dream or a vision. Helen went into the bathroom and cried.

Chapter Thirty

When Helen had cried herself out, she straightened her clothes, retrieved her purse and exited the room, locking the hotel key inside. She would not be coming back to the Cozzzy Inn.

Hers was the only car in the parking lot. It crouched under the single streetlight that illuminated the lot. As Helen approached, she cursed. A flat. Just what she needed. She took out her phone and dialed AAA. As she waited for the automated voice to give her instructions, she noticed that it was not just the tire closest to her. Both back tires had gone flat.

The AAA operator came on the line. "Are you in a safe location?"

Helen walked to the front of her car. The front tires were also flat.

"I'm not sure."

The bar had closed. One pickup truck remained parked in what might have been a handicap spot if anyone had bothered to pave and mark the lot. It looked like it hadn't moved in years. In the front office of the Cozzzy Inn, the desk clerk spoke to a man seated in the lobby. The surrounding forest was dark and motionless. No traffic disturbed the rural highway.

"I think my tires have been slashed," Helen told the operator.

Once the dispatcher had arranged a tow and given her an estimated wait time, Helen hurried to the light and safety of the lobby. *It just doesn't feel right.*

"Checking in?" the clerk asked when Helen entered.

Did he not remember her? Or was "forgetting" the specialty of the house? She explained the situation.

The clerk fumbled with a cigarette pack and extracted a flattened cigarette. He had weathered hands and wore a baseball cap advertising a diesel repair company.

"Dang kids." He held out the pack to Helen. She shook her head. "That's the third time someone's messed with the parking lot this month. Jimmy–O got his truck all keyed up. Then Sally Jenkins left her window open, cause it was so hot, and came out after her shift to see some crazy, old coot pissing in the backseat of her 4-Runner. Right through the window."

The clerk picked up a small, no–smoking plaque from the counter and placed it face down. He lit his cigarette.

"That shit will kill you," his friend said. To Helen, the friend added, "Sorry about your tires, Miss. This place is no good. I only come here 'cause my wife says she can't stand the smell of beer on me. Gotta spend a few hours with this asshole anyway." He jerked his thumb toward the clerk.

The clerk glared at his friend from beneath wiry eyebrows.

"Did either of you see anyone near the black Lexus?" Helen asked.

"Well, shit, a Lexus," the clerk said. "No wonder you got your tires poked. No one drives cars like that around here."

"Did you see anyone?"

He looked away. "Nope."

Helen took a few steps toward the counter, so that she could look him directly in the eye. The clerk played with his cigarette, rolling the glowing tip around the rim of an ashtray without looking at her. He was lying. She was certain.

"Are you sure?"

"I can't see nothing from in here."

Helen looked. Her car stood out like a single player on a spot–lit stage.

"I saw him," the friend chimed in. "Buddy here is a pussy. Doesn't want any trouble with the locals. He saw him too. Some college kid. I didn't get a plate. I figured he was working up the nerve to go see a hooker. He pulled in. Sat in his car. Then left. Then came back about an hour later. I noticed 'cause he never went in the bar, and he was driving this big, yellow truck. More like a Jeep. Bright yellow. Like those Tonka toys my boys used to have when they were growing up."

It was late at night, and he was alone. He flipped through a hardcover book of antique medical equipment. The hemorrhoid forceps. The hysterotome, for amputating the cervix. The tonsil guillotine. These were just toys. He was looking for tools.

Finally, he found the knives. The curved amputation knife of the 1700s, the straight saw of the 1800s (such an innovation, despite the decorative engravings which were a breeding ground for infection). If he wanted to keep Ivers alive, he would have to be more skillful than he had been with the others. But there would be no electricity and limited light. He had to look to the forefathers. They had amputated without blood transfusions, sutures, or anesthesia. Some of their patients had lived. He would sterilize everything as best he could. That was already an advance over technology of the past. She might live for weeks. He dared to hope. Perhaps for years.

Chapter Thirty-one

Helen felt the campus watching her as she walked toward Meyerbridge Hall. There were eyes in the windows of passing cars. Eyes in the darkened windows of the basement computer labs, glinting through the shrubbery. They knew. They saw. It had been Eliza's perennial complaint. "They're watching me." Now Helen felt it too. She had showered at the Pittock House, but she could still smell Wilson's sweat on her skin.

At his desk, Patrick wore a knowing expression, a smile that said, "I see you."

"How are you, Helen?" he asked. "I heard about Adrian Meyerbridge. That must have been a shock."

This is the end.

When Helen passed Drummond's office, Drummond pointed at her. He was on the phone, but he covered the receiver. "Wait."

Helen's blood ran cold. The smell of sex clung to her hair. It was under her fingernails. Her mind raced ahead, looking for an argument in her defense, but there was no defense. She could still feel Wilson's body clasping her from behind. She had wanted it. Maybe she had even known it was Wilson. Maybe that was part of the thrill. One chamber. One bullet. *I want to forget.*

Drummond hung up the phone.

This is it.

But all Drummond said was, "Arts and Letters faculty meeting this morning. Patrick just put it on your calendar."

Helen hurried to her office and closed the door like a woman pursued. *They're looking at me!* Her breath came in deep huffs. She pressed her hand to her chest, as though the pressure could slow her breathing. She was taking in too much air, drowning in it. Her head swam, the oxygen expanding her mind and consciousness until she felt like she filled the whole room. She filled the campus with its many eyes. She felt it, and somewhere far outside her body she heard a whisper. *Help me, Helen. Help me.* This time, it was not Eliza. It was Carrie Brown.

The phone rang, and Helen jumped. She held her breath for a moment, trying to stop hyperventilating, to contract her mind back into her body. The number on the caller ID was from out of town. She picked up the phone. "This is President Ivers."

It was Meyerbridge's lawyer. "Good morning, and good news for you." He had a voice like a genial grandfather. "Everything is in order to the best of my knowledge. Very generous of Mr. Meyerbridge to make this gift, I'm sure. Such a good cause too. You know my granddaughter went to Pittock."

Helen tried to focus. The sooner she could finalize the Meyerbridge gift, the better for Pittock. The college was close to running a deficit. She could do this much for the college. She could at least finalize the gift transaction before she was discovered.

"When can you write the check to the Pittock foundation?" she asked.

"Oh, I'm not the trustee. I drafted the will, but Mr. Meyerbridge's trustee is..." The attorney shuffled some papers. "Here it is." He read aloud. "The entire donation will be granted in unrestricted funds. Investments to be liquidated upon the grantor's death. Established at the request of Adrian Meyerbridge. The trustee is Marshal Drummond, your provost if I'm not mistaken. That will be convenient, won't it?"

"Very," Helen said.

The attorney chuckled sympathetically. "Well that's done, then."

"Wait, I have a question." Helen exhaled. "How do I put this?"

"Say it plain," the lawyer suggested.

"Are you certain Mr. Meyerbridge did not make any provision for a gift to the ALS Foundation?"

"There is nothing in the will. Why do you ask?"

"We talked..."

Helen stopped. There was no point in sharing Meyerbridge's last words. A conversation at a cocktail party would never supersede a legal will. If the college had been on the other end of the situation and the ALS Foundation had laid claim to Meyerbridge's estate, Helen would have taken the issue to court.

"Never mind. I'm sure everything is in order."

At a quarter till ten, Drummond knocked on Helen's door. Together they made their way across campus.

"The faculty will want to talk about the budget, professional development grants, and curriculum," Drummond said as they walked. "We will have to debrief about the legs, of course. I think that is the most important thing: to reassure them that the legs are a closed case. The less they worry, the less the media can feed on their fears. The less attention it will draw to the issue."

"The sooner we can proceed with our real lives," Helen added.

Inside her skull, Carrie clamored for attention. *Help me, Helen. Help me.*

The Arts and Letters affair was a simple meet-and-greet, but Helen's heart raced as she surveyed the crowd in the library reading room. In the back of the room, leaning against one of the built-in bookshelves, Wilson stood with her hands in her pockets. Helen tried not to look at her, but her eyes were drawn back repeatedly. Wilson's presence was commanding. Even her colleagues seemed to move in her orbit. Deferential. Enamored.

She wore her usual cargo pants and t-shirt, but this was no Dockers-and-Fruit-of-the-Loom outfit. Everything she wore was beautifully tailored. The clothing clung to her body in sumptuous gray and beige, as though made of heavy, un-dyed silk. On her fingers, she wore several silver rings. They were hand-forged art pieces, not costume jewelry. When Helen finally met her eyes, Wilson cocked her lips in a faint intimation of a smile. She was gorgeous. And Helen felt Wilson's body pressing into her back, the holster of the gun hard between their ribcages.

At Helen's arrival, the audience settled. Helen outlined her improvements to campus security. She mentioned the discovery of the torso in the Pennsylvania train yard, keeping her description as bland as possible.

"What does this all mean?" one of the professors

asked.

Helen felt Drummond's hand on her shoulder. "What Dr. Ivers is saying is that the mystery is solved. We have every reason to believe this was the result of a tragic nexus of opportunity, accident, and mental illness. The tragedy brought a lot of media attention, but it is over."

Wilson's eyes flared. Her face grew pale.

No, Helen mouthed, her eyes locked on Wilson's.

Wilson relaxed. Beside her, a professor in a tweed jacket stood. "John Hodson. Music and Performance." He gestured toward Wilson. "Dr. Wilson has been very discreet, but I have to bring this up. For three years, the budget has included a $10,000 allotment for theater refurbishments, but by the time the school years starts, that money is always gone. Can you tell us where that money is going?"

"I was just reviewing the budget from last year. The theater got new rigging. That was an expenditure of over $10,000, the largest capital improvement of the season," Helen said.

"That's simply not true!" The professor sounded irate. He turned to Wilson to rally her support. "Is there any truth in that?"

Wilson touched the professor's arm and whispered something. He looked reluctant, then nodded.

"Forget it," he mumbled and sat down.

On her way out the door, Wilson tried to stop Helen. Her fingertips grazing Helen's hand, sent a shiver of sparks across Helen's skin. "Not now," Helen said, and glided past Wilson, speaking without stopping. "I will handle this."

A second later, a hand tapped her shoulder.

Helen whirled, ready to chase Wilson away. It was only old Professor Lebovetski. He stared up at her, his eyes gleaming within wrinkled lids.

"What can we do for you, Dr. Lebovetski?" Drummond had appeared at Helen's side. He put his hand on Lebovetski's back. "How is your research going?"

Lebovetski lowered his voice. "I have to talk to you, but not here. Come to my office in Boston Hall. This has to do with our little 'administrative issue' in the woods. You see, there has been a development, and I fear I am at the center of this new occurrence."

Lebovetski smiled. He was loving every minute of this. To Helen's surprise, Drummond seemed as eager to talk to the professor as Lebovetski was to bend their ears.

Reluctantly, Helen followed the two men to Boston Hall, a small colonial-style house nestled between the library and one wall of the science building. Inside, Lebovetski led them up a flight of stairs. He clung to the railing with one hand. In the other hand, his cane marked each step. When they reached Lebovetski's office, Lebovetski flung open the door. Helen gasped. The place had been ransacked.

"You see, someone has been in my office. They're looking for something," Lebovetski said.

"Have you called the police?" Helen asked.

Lebovetski laughed. "Oh, this?" He waved a dismissive hand at the disaster. "This is just an old man paying attention to the more important aspects of life. To scholarship!"

Lebovetski motioned for her to follow him. With

surprising dexterity, he picked his way across the floor. "I want to show you *this,* lovely lady."

He led them to a door in the corner of his office. Helen had not noticed the door among the clutter of bookshelves and overstuffed furniture. From his pocket, Lebovetski withdrew a key and turned it in the lock. The door opened into another, smaller room. A table rested in the center. Along the walls, stood several chests of drawers. On the floor lay a pair of white gloves. Other than that, the second room was as clean and sparse as the first room was messy.

"Careful," Lebovetski said. "Look here." He motioned to the light switch. "The light is on. I always turn it off." He pointed to the gloves. "On the floor. I would never. But this is what worries me most." He moved to a chest of drawers. "Look how each drawer has been pulled out."

To Helen, the drawers looked closed. Lebovetski followed her gaze.

"Ah, you must think I have gone crazy. Come. See how I push this drawer back. A quarter of an inch. The lock prevents it from coming out more than a little bit, but I always push the drawers in until they sit. Otherwise, you get moisture, dust. A historian knows, a quarter of an inch is a mile when you are preserving old documents."

"Is that what's in here? Old documents?" Drummond asked.

"Yes, documents, and someone has been trying to get into these drawers. Someone has been in my office."

Helen glanced at the open door that led to the larger office and then back at Lebovetski. He was ninety years old if he was a day, and the outer office looked like it had been hit by a tornado.

"This is very interesting, Dr. Lebovetski, very interesting work," Drummond said. "Tell me... which documents?"

"A fine question! I tell you."

Helen groaned inwardly, even as she admired Drummond's patience. Now was not the time to fuel the fire of academic scholarship.

"All the primary research for my grand œuvre, 'Buried Practices: The Unclaimed Dead of Kirkbride Asylums from 1855 to 1955,'" Lebovetski said, warming to his favorite subject. "Doctor's logs. Diaries. Funeral programs. Maps. It is all within."

"Which maps?" Drummond asked. "Where did they come from?"

"The rare book room." Lebovetski's eyes grew brighter. "And someone has been asking for them back, but I will not yield." He carefully pushed each drawer back into its appropriate spot. "Do you think there is a connection between the Pittock legs and this break in?" He looked pleased with the idea. "Two such strange occurrences within a few weeks of each other? Will you help me, Dr. Ivers? I must keep these treasures near me. I have so much work to do."

Drummond bowed to Lebovetski. "Doctor, I must implore you to return these books to the library. At least give us a recording of what you have. They are clearly not safe here, with someone riffling through your office."

"Dr. Ivers?" Lebovetski asked.

Helen glanced at Drummond. He shook his head a fraction of an inch.

"I trust, Mr. Drummond," Helen said. "If he thinks you should return them to the library, I concur."

Chapter Thirty-two

A few hours later, Helen headed downtown, feeling like an adulterer. Darting. Furtive. Guilty. She'd told Drummond she was popping home to check something on her laptop. She had told Patrick she was available by phone, then switched off her cell and dropped it in her purse.

Arriving at the police department, she looked both ways before slipping inside. There she found Chief Hornsby eating lunch at his desk. It looked as though he had lost his appetite, and eating the sandwich depressed him. His uniform, which had been crisply pressed when they first met, was wrinkled.

"What now?" he asked by way of greeting.

Helen remembered that Hornsby's wife was dying and spoke formally, politely. "Good afternoon, Chief Hornsby."

"I'm sorry," Hornsby mumbled, wiping his hand on his pants before extending it to her. "Dr. Ivers. What can I help you with?"

Helen pulled up a chair. "I have some concerns about the Pittock legs. I wonder if you can put my mind at rest."

"Everybody's got some concerns about the legs," Hornsby grumbled.

"I'm sure they do. You'll have to address mine right now. I know you don't have definitive answers, but I want to understand the questions and the pieces of this puzzle."

"Which pieces?"

She relayed Sully's allegation that the victim had been alive several days after the discovery of the legs. She told him about Wilson's over-exposed cell-phone photograph and her conviction that the legs had been scarred. She finished with Wilson's investigation into the trains and her own growing fear for Carrie Brown.

"I have called and emailed her and made it very clear why I am contacting her. And nothing. Not even a 'leave me alone' or a new message on her voicemail. It's like she has disappeared." Helen waited. "I *will* understand this," she added when Hornsby said nothing. "If it's true, or even possible, that two women were killed the same way, we need to find out who did it. Our students—my students—are in danger. I have to protect them. I cannot let anything come between me and my obligation."

Except Wilson. Tell him where you were last night.

In the silence of Hornsby's office, a clock ticked. Hornsby folded his arms across his chest. He stared at his desk.

Tell him. A words repeated in Helen's mind, adding to the clamor of voices that had become her constant companions. *Help me, Helen.*

"You want to look at the medical examiner's report?" Hornsby asked finally. "You want to do my job?"

His eyes were watery and red. There was a fleck of mustard on the corner of his mouth. His cheeks sagged, as though he had aged since she last saw him. *He's falling apart.*

"There were no unusual marks on the legs," Hornsby said adamantly. "Carrie Brown is at UMass, failing calculus and paying her rent on time. And Sully...she's told us *everything* over the years. UFO landings. Political assassinations. She predicts it all. Sully would say anything for a hot meal and a fiver."

"What about the torso?" Helen asked. "Does it match the legs? Can you check the blood type?"

"You want the medical examiner's office to rush results when they have a hundred other cases, and we know this girl was homeless and mentally ill?"

She shot Hornsby a warning look.

"Fine. I checked the blood type." Hornsby exhaled heavily. He had run out of steam after his short burst of outrage. On his desk, the sandwich glistened, deconstructed on its paper wrapper. "The blood type for the legs matched the torso of the homeless woman found under the train."

Helen saw Thompson and Giles lingering outside Hornsby's office. When they caught her watching, they disappeared.

"The blood type matches. The wounds match," Hornsby added.

"DNA matches?" she asked.

"We don't have the results yet, but she had the same plastic ties on her person as we found on the legs."

Helen wished she could talk to Hornsby about the yellow Jeep. In Pittsburg she could have told the police that her tires had been slashed in the parking lot of a one-night-stand hotel. Vandusen had a good working relationship with the Pittsburg police, but the police had a thousand other businesses under their jurisdiction. The president of a small college was nobody to them. In Pittock, Helen was the most interesting public figure for fifty miles. If she enlisted the police department's help in discovering who slashed her tires, they would need to know why she was at the Cozzzy Inn and who was with her.

"What about the emails from the group in Boston? The devotees?" Helen persisted. "They say some guy is attacking them online."

"A creep." Hornsby shrugged again. "Every pervert west of Holyoke has something to say about the case." Hornsby dug in a desk drawer. He came out with a large binder. "Look." He opened to a red tab. "These are Internet alerts. It's stuff people send me, stuff I found on my own. It's sick."

Helen flipped through the pages, reading at random. One writer extolled the beauty of the Pittock feet. Several accused the victim of being a sexually promiscuous, drug addict who deserved what she got. "God will rain down punishment on the wanton," one wrote.

"When you've been in law enforcement as long as I have, you see things." Hornsby said. "Even in Pittock. I wish I could say this all came as a surprise to me, but it didn't. Bad things happen, especially to the homeless. It's hard out there, and it's hard for us to protect them because, quite honestly, they don't always want us to. There also isn't a lot of money for pursuing cold cases."

"The legs were discovered less than a month ago. That's not a cold case."

"Yesterday, Springfield PD found two women in a dumpster." Hornsby pushed some papers aside. "Boston had a John Doe wash up in the harbor. In Holyoke there was a gang shooting that injured three minors."

There it was again, that weariness, as if Hornsby

could barely manage to speak. Helen shook her head. She felt as tired as Hornsby looked. *A yellow truck, like one of those Tonka toys.*

"Is there any suspect you haven't investigated? *Anyone* whose alibi is questionable?"

Hornsby picked up a pencil and twiddled it between his fingers. He squinted at the watch on his wrist, then looked out the front window. "Are you asking about Ricky?"

Helen nodded slowly.

Hornsby shifted in his seat. "Ricky had nothing to do with this. Marshal Drummond told me himself. Ricky was at home that night playing computer games. We have records of his log-in and log-out. That's as good an alibi as we've got for anyone. Adair Wilson doesn't even have that good an alibi." Hornsby shrugged, as though something had crumbled inside him. "She didn't call anyone that night. She didn't buy anything. Didn't send an email. She lives alone. No one saw her go in her apartment. No one saw her leave."

Chapter Thirty-three

No one saw him cut the rusty padlock with a pair of bolt cutters and enter the asylum. It was 4:30 a.m. The morning joggers would not be up. The homeless slept in their camp. Still, he moved quickly and quietly. He stepped inside, closing the door behind him.

Memories rushed back: The smell of bleach. The echoing halls. His legs raw from Father's belts. The nurses hurrying past him without seeing. Carla Braff screaming from her wheelchair. The schizophrenics in Ward C, shuffling across the floor, their tongues protruding, their shoulders twisted around their ears.

"All a product of the medication," Father had said casually. "It's better. This way we can see them. They are more manageable if we can identify them by sight."

"Does it hurt?" he had ventured, when he saw one of the men pounding his head on the ceramic tile wall.

"Does it matter?" Father countered.

He understood now. Some things were more important than pain. Helen Ivers would suffer more than the others, because she would live. This did not matter because she would soothe the need. He would keep her, and she would fulfill him.

The asylum was built in wings. All were in ruin, but when Father had been the administrator, the central wing—where he stood now—had looked like an upscale hotel, complete with chandelier and marble staircase. The farther one moved from the center, the more the asylum resembled a prison.

He had to find the right place for her surgery. He hoped it would be Father's old office. Once he found it, he cursed. He'd thought it was on the second story, high up and secluded. Here it was, on the first floor, near the central nurses' station. The windows looked out on the garden, almost at ground level. This would never do.

He climbed the stairs to the second floor. The floor was spongy in places and completely disintegrated in others. Vandals and weather had broken the glass in all but the highest window panes. He could not take the risk. If Ivers crawled to the window, she could call through the iron grating.

An hour later, he found his way to the theater with seats going up in rows. He liked the space. After all, he was producing a love story. Unfortunately, a dozen entrances led to the theater. Too many variables. He would have to go underground.

He was just about to leave, when he noticed a white, metal cupboard, lying on its side near a window. He opened it. On one side were several syringes, a box of tongue depressors, a brown bottle of unidentified fluid, still preserved by a rubber cork, and one pair of pliers. The pliers were rusted orange. On the other side of the cupboard, sat the bulk of a folded straitjacket. He picked it up and shook it. The buckles had rusted like the pliers, and rust had stained the canvas. It would make a nice souvenir. He picked it up. It would make a nice gift.

Helen waited anxiously for the second Tuesday of the month, when the devotees of Boston met. Under the guise of visiting alumni, Helen left the Mass Pike for the narrow streets of Boston.

The site of the meeting was a church, stuck between row houses. The stairs were warped, the paint peeling. A faded banner read, “Holistic Wellness and Conference Center.” The door opened onto a hallway with rooms on either side. Some of the doors were open. One door bore a plaque reading, “Meditation Lounge.” The orange sofas within looked like they'd been salvaged from an airport waiting room. A hand-written note taped to an easel read, “Devotees/Wannabes/Pretenders downstairs. Free coffee.”

Downstairs, it looked like the setting of an AA meeting. A few people sat in a circle on folding chairs. On a table by the door, the coffee pot sputtered.

A young man in a green vest caught sight of Helen and smiled too broadly. “Devotees, wannabes, and pretenders?”

She nodded.

“Come in. Come in.” He gestured expansively, as though welcoming her to a party. “Coffee's ready. I'm Blake.”

“Helen Ivers.”

Blake's smile vanished. “Helen Ivers from Pittock?”

She nodded.

“Who told you to come?”

Helen could not tell if he was angry or frightened. “You did,” she said. “I wouldn't have had to drive to Boston if you'd just answered my calls.”

Blake looked down. "We have a confidentiality policy in this group." His voice took on the same indignant tone Helen had heard on the phone. "This is a safe space."

Helen said. "I'll do my best to respect that, but I need to ask some questions."

The door opened and a man in a motorized wheelchair arrived, bellowing a greeting. Helen and Blake made room for him to pass. The man took a place in the circle of chairs and proceeded to recount a recent run-in with a grocery store manager. His face was animated. The rest of his body remained frozen.

"You know what the manager said?" The man had a thick Boston accent. "He said 'I thought welfare put people like you in a home.' I nearly jumped from my chair and clocked him."

There was a ripple of laughter among the people in the circle.

"That's Chuck," Blake said quietly. "He's the only wannabe in the group right now. He identifies as a C5 quadriplegic. He really wants to go through with it."

"Go through with it?"

"Become a C5," Blake said. "This group is for devotees, wannabes, and pretenders. I'm a pretender. I'm not in my chair today because I'm having a new seat put in. Plus, I have a job interview this afternoon, and I take the train. I couldn't very well park it outside my interview."

"What do you do?" Helen asked. The whole scene was surreal.

"I'm a machinist. That's why I'm not a wannabe. I'd have to totally retrain if I wanted to work at a desk. That's a big mistake people make. They think we want to live on welfare because we want to use our chairs. It's not true. We just want a society that makes it possible to live a productive life with a disability."

"Some people here would like to be disabled in reality?" Helen kept her voice low.

"Absolutely." Blake had no compunctions about discussing his condition. "Being disabled or being with handicapped people frees us to be who we really are." He rubbed at a pimple on the side of his jaw. "Although most of us aren't ready to make the ultimate commitment. It's hard to do it safely. That's why we are so concerned about that girl in Pittock. She must have been one of us."

Helen nodded toward Chuck. "So he's going to make himself a quadriplegic. How?"

Blake shook his head. "He doesn't know. There are doctors in other countries who will do it sometimes, but it's difficult. You have to find the right person. Even in Third World countries, it can be expensive."

The meeting was starting. The room had filled with fifteen people.

"Can I talk to your group?" Helen asked.

Somewhat reluctantly, Blake introduced her.

"Wait a second." A girl with dyed black hair and a black polyester dress spoke. "You said we wouldn't have any media here. No cops and shit."

Next to her sat a young man in jeans and a white t-shirt. Half his left arm was missing. On his other side, a pretty woman in a business suit cradled the stump in her hand.

"Yeah, who are you?" the business woman asked. "How do we know you're safe?"

"Blake contacted me," Helen said. "He told me about Cutter and asked for my help. Then he hung up on me." She raised her eyebrow in Blake's direction. "It would be irresponsible for me not to follow up. If your fears are correct, my students are in danger. I'm here for them. I'm not here to out you or threaten you."

"How do we know that?" a woman in leg braces asked.

Helen shrugged. "How do you know anyone is safe? You don't. But you're going to have to trust me if you want my help."

Beside Helen, a man in an embroidered tunic sat cross-legged on his chair. "I trust her," he said in a dreamy voice. "She has a strong aura."

To Helen's surprise, this seemed to satisfy the devotees.

Blake said, "Why don't we go around the room and say our names. Then we can talk to Helen about the website." He began the introduction, placing a hand over his heart. "I'm Blake. I'm a devotee."

As soon as the introductions were made, Chuck, the C5, spoke. "What are you going to do about this guy?"

"We're not safe as long as this asshole is on the loose," the girl in black added. "What if that girl didn't want to do it? What if she wasn't ready?"

Blake spoke with the somber tone of a public service announcement. "Because so many of us are closeted, we often turn to the first person we can talk to. They're not always from a supportive group like this. Sometimes it's just a pervert, a creep, like this guy. That poor girl probably thought she had no options."

Helen looked at their worried faces.

"What are you going to do?" Chuck demanded again.

"I don't know," Helen said. *I don't know. I don't know.* "I've urged the police to look into this. It's hard.

People are allowed to post in public forums. They can post awful things. That, in itself, is not a crime."

"That forum is our lifeline," the woman in the business suit said, still clutching the stump of her companion's arm. "Wren and I talked on the forum for six months before he came to his first meeting."

The man next to her nodded.

"He would never have had the courage otherwise, and he would never have realized what this group is about. We can't let someone like Cutter ruin this group. For some of us, it's all we've got."

Blake added, "A lot of amputees are reluctant to contact devotee groups because they think we're a bunch of fetishists, who just want to handle their stumps or worse. A person like Cutter sends all the wrong messages."

"A devotee is…?" Helen asked.

"Someone who loves amputees," Blake said.

"Sexually," the Goth girl added.

Blake shot her a disapproving look.

"Well, it is! We *are* fetishists in a way. I love women with above the knee amputations, but society says that's wrong. Other people have fetishes for hard abs or big breasts or blonde hair. We're told not to look at handicapped people like that. I am a fetishist, but it's an innocent fetish. I would never hurt anyone."

"I've been an artist for over ten years," the man in the green tunic said. Everyone turned to face him. "At first, it started as an aesthetic challenge. How do I paint someone whose body doesn't conform to our expectations? Either I hide or objectify, but neither choice is right. The amputee does not avoid her arm, nor does she make it the focus of her identity. I wanted to make the viewer as comfortable with the different body as the amputee herself."

He touched the tips of his fingers to his thumbs and rested them on his knees.

"It all came together when I went to China and met Bao Yu Lee. She was starting a chapter of the Foot and Mouth Painters International in China, and I was a graduate student visiting her university. She had been born without arms. She was so elegant in her cheongsam, I didn't notice that she was armless nor did I *not notice.* She did in real life what I had wanted to do in my paintings; she let her reality stand without comparison to other people. She simply was. Once I realized that all that grace came along with a double loss, I was in love." He smiled and closed his eyes. "Of course she was a beautiful married woman, and I was a silly American trying out my few phrases of Mandarin. She made me a devotee."

There was a ripple of agreement among the gathering.

The women in leg braces spoke. "This guy, Cutter, he's different. He's a predator."

"I read the emails Blake forwarded me," Helen assured her.

"He's still at it," Blake added.

"Send me any new messages you receive, and send them to the police too." Helen felt helpless. "I'll do what I can."

For a while there was silence. Helen wondered if the meeting had an agenda that would begin now.

"Poor, Carrie," the Goth girl said, readjusting her stiff, black gown. "I feel like I know her. I know what it's like to have these desires and not be able to tell anyone. She could have been my friend."

"What did you say?" Helen asked, suddenly alert.

"She could have been my friend."

"What did you call her?"

"Carrie."

"Why Carrie?"

"I've been helping Blake monitor the forum. In the last couple of messages, Cutter called the girl Carrie. I don't know if that's her real name, but I keep thinking of her as Carrie. You know, she was probably just another girl. Like me. Like anyone. She probably grew up in the suburbs. Then she got mixed up with this asshole."

Carrie. Helen's mind raced. Had the name Carrie been in the news?

"You know, she was pregnant," the girl added. "I think that had something to do with what happened. She was going to tell her guy, but she was nervous about what he would say. No." The girl stopped. "Not nervous. Scared."

Chapter Thirty-four

On the street outside, Helen called Terri. "Long time, no hear," he said amiably. "How's our latest PR crisis?"

"I need your help, Terri."

Terri's voice grew serious. "What is it?"

"I need to know if any media source mentioned the name Carrie or Carrie Brown along with the Pittock legs."

"I'll get someone on it right away. What are you thinking?"

Helen stepped off the sidewalk. In the narrow space between the church and the next building was an old cemetery. She stepped through its wrought-iron gates and looked for a bench.

"I just met with the Devotees of Boston. It's an amputee fetish group. Don't ask. They've got a web forum, and some guy named Cutter has been flaming them. They say he mentioned a girl named Carrie."

"That's the one your professor was worried about."

"Yes. Carrie Brown. If it was in the media, it doesn't mean anything. Some creep heard the name and used it. But the police didn't take Wilson seriously, and if no one publicized the name 'Carrie,' then there's a good chance the guy who's posting to the forum knows about the Pittock legs."

"And your crazy professor isn't so crazy."

Or crazier than we can imagine. Helen felt the holster of Wilson's gun pressed against her ribcage.

"Wilson is worried about Ricky Drummond. He dated Carrie. Then Carrie transferred to UMass, where they have 25,000 students and no official record of who goes to class. Apparently, she's living off campus."

At her feet, a weathered headstone read Jonathan Broen 1879—1921. Beside it rested his "beloved wife" and "loving son."

"There's something else," Helen said. "My tires were slashed."

"Oh hell." Terri was animated.

"Someone saw the culprit drive away in a bright yellow Jeep. That's the kind of car Ricky Drummond drives."

"What did the police say?"

Helen kicked a dry clod of dirt at her feet, sending particles skittering across a flat tombstone. "I didn't tell them."

"What?"

"I was at a hotel." Helen paused. "I've done something stupid."

"I'm listening."

"I slept with someone I shouldn't have." Helen glanced around as she spoke, but the cemetery was empty. Only the cicadas and the sound of traffic broke the silence. The grass grew in long tufts between the tombstones. Whoever tended the cemetery had neglected it for some time.

"A student?" Terri asked. He was no stranger to college scandal.

"Give me some credit."

"It's been done. Was it a minor?"

Terri was a man of integrity, but his job required

that he handle the shady side of life, and he did this with aplomb.

"A professor," Helen said reluctantly.

"Consensual?" Terri sounded like he was going down a checklist: PR questions for lascivious administrators.

"Not exactly," Helen said.

Terri's voice was urgent. "Did he attack you, Helen?"

"Nothing like that. It's just I didn't know...she was a professor at the time."

"A woman, eh?"

Helen could almost hear Terri lower his hackles.

"Yes."

"That's hardly scandalous anymore. If you're trying to shock me, you're going to have to do better. What does she teach?"

Helen leaned her elbows on her knees, cupping her phone to her ear. She stared down at the dry ground.

"It was Adair Wilson. And there's more. She has a history of discrediting administrators with allegations of sexual misconduct. According to Marshal, she has a history of blackmail."

Terri was listening closely. "Tell me more."

"Marshal says she got her first teaching position by blackmailing her thesis advisor. Then she tried to get Drummond fired with some trumped-up sexual harassment charges made by a janitor who didn't speak English. He says Wilson wanted to sleep with this woman, and when she couldn't woo her the ordinary way, she helped with her harassment case. I can't believe I did this, Terri. I can't believe it."

❧❧❧

There was always a moment of realization when the woman he was making grasped what she was to become. In those seconds, he was her god, and she was clay in his hands. It was glorious, and for Helen Ivers, that moment would go on and on.

Slowly, reverently, he placed the box from Generations Medical Supply on the basement workbench. He smiled and picked up his box cutter. The blade flicked out like a snake's tongue. He slit the clear membrane of tape from one end of the box to the other. He could have ripped it open, but he wanted to practice. The tape was like skin. Inside, a card told him that Operator 436 had reviewed his order and packed his supplies. They rested in a nest of Styrofoam peanuts: gauze, rubber tubing, absorbable gut sutures. Nothing that would raise police suspicion. The bone saw would have to come from the asylum.

A single, narrow window cast a bit of dusty sunlight. He thought about filling in the brick-lined shaft that allowed it to reach the basement. Then he could bury the window. He could make Ivers here, in the same basement where Father had tortured him while, above their heads, Mother drifted from room to room in her oyster-gray evening dress. It would be appropriate. Poetic even. Everything coming full circle.

He wrapped the rubber tubing around his hand, to feel what Ivers would, then pulled the tubing tighter. He wanted her here. Now. But he had to wait and prepare.

The next step would not be as exciting as inventorying his equipment. He had to rent Ivers an apartment, and, for that, he would go onto campus. In the unlikely event that someone got suspicious, there could be no link between his computer and Ivers's well-appointed but isolated rental.

UMass was halfway between Boston and Pittock. Helen expected the visit to take only a few minutes. As it turned out, traffic on the narrow rural highway was backed up bumper to bumper. When she finally got to Amherst, she realized that the address for Carrie Brown was one town away, in Hadley. There, she found a large, white, clapboard house converted into six apartments. On one of the mailboxes, the name "Carrie Brown" was written in cursive script.

She climbed a rickety exterior staircase to Unit 4 and knocked. There was no answer. The Venetian blinds were drawn. She knocked again. The heat of the day was stifling. Below the staircase, several trashcans exuded a rank odor. She knocked again. On the other end of the porch, the door opened to Unit 5. A woman in a housedress waddled out.

"Excuse me," Helen said. "Have you seen Carrie Brown?"

"Don't know no Carrie Brown," the woman said. She jerked a thumb in the direction of the door on which Helen had knocked. "But if you're looking for him, you ain't gonna find him here."

"Him?"

"Him. Her. Don't know." The woman lifted both hands, as though the issue exhausted her. "Must be a vampire or something. I never see anyone come or go. Quiet neighbors. I'll tell you that. These walls are paper-thin. I don't think anyone shits in that apartment. I've never heard the john flush."

"Do you know who pays the rent?"

The woman pushed a cat back into her apartment and closed the screen door behind it. "You the police?"

"No. I'm just looking for a student who might be in trouble."

"Hmm," the woman grunted. "No student lives there. I know if they're students. Students always loud. I don't care if they say they're studying. They breathe loud."

The neighbor was not the only person to whom Carrie Brown was a mystery. Helen was leaving her car in the Pittock parking lot when Terri called.

"I put my best people on it," Terri said. "I don't see the name Carrie anywhere. It's possible it turned up in private forums, blogs, Facebook, but I doubt it. Anyway, if it did show up behind a password that would still mean the flamer you're looking for is someone close to the campus community. That doesn't mean the guy killed her, but he's interested. I read the emails. He's scary."

Chapter Thirty-five

He watched her get out of her car. He knew her silhouette. Assertive but worried. He wanted her to relax, to lie back and be his. Though she might not realize it yet, she wanted that too. He could see it in the weary way she pulled her hair into a band when she thought no one was looking. As though she was getting ready for some unpleasant task, scrubbing the floors or cleaning a tub. A woman of quality should never have to do that.

When the Pittock Asylum was founded, doctors believed that too much exercise or intellectual stimulation would drive women mad, Father had told him. Doctors prescribed more time with infants, less conversation, and more needlepoint. When the asylums went public, women from the factories lined up, complaining that physical work and their husbands' abuse made them ill.

"It was the downfall of the asylum," Father had said. "Now we have this." He had gestured toward the occupational therapy room, where several schizophrenics were performing their agonized dance. Stand up. Shuffle. Sit down. Stand up. The nurse was trying to get them to make clay pinch pots.

He would bring back the old asylum. The place of peace. Once he made her, she would not have to rush across campus in those high heels. She would never have to bind her hair behind her head. She would never have to rise. In some ways, even the pain would be gift. She could not think with that much pain. She would just be. His. Made.

He carried the straitjacket in a leather briefcase at his side. Tonight was a good night to leave it for her, a promise of what was to come.

Back at the Pittock House, Helen poured a glass of vodka. She had just lifted the drink to her lips when a knock at the door startled her. She retraced her steps and opened the door. An electric thrill ran down her spine. Wilson leaned against one of the porch columns, her clothes clinging to her body with casual grace, her pale eyes set off by her soft tan. Helen could not look at Wilson without remembering the orgasm shuddering through her body. She also felt a sudden and uncomfortable certainty: Wilson had been watching her door, waiting for her to come home.

Helen stepped onto the porch and closed the door halfway behind her.

"What can I do for you, Dr. Wilson?"

"I need to talk to you." Wilson appeared to deliberate for a moment, then she said, "Some of my students got into Carrie's room last night."

"Got in?"

"Broke in." Wilson's shrug was just a ripple in her silken t-shirt. "They're old buildings. It doesn't take much."

"You do understand that students on a college campus have a privacy right..." Helen stopped.

Wilson was watching her intently, waiting for her to finish. "It doesn't matter, does it?"

You're invulnerable. Helen remembered Wilson's description of the invulnerable Drummond family. *I come from a family like that.* She heard Drummond's voice: *You can't touch Wilson.*

Wilson shrugged. "Do you want to know what we found?"

Helen sighed. "Yes."

"Are you going to let me in?" Wilson took a step closer.

"We can talk out here."

"You just use women?" Wilson's voice was flirtatious, but a trace of melancholy touched her eyes. "You can't even sit down with me? You won't even let me in your house?"

Wilson was standing so close; Helen could smell her cologne, see the fine sheen of perspiration at the hollow of her throat. She could not let anyone see them like this.

"Okay. Come in."

In the kitchen, Helen took a sip of her drink. She offered the bottle to Wilson, who shook her head. Helen sat. Wilson leaned against the counter

"She hadn't packed, Helen," Wilson said without precursor. "It was as if she had just stepped out to use the bathroom. Her computer was on. There was half an apple on her desk. There were empty suitcases under her bed. Maybe she was getting ready to go somewhere, but she didn't get there. She never left."

Help me, Helen. Help me.

"I know." Helen rotated the glass in her hands. She had to decide: throw Wilson out with a lecture on college procedure and call Hornsby or tell Wilson everything. Carrie. Sully. The slashed tires. The devotees.

"I know. I know. I know." There was really no question. Not anymore. She had to tell Wilson. "I was at her apartment today, the one she supposedly rented to go to UMass. The neighbor said she'd never seen anyone go in or come out. Never heard the toilet. There was no one there."

"Do you see now?" Wilson asked. "The police aren't looking. Someone doesn't want us to know what happened."

"I don't know what this means, but…" Helen told Wilson about Sully and Crystal Evans. She described her meeting with Hornsby, and told her about the devotees and Carrie. Wilson listened, rapt. Reluctantly, Helen added, "After you left the Cozzzy Inn… my tires were slashed. The hotel clerk said he saw someone near the car. A man driving a yellow Jeep."

"I've seen one on campus. We can find it, find out who owns it," Wilson said.

Help me, Helen. She could not stop the voices anymore. *You can't touch Wilson. They don't let boys like Ricky Drummond go down for anything. I know. I come from a family like that. Help me, Helen! Help me.*

"Ricky Drummond drives a yellow Jeep," Helen said.

Wilson put her face in her hands. "I have to see the legs."

Helen had planned on driving them to the medical examiner's office in Holyoke. But when they arrived at the staff lot, Wilson put her hand on Helen's arm.

"You must be tired. I'll drive," Wilson said.

Wilson was right; she was exhausted. Her head pounded.

Wilson removed an electric key from her pocket and clicked in the direction of the parking lot. Helen looked for taillights. Nothing.

"Behind the sedan," Wilson said.

Her car was a platinum-colored BMW convertible. Helen recognized the model because she had entertained the idea of getting one before she realized that a year's salary would not begin to cover the cost.

"How does a theater professor afford a BMW M6?" Helen asked as she lowered herself into the sleek interior. It was a lovely car.

Wilson shifted into second gear, and the car purred out of the parking lot.

"Family money." Wilson kept her eyes on the road, a slight smile turning up the corner of her lips.

"That's a lot of money."

"I have a lot of family."

Helen stared out the window as they pulled onto the highway that led out of Pittock. The sun was setting in long, orange fingers. The scene was beautiful, but the light hurt her eyes. Her headache was threatening to become a migraine. She pressed her fingertips against her forehead. Wilson glanced over.

"You okay?"

"Fine."

"You want an oxycodone? There's some in my bag in the back." Wilson gestured backward with a nod. "You won't feel a thing."

"No. I'm fine."

"You know, you don't always have to be in control." Wilson reached for the satchel with one hand, while keeping her eyes on the road ahead. She pulled out a prescription vial and tossed it to Helen.

"Here."

Adair Merrill Wilson, Helen read on the bottle. *This is the end.*

The drug took affect almost immediately. The pain in her head became irrelevant and then disappeared altogether. Helen felt her limbs relax. Her body sank into the soft leather. She was vaguely aware of Wilson running her fingertips back and forth across her thigh. She felt her body flush at the touch, and then she was asleep.

Chapter Thirty-six

When Helen woke, it was night and they were in front of a brick building on the side of a divided highway.

"The medical examiner's office," Wilson said.

The building was four stories high. It looked squat because its length was so much greater than its height. The bricks reminded Helen of the asylum, without its antiquated grace. Inside, florescent lights reflected off linoleum floors. On the walls, posters invited them to take a bite out of crime and check for radon. Helen thought that if she had ever been in a building where she feared radon poisoning, it was here.

It took her almost an hour to convince the receptionist to let her speak to the medical examiner on duty. The man who finally appeared was in his early fifties, with a boyish face and silver hair. His lab coat fitted him well, and he looked pleased to see them, shaking first Helen's hand then Wilson's.

"I went to Pittock for two years. Best two years of my education. What can I do for you ladies?"

Helen explained the situation.

"Ah! You would like to help the police investigation."

Helen nodded.

"I'm sorry. I can't accommodate you, Ms. President. I'm flattered to have the president of Pittock here. If you would like a tour of our office, I could arrange that for you, during working hours, but I can't let you see the legs."

"Why not?" Helen asked.

"Completely nonstandard procedure." The medical examiner smiled jovially. He had the confidence of a man in his element. This was his world. Whatever Helen did on the outside, he ruled this fiefdom. "We don't let random civilians in to see body parts. Ever. You know that scene in the movies where the family goes into a viewing room and they wheel out the body? We don't even do that. No one looks at those bodies besides us. If anything, we'd take a Polaroid. "

"Can we see the Polaroid?" Wilson asked. "I have to see her."

The medical examiner shook his head.

"All that is police business. I'm sure the investigator assigned to the case has the information he needs."

"But he's not investigating!" Wilson said.

"I wish I could take you back. Everyone should see a few dead bodies. All young people…" He gave Wilson a pointed look. "…should visit the morgue a few times. It's better than joining the Boy Scouts. Very edifying, but we don't provide that service here."

He steered them toward the door, not quite touching their backs with the tips of his fingers.

"Thank you for coming, ladies. Good luck with your quest."

Outside, Helen and Wilson stood in the halogen glare of the receiving bay. As they pondered what to do next, an ambulance pulled up, its sirens muted, its lights dark. There was a large crack in the back window. A piece of silver duct tape traced the break.

Helen thought of the poem she had chosen for

Eliza's memorial service. W. H. Auden, "As I Walked Out One Evening," with its dark evocation of horror lurking behind the artifacts of everyday life. In the cupboard. In a cracked teacup.

Eliza would have liked the 23rd Psalm. Eliza was always going on about "sweet Jesus" and angels, although she never set foot in a church. It was the last gift Helen could have given her, a ceremony that affirmed Eliza's belief that Jesus loved her and waited for her. Instead, Helen had given the priest a copy of the poem. "Are you sure?" he had asked.

The back of the ambulance opened, and two EMTs rolled out an empty stretcher. The wheels rattled on the rough pavement. The medics walked with their heads down. For a moment, Helen felt the urge to pull Wilson to her and kiss her violently on the lips. The parking lot was so stark, the building so institutional. Behind the swinging double doors worked men and women who had become inured to death. In the examiner's trays, lay men and women reduced to less than human. And then there was Wilson, so young and beautiful, her skin flawless, her muscles visible in the artificial light. She was so alive; Helen wanted to crawl inside her skin.

The diner that Wilson drove them to was as bleak as the medical examiner's office, and Wilson looked just as stunning. She leaned back in her seat, one arm draped over the back of the ripped vinyl booth. Behind her head, a faded Precious Moments print looked even more mawkish against her aggressive beauty.

The waitress arrived with coffee and menus.

Helen waved away the menu, but Wilson ordered a plate of pancakes.

"With two forks," Wilson said. "And extra syrup and butter, plus whipped cream if you have it."

The waitress, a haggard woman with straw hair and a dry cold sore on her lip, shot Wilson a contemptuous look. Helen understood. Wilson looked like a model in an avant garde photo shoot, posed in this diner because its unremitting ugliness showcased her beauty. She probably ate whipped cream every day and stayed as lean and muscular as a race horse.

Helen felt Wilson's eyes on her.

"What now?" Helen said to break the silence.

Wilson sucked her lower lip. "If the medical examiner won't talk to us, maybe he will talk to someone else."

"I don't trust Hornsby."

"What about Darrell or Tyron?"

In Helen's mind, the two young officers had become Tweedledee and Tweedledumb. She furrowed her brow. "Do you trust them?"

"Think about it. They're young." It sounded funny coming from Wilson. "They don't know all the rules yet, and you're as much an authority figure in Pittock as Hornsby. The college and the town are like this." Wilson held up her crossed fingers. "Ask a personal favor. Can it hurt?"

Helen thought about her slashed tires. Everything could hurt and would eventually, she was certain. Wilson pulled out her phone and touched the screen.

"Ready?" She tapped out the number and held the phone to her ear. "Is Officer Thompson there? Just a friend." A second later she said, "Tyron. It's Addie from Pittock. I have a friend who needs a favor."

Wilson passed the phone to Helen. It was still warm from her touch.

"Is there a way you could check on the Pittock legs case for me?" she asked. "I need to know about a picture, a Polaroid you got from the medical examiner's office."

"Of course, I can look into that for you." He sounded very grave. "It's about time someone took this seriously."

"What do you mean?"

Thompson hesitated. "I mean, Chief Hornsby has a lot on his mind, what with his wife being sick."

Thompson was not giving Helen the full story.

"Can we keep this between you and me?" she asked.

"And Darrell?"

"Sure."

"Yes, ma'am. I'd rather do that. I'll look, and call you right back."

Helen ended the call and placed Wilson's phone on the table between them. The screen saver showed a picture of students in the colorful garb of a theater production.

"What play was that?" Helen asked.

"*Brigadoon.*"

"Whose choice?"

"Mine. Why?"

Helen laughed. "I would have pinned you for *Rent.*"

The waitress returned with the pancakes, and Wilson pushed them toward Helen.

"Eat something."

Helen had just taken a bite when the phone rang.

"Strange thing," Thompson said. "There's no

photo in that file. There's almost nothing in that file. I mean there's a lot of paper, but half the medical examiner's report is missing. The other half has been redacted like an FBI cover up. Most of the photos we took at the scene are missing. Someone gutted that file."

Helen relayed to Wilson what Thompson had just said. Wilson gestured for the phone.

"Tyron," she said. "You've got to help us. We've got to see that medical examiner's report. Can you or Darrell get out to Holyoke to the medical examiner's office and get another copy *without* Hornsby catching on?"

Two hours later, Thompson joined them at the diner, a manila envelope tucked under one arm.

"Coffee, officer?" The waitress asked. "I sure feel safer with you here. I hate working the midnight shift, but I get off in an hour."

She was flirting. Thompson looked up, as though he had never wanted coffee in his life.

"Just leave a pot on the table," Wilson commanded.

The waitress glared. Helen could read her mind. It was bad enough Wilson had taken up a table for hours, looking gorgeous and drinking coffee at a superhuman rate. Now, for the first time that evening, maybe that year, a handsome man walked into the diner and Wilson got him all to herself. *If only she knew.*

"Are you ready?" Thompson opened the flap of the envelope.

Helen nodded.

Thompson extracted a picture and laid it on the table before them, shielding it from the view of the other diners with his arm. Between them lay a high quality scan of a medical examiner's picture printed on glossy paper. Two legs, viewed from four different angles. Each angle, showing a messy tangle of scars as though someone had tried to carve the leg with everything from a razor to a fork.

Chapter Thirty-seven

Helen caught a few hours of sleep when they got back to Pittock and dreamed about Eliza. Eliza was locked in a bathroom at their parents' house. Helen threw her shoulder against the hollow core door and pushed until it gave way with a crack. Inside, the bathroom was filthy, the drain submerged beneath brownish water that spilled onto the floor. Eliza stood in the shower, naked from the waist up, her breasts and belly bloated from her medications. Her wet sweatpants clung to her enormous thighs. She held her hands away from her body as though afraid to touch it.

"Help me, Helen."

Suddenly their parents stood in the doorway, her mother in a faded, blue jumper, her father in his painting clothes. Even as she felt the glow of recognition, Helen knew they weren't her parents. They were the Browns.

"Where is our daughter?"

"I'm here," Helen said.

Eliza tried to speak, but her words sounded muffled. Helen turned. Eliza's mouth was full of hair, a wad of gray hair. It was getting bigger and bigger, filling Eliza's mouth

"Where is our daughter?" the Browns asked.

Eliza was choking. Helen tried to pull out the hair, but it kept growing. Then the hair turned to blood, and Helen was back in Eliza's kitchen.

Helen was still rattled the following morning, when she entered the kitchenette in Meyerbridge Hall to make another pot of coffee. The coffee can was empty.

"Patrick?" she called down the corridor. "Is there any more coffee?"

"In the closet. Do I have to do everything around here?" he answered genially.

Helen opened the workroom closet and scanned the shelves. Office supplies. Copy paper. Plastic cutlery. Lost and found umbrellas. Coffee. She reached for the coffee. Then something caught her attention. On a hook in the small closet hung an unfamiliar garment. A workman's jersey or a painter's smock. She pulled it toward her then released it as though the fabric was hot. The arms on the shirt draped well below the hem. It was stained and stiff. Brown streaks crossed the back like whip marks. The belt on the garment jingled. Only it wasn't a belt. She looked again. There were buckles on the sleeves. Long arms. Buckles. All the times Helen had taken Eliza to the hospital for observation, Helen had never seen a straitjacket, but its iconic shape was unmistakable.

"Patrick!" She heard the fear in her voice, shrill and trembling. "Patrick, come here."

"If you can't make coffee, you can't run this school," Patrick said as he trundled down the hall. "I swear…" He stopped when he saw Helen. "What happened?"

"What the hell is this doing in here?" She pointed.

Patrick reached for the straitjacket.

"Don't touch it," Helen said, stepping back.

Patrick ignored her, taking out the garment and stretching it between his hands. The smell of mildew drifted up from the sleeves. Mildew and something Helen could not place. Something that reminded her of Eliza.

"I'm calling the police," she blurted. Even as she spoke, she realized she couldn't. Who would she talk to? Hornsby?

"Don't worry. This has probably been here for years," Patrick said.

"Why would anyone leave something like this?"

He shrugged. "Maybe it's a prop, a retirement gag gift. No one uses this closet."

"I looked in here last week."

"Maybe you didn't see it."

"Someone left it for me," she said. Someone knew about Eliza. The message could not be clearer: you're just like her.

"You've been here long enough to see," Patrick said. "Every cupboard in this place is full of creepy antiques someone thought were a valuable Pittock tradition."

"Who's been back here?"

"You. Me. Mr. Drummond. Probably the janitor. Helen, it's nothing."

Patrick's look of concern frightened her almost as much as the jacket with its nightmare sleeves. She had worn that look. *Come on, Eliza. No one is going to hurt you.*

"It *is* creepy," Patrick added. "It's creepy as fuck, but this is Pittock. You've got to get used to it."

The last thing Helen wanted to do was put on a cheerful face and explore the Pittock Harvest Festival. However, this two-day conflagration of local bands and fried dough was Pittock's one, town-wide celebration and, as such, possessed iconic significance. "This is who we are. This is Pittock," the mayor had told her when he had called to extend a personal invitation. After work and after a quick shower, Helen stepped out of the Pittock House into the hot twilight. At least she would not be alone.

All of Pittock had come out for the Harvest Festival. At the intersection of Main and Ferry, just beyond the Grandville Hotel, the road had been cordoned off with sawhorses and caution tape. Vendors sold hot dogs from concession stands. A Ferris wheel bearing the logo "Carne-Traveler: Rent the Stars" flashed and rumbled. Occasionally, another ride would lift passengers above the crowd, their screams mixing with the screams of the movie playing in large format on the side of Harold's Hardware. On the front steps of the church sat Sully the fortune teller—the only character who hadn't come straight out of a Norman Rockwell painting—with a hand-lettered sign reading, "Fortunes. $5. Know your future."

Helen found the mayor's tent and shook his hand. He was younger than she expected but he wore the same boxy sport coat that completed every outfit Drummond had ever worn. It was the uniform of old money in a small town.

"You're lucky to be working with Marshal," he said, cheerfully. "He's a good man. His father and my father were friends. A good man."

"Yes," Helen said, staring out at the crowd. "He

is a good man."

The mayor followed Helen's gaze and pointed to the center of the crowd.

"See Mad Mary?"

In the center of the crowd stood a paper mache effigy, about a head taller than a real human. The sculpture had wild, orange hair and green eyes the size of saucers. Her body was wrapped in canvas sheets.

"She represents an asylum patient. It's an old tradition. At midnight, they burn the statue as a warning for Mary and the other patients to stay away for another year."

Helen thought of Eliza huddled on her sofa, surrounded by junk she had bought from television: dolls and teddy bears and sundresses. For a moment, the effigy's face seemed to flicker to life, her mouth opening slowly. Helen blinked to clear her vision.

"Do you want a glass of wine?" the mayor asked.

Helen shook her head. "I think I'll just walk around, take it all in."

The street was crowded. People jostled each other in the gathering darkness, their faces appearing and disappearing as they passed the lights of the concession stands. Helen noticed a news camera sticking out above the crowd. She listened to the buzz of conversation around her. It was all about the Pittock legs. They were in every conversation, adding a thrill to the evening.

Helen sighed. One of the news reporters was making her way through the crowd, microphone in hand.

"Dr. Ivers, are you enjoying the festival?"

Helen recognized the trick question. Say "yes" and she was frolicking in the beer garden while women were dismembered in the woods behind her campus. Say “no” and she had no interest in the town and its provincial offerings.

“I felt it was important to be here.”

“Do you know the identity of the legs found on campus? Are the police any closer to an explanation? Do you think we are in danger?”

A few people in the beer garden waved at the camera. She could almost hear them. “Over here. Hi Mom! Red Sox rule!” It was all carnival to them. The beer. The fried dough. Mad Mary. The Pittock legs.

Another tragedy.

“But not mine,” the drinkers seemed to holler.

“Can you tell us what the police have learned so far?”

Helen was about to speak when something caught her attention. The beer garden crowd had stopped waving and was watching something.

Chapter Thirty-eight

Two young men circled each other. The crowd parted, hoping for a fight. In the space they provided, the men faced each other. One was lean. The other was built like a bull, with a sweet, baby face.

"She was our friend, and now she's gone," the bull yelled. "And you killed her."

"I did not, you fucking asshole." The slender boy swung a punch. He was half the bull's size, but he was fast and struck with a rattlesnake's speed. "You had better shut the fuck up. Everyone is saying that, and I didn't touch her."

"How do I know that?" The bull's voice was too soft for his massive body. He sounded frightened. "You… you had sex with her."

"Well that's more than you can say, Marcus. You fucking faggot! You wish you stuck it to her. You wish you did."

The slender boy came into view. *Ricky. Ricky Drummond and Marcus Billing.*

"Take it back," Marcus yelled.

"What? Faggot? Or faggot who wanted to fuck Carrie Brown and couldn't get it up."

Marcus tapped Ricky's jaw, not a real punch, just the threat of one.

"He hit me," Ricky cried. "Somebody help me." But he was not scared; his eyes were bright in the flickering light, black and full of malicious glee. He was having fun. He was winning, and he knew it.

Ricky lunged at Marcus, plunging his head into Marcus's chest. The boys locked shoulders like wrestlers. Neck to neck. Skin to skin. A headless beast. Staggering. At war with itself. Someone in the crowd cheered.

A woman cried, "Call the police," but made no move to do so herself.

A drunk man to Helen's left, slurred, "He's not putting his back into it. Man up, boy!"

Ricky's punch flew up from beneath the headlock and connected with Marcus's jaw.

Helen did not stop to think. She pushed her way through the crowd. "Stop. Break it up!"

A second later, she had her hands on the boys' shoulders. When they did not immediately release their grips, she raised her voice. "You will stop this now."

She grabbed a fistful of Ricky's hair and pulled him back. Beneath her other hand, she felt Marcus's shoulders soften. A moment later, three men from the crowd leapt forward and put their arms around the boys. Helen stood between them, arms outstretched, her fingertips resting on their chests. Ricky clutched his belly.

"Arrest him," Ricky cried, a grin barely concealed beneath his look of mock outrage. "He hit me."

"I didn't hardly touch him," Marcus pleaded. He really did look bovine, with big, wide-set eyes and shoulders like low foothills.

"That's enough, Ricky."

"He started it!" Ricky yelled the familiar playground cry.

"That doesn't matter. You're the provost's son, comport yourself."

"Yeah!" The drunk in the crowd yelled. "Dig–ni–ty!"

"Marcus." Helen turned to the other boy. Marcus's face crumpled into a look abject apology. "Carrie Brown is not dead. She transferred to UMass."

"But Professor Wilson said..." he mumbled.

Marcus looked past her. Without taking her fingers from the boys' chests, Helen turned to see what Marcus was watching.

"Marcus! Are you okay?" Wilson broke through the crowd and threw her arms around him, pulling Marcus away from Helen and stepping between them, as though ready to take a punch for Marcus. "Ricky Drummond, if you hurt him, I will see you flayed."

Helen grabbed Wilson's arm but with a lighter grasp than she had used on either of the boys. Wilson's bare skin was hot to the touch.

"Come with me," Helen said between closed teeth. To the boys she added, "You two! Break it up and go home."

She led Wilson through the crowd, then marched her down a narrow side street.

"Did you tell Marcus about Carrie?" she said when they were out of earshot of the crowd. "Is he out there because he thinks Ricky killed Carrie or because you told him?"

The street was darker than Helen had expected. Night had reached the alley first. Still she could see Wilson's strange, ice–blue eyes travel up and down her body.

"We can't hide the truth."

"Yes, we can," Helen said. "We hide it from our students to protect them. No one can know what we're thinking."

I want you, Adair.

"I trust my students. They know this campus."

Through the gap between buildings, Helen could see the effigy of Mad Mary swaying above the crowd. As she watched, the puppeteer turned Mary, and Mary's eyes were suddenly in shadow, like great gaping holes. Helen felt dizzy. She leaned against the wall behind her.

"What is it? You're not okay," Wilson said.

"I'm fine."

"I live right over there, at the Grandville. Come upstairs."

"It's just a touch of asthma, the heat." Helen sat down on the curb. "You're right. I don't know what to do."

"What is it?" Wilson sat beside Helen and put an arm around her shoulder.

"Someone left a straitjacket in Meyerbridge Hall."

"A straitjacket?"

"In the closet. And it was old. It was used." Helen could still smell the must coming off the fabric. She could feel the arms of the jacket closing in. "It's a sign."

"Of what?"

Helen felt her body go cold. She made a move to stand, but Wilson held her back.

"Of what?"

"I don't know."

Helen tried to slow her breathing. It came in frantic gasps. She had to stay calm. "I need to do something. Someone has to know."

"Back in your office, when I showed you the picture of the legs," Wilson said, "what were you looking for? You fell to the floor, and you said, 'Help me.' What do you need? Let me do something." Wilson's voice was earnest. "I want to protect you."

"No." Helen rose, stepping away from Wilson. She had to get out of the heat, out of the alley, out of the shadows. In the distance, she saw an orange glow surrounding Mad Mary. They had begun the burning. The crowd cheered.

"At least let me get you a piece of fried dough, a beer, a glass of water. Something. You look pale. You should eat. Come home with me."

Wilson was on her heels.

Helen spun around. "You're so lovely." It came out like an accusation. She had meant to say *leave me alone*. She had meant to say *go away*. She'd meant to lie. Instead, she fell into Wilson's embrace. Wilson's arms closed around her, warm and safe. She smelled Wilson's rich, exotic cologne, like the smell of frankincense and springtime and sex and chandeliers hung over marble floors.

"I can't do this," Helen whispered into Wilson's shoulder. "I can *never* have a drink with you. I can *never* eat fried dough with you. Ever."

Helen felt Wilson's smile against her cheek. "I bet those are words you never thought you'd have to say." Her voice was very tender.

"You need to understand."

"I don't understand." Wilson pulled her closer. "I won't understand." Her voice dropped to an even softer whisper, barely a breath. "I want to fuck you, but I'm also trying to be your friend."

Helen shook herself loose and pulled at the edge

of her suit jacket, feeling the shoulder pads settle. The façade and the real: so hard to distinguish.

"I have to focus on the college right now."

"Is that the price you pay for your position? For being president?"

"It just is." Helen heard the sadness in her own voice.

"If you don't fraternize with your subordinates, what do you do?"

"What do you mean?"

"Do you even have friends? Do you have a hobby?"

Hobbies? Helen saw Eliza's visage flickering on the faces of the crowd. Always on the periphery of her vision, always dissolving when she looked closely. Always there. The eye sockets empty.

Helen had never had any hobbies. No ballet lessons. No high school track. No piano. Only Eliza screaming in her bedroom, and Helen waiting for the panicked footsteps, the car engine starting again. Another flight to the hospital. The mad house. Their mother had begged Helen not to call it that, but she refused to give Eliza the dignity of a euphemism.

"I don't have time for a lot of hobbies," she said.

"Nothing," Wilson pressed. "Hiking? Scrapbooking?"

God no. What could she possibly want to save from the past?

"I've been thinking about redecorating the Pittock House." She had to say something. Hobbies were normal. A woman with no hobbies, no pleasures, no gentle leisure time—that was a woman on the edge. "I want to do it all in white."

She was hurrying out of the alley, barely glancing

at Wilson, talking to keep from telling the truth.

I want you.

"There are some great antique stores in the area, but last thing I need is antiques." She reached the street, where she could see the flames consuming the last of Mad Mary. "I want white carpet, white sofa, white art, white vases with white flowers."

"It sounds like a hospital."

"It sounds clean," Helen said and rushed away from Wilson, until the crowd separated them and she could not hear Wilson's reply.

Helen stopped a block later. She could still hear the noise of the festival, but beneath that, footsteps sounded close behind her. She thought, for a moment, that Wilson had followed her.

"Wilson?"

A shadow merged more fully into the black mouth of a recessed doorway. Then the street was still.

"Adair?"

Nothing.

Helen hurried back to the Pittock House, thankful for the extra lighting installed by security. She paused when she got to her porch. There was no one in sight, no motion in the darkness, and yet she felt a human gaze slide down her body. *It's nothing. Don't give in.*

A window in the peaked roof of the Pittock House, gave him a clear view of the president. She sat at a desk, her dark, red hair glinting in the glow of a laptop, like the color of blood in the moonlight. He tried to imagine that, instead of sitting at a desk by the window with the lower half of her body obscured by the wall, she was sitting in a wheelchair. Better yet, she was sitting on a little platform, right at window height. Nothing below. Just the stumps of her legs, serving as a pedestal for her torso. He felt the need. Without thinking, he drew nearer, ducking into the shadows of the bushes.

The branches around him rustled, brushing the side of the house. Ivers stood up. *No!* He could see the tops of her thighs. She walked to the window and pressed her face to the glass. The stumps were gone, his imagination replaced by the reality of her complete body silhouetted against the window. She closed the blinds.

Her face remained frozen in his mind, a photograph burned into his retina. She was much prettier than Carrie, older but far more beautiful. He eyed the front door. It would be easy to force his way in. Any one of the windows or doors would give way at the thrust of his shoulder. He could even request a key if he wanted. Just turn the key and step in.

The problem was the students. It was always the students, each one an insipid fool. There were so many of them. In the Ventmore dormitory, directly across the Barrow Creek, thirty windows stared into the night. At any one, a girl might be talking on the phone, a boy might be blowing out cigarette smoke. The building had a hundred eyes. He would have to think of another plan.

He pulled a twig off the holly bush at his elbow. The bark peeled away like skin, bloodless at first. There was always a millisecond before the blood started, as though it took the body a moment to respond to the wound, to recognize the end. Ivers was living in that moment. He slipped from behind the bush and placed the broken twig across the bottom step of Ivers's porch. Just a token. A foretaste.

Chapter Thirty-nine

The next day, he waited as Hornsby made his way across the Pittock campus, toward the Barrow Creek bridge. Hornsby moved slowly for a police officer. It was hard to imagine a criminal who *couldn't* outrun him. Still, when Hornsby arrived he drew himself up to his full height like some real man. Mr. Cop.

"Thompson saw the medical examiner's report," Hornsby said.

"I know."

"He's alerted the media."

"I know."

"There was nothing I could have done. He ordered another copy of the report. He forged my signature on the request."

"How are you going to fix this?"

"I can't do anything more," Hornsby said. "If I cover it up again, he'll suspect something. He'll call someone in. Just let it go. If Thompson finds something, great. If he doesn't, fine. I did everything you asked."

"I said make the legs match the body."

"You can handle the PR! People will lose interest. This isn't the end of the world."

"I told you to make this go away."

He could tell by the look on Hornsby's face that the truth was finally dawning. How quaint. How innocent. He had not even thought about it.

"You...you didn't do it?" Hornsby asked, his breath a gasp. He took a step back, tripping on a loose board. "Tell me you didn't. You wouldn't. That's not what this is about. Tell me that's not what this is about."

"You still want to sleep at night, don't you?" He put his hand on the back of Hornsby's neck. "You want to be the good cop who keeps us safe."

"If I find out you....If it was Ricky...No one is going to get away with this."

He squeezed Hornsby's neck until tendon pressed against bone. He had only a moment to decide. He could move his hands around to the front and press until Hornsby's body fell limp. Surprise would slow Hornsby's movements, surprise and disbelief. He would go down wondering how the world could be so bad. Then one quick shove and Hornsby would be over the rail. He wouldn't even have to kill Hornsby on the bridge. As long as Hornsby was unconscious, he would drown in the shallow water. He looked up and down the bridge. The playing fields. The library. Boston Hall. The Ventmore dormitory. There were so many eyes. He released Hornsby.

"I had better call Dr. Le Farge and tell him to cancel the study."

"You can't do that. Alisha left this morning. She's probably in Switzerland by now." Hornsby's voice shook. "The treatments start in a week. You said they're expecting her."

"I've run out of money."

"You haven't!"

"No. I haven't. In fact, I just received a rather large windfall from an old friend. But Dr. Le Farge has no way of knowing."

"They won't take her off the study. They need

her for science."

"Do you think it would be hard to find someone to take her place? Do you think there is any shortage of wealthy women who would pay for a second chance at life?" He leaned close enough to smell the police chief's breath. Coffee. Bile. "Le Farge is offering a miracle, not some new chemotherapy that will extend her life another six months while she vomits up blood. This is the real thing, and it comes at a cost. The cost is your soul."

"I'll think of something. I'll figure something out." Hornsby had gone pale. "Please. Don't take Alisha off the study. She has nothing to do with this. It's not her fault. Blame me. Hurt me."

I still might. He watched Hornsby hurry away, almost running. Hornsby just needed a little fear to put the hustle back in his step.

He dug his nails into the wood of the bridge railing. He had to move quickly. In a few days, Alisha Hornsby would show up at the Hôpitaux Universitaires de Genève and find out there was no study. There was no Dr. Le Farge, no miracle cure. Then Hornsby's honor might win out over self-interest, although he could still be blackmailed. There would be Giles and Thompson's youthful optimism to contend with. But if everything went according to plan, none of that would matter. If everything went according to plan, Helen Ivers would disappear as quickly and completely as the whores in Battambang.

On Monday morning, Helen was surprised when the first telephone call came from Robert Hornsby.

"Heard you were talking to Officer Thompson about the legs," he said gruffly.

"Do you have some news for me?" Helen asked. She wasn't going to a debate whom she talked to and why.

"Look, I know you and I got off to a difficult start," Hornsby said. "I called to say I'm sorry. What with my wife being sick, I haven't been myself." His apology was as warm as a frozen lake.

"This is unprecedented," Helen said.

"I just want to repair relations with the college. We've all been under a lot of stress, trying to solve this case." Hornsby coughed. "And I've got some news for you."

"Yes?"

"You were right. The DNA on the legs matches Carrie Brown, and we're pretty sure it was a suicide. The torso belongs to another woman. We got a positive ID on a homeless woman. Crystal Leigh Evans. Probably another suicide. It's not her first attempt. I talked to a therapist who used to see her when she was at the asylum. He said this didn't surprise him."

"What didn't surprise him?"

"A suicide. Crystal saw the media attention and, in her mind, that meant Carrie Brown was a star. She wanted that. We got the Berkshire–Western people looking for the bodies. We figure the same thing happened twice. First time, the train lifted the body. The second time it was the legs. Could be coyotes, though."

"Mr. Hornsby, you'll forgive me, but this sounds farfetched. Two suicides?"

"It's not that unusual. When there's a widely publicized attack or suicide, next thing you know, someone's trying it themselves. We saw that with 9/11. The Trade Center went down and then, don't you know, some idiot with a two-seater flies his plane into the side of the U.S. Bank building in Seattle. Gets the plane stuck and has to have the building's security staff help him out."

"You're telling me two women committed suicide on the train tracks and each time their body—or half their body—was carried away or...?"

"Eaten. It happens."

Helen paced across her office, stretching the phone cord until it almost pulled the phone off her desk. "I just don't believe it."

"You haven't worked in law enforcement. You don't understand this town."

Helen was about to say, *I don't need to understand this town to know when I'm hearing bullshit.* Something in Hornsby's tone stopped her. She had believed him until now. She had believed the dying-wife story. He was an old man, in over his head, with two rookie cops underfoot. Gross negligence, shielded by Rotary Club loyalty, in a town where people were defined by their grandfather's property lines more than their own accomplishments. Or failures. Now there was an edge to Hornsby's voice that stiffened the hair on the back of her neck.

"Is Officer Thompson helping you with this?" Helen asked.

"He's away."

"Away?"

"He's looking into some poachers; guess they're hunting mountain lions. Some environmental protection group is up our ass about it."

Poachers?

"What about Darrell Giles?"

"Officer Giles is on administrative leave for discharging his firearm without cause."

"Who did he shoot?"

"It was at a Fourth of July party this year. He fired a police-issued weapon seven times. Shooting cans off a stump. He could have killed someone."

"Shooting cans. That's…" Helen stopped.

You don't understand this town.

"I'll call Carrie Brown's next of kin this afternoon," Helen said. "Thank you for contacting me. I hope your wife is all right."

"Carrie's dead," Mrs. Brown said, before Helen had a chance to speak. "The legs. Of course. We knew. We saw it in the news." Then the woman let out a soft cry, like the last breath escaping a sparrow.

Helen pressed the receiver to her ear, as though she could somehow press her sympathy onto the Browns. They reminded her so much of her parents.

"Deidre, please put down the phone," Mr. Brown instructed his wife. "Tell me what I need to know, Ms. Ivers."

"DNA confirmed that the legs belonged to your daughter, Carrie."

Helen hated delivering the news. She hated the fact that the Browns must hear about their daughter's death and understand that even that news led to another tragedy. The freakish manner of their daughter's death would taint the sympathy they received. Even as the neighbor's consoled them, they'd be thinking about Carrie's naked legs bound to the train tracks.

"I'm so sorry," Helen said.

"Oh, Carrie," Mr. Brown said.

In the background, Mrs. Brown cried quietly.

"How do we go about arranging for the body to be sent out? We don't want to fly to Massachusetts."

The body. Helen had been dreading that question.

"The police have not recovered the body. They believe it may have been transported by the train."

"Damn her," Mr. Brown said. It was not a passionate outburst. Something in his calm piqued Helen's curiosity.

"Are you surprised?" Helen asked as gently as she could.

"We knew this was coming. We just didn't know when. Carrie was sick," he said, his voice flat.

Helen had a vision of her own father trying to make sense of Eliza's illness, words like "schizoaffective disorder" and "atypical antipsychotics" catching on his tongue like the answers to an exam.

"I know this is hard. Can you tell me about Carrie and why you thought this might happen?"

The phone crackled and Helen closed her eyes to listen.

"When Carrie was five, her aunt broke a leg." Mr. Brown spoke slowly. "Carrie was obsessed with it. She wanted to touch the cast, to put her fingers under the plaster. Finally, she started pretending her leg was broken. So what, we thought. We gave her an old pair of crutches. She was just a kid playing pretend. We said she wanted to be a doctor. That's what we told our friends." He gave a strangled laugh.

"Then when she was about ten, there was a boy in her school who was missing his left leg. A birth defect, you know. She talked about him all the time.

We thought it was a crush at first. But it wasn't right. The things she said. The way she said it. Like she was hungry for it. She wanted to talk about it all the time, and we got strict with her. Told her we didn't want to hear that kind of garbage. Maybe we should have been softer on her. Maybe if we had got her help right then..."

Helen could tell he had asked these questions a thousand times before.

"In high school, she cut up her legs real bad." The man's voice wavered. "It was awful. We had some friends. Their daughter used to cut herself, little perfect razor marks. So clean, you could barely see them. This wasn't like that. It was like she was trying to carve her bones out.

"She used one of my hunting knives. I was always so careful with my rifles. Not even Deidre knew the gun safe combination. I was never going to be one of those fathers who leaves his loaded rifle out for his kids to play with. But the knife. It wasn't even a real hunting knife. It was a souvenir. The psychiatrist said it was a plea for help. He said if we spent more time with her, took an interest in her hobbies, she'd get over it." He was crying now. "But I know she was trying to cut her legs off.

"She was always so tall and graceful. She never put on an ounce of weight. Everyone at church always said she should be a model for J.C. Penny's. But Carrie wanted her legs cut off. She wanted to go around in a wheelchair for the rest of her life. She ran away when she was seventeen. We tried to find her, but what were we going to do? How can you understand a beautiful, healthy girl who wants to cut her own legs off? He raised his voice. "Were we supposed to get her a wheelchair? Fix the house so she could get around? What she wanted was an abomination."

"Had you been in touch with her recently?"

"She ran away when she was seventeen. She got back in touch when she was twenty-three, came home for Easter one year. We were proud that she put herself in college, but we weren't really a family. We didn't talk to her but once or twice a year. I knew she still wanted to do it, to cut off her legs."

Helen thought about Blake and the devotees. The "ultimate commitment" he had called it. *Being disabled frees us to be who we really are.* But it hadn't freed Carrie. It had killed her.

After she talked to the Browns, Helen called Eliza's psychiatrist.

"Helen!" She could hear Dr. Linda Crestwell shushing her receptionist and closing a door behind her. "How are you?"

Helen resented Crestwell's overweening sincerity. A professional hazard, Helen guessed. Nonetheless, Crestwell was the best in Pittsburg, maybe in her field.

"I'm absolutely fine," Helen said. "I'm calling with a professional question."

"Ah. The Pittock legs. I've been following the case," Crestwell said. "Body Integrity Identity Disorder, that's my diagnosis."

"Body…?"

"Body Integrity Identity Disorder. BIID. You've heard of transsexuals, yes? They possess the body of, say, a man, but feel as though they were meant to be a woman. It sounds strange, and, of course, we don't like to think that our gender defines us, yet it does. Men can be nurses; women can be doctors." Crestwell chuckled. She was proof. "I'm not talking about those kinds of distinctions. Deep inside, however, our gender does determine a great deal of our experience. And it's more than your parts. It's DNA. It's in utero hormone exposure. It's properly developed sex organs. One aberration in any of those factors, and it's possible the individual's body won't match their neural map. So, you get a transsexual. His body is male, but his…or her…mind is different."

Helen tapped the end of her pencil against her chin. "But we don't wake up every morning and think 'I feel like a woman' or 'I feel like a man.'"

"No. But close your eyes. You still know where your hands and feet are, yes? Even if you can't see them. Even if nothing is touching your skin. You *know* where your body is. We call it proprioception. Proprioception works, in part, because the mind has a map of the body that is separate from just feeling things on your skin. Your map matches your body, but what if it doesn't? Imagine your neural map has a penis."

"That's hard to imagine."

"For you. For a transsexual woman, that's everyday life."

Helen tucked the phone under her ear, twisted her hair into a knot, and secured it with the pencil.

"So what does this have to do with the Pittock legs?"

"People who suffer from BIID have a neural map that ends above the left knee or at the left wrist. You can have right-sided BIID or dual BIID, but it's less common."

"Do you think it's probable this was a case of

BIID?" Helen asked.

"Possible."

"The police say there were actually two cases. First the Pittock legs and then a suicide."

Helen could almost picture Crestwell brushing her coarse, gray hair off her forehead. She would wear a sympathetic, no-nonsense expression.

"It's possible," Crestwell said. "Copycat suicides, copycat crimes... that's not a stretch." She paused. "But, really, how are *you*, Helen? How are *you* doing?"

Helen gave Crestwell a brief rundown on the college's financial problems, her plans for a capital campaign, and highlights from her alumni visits.

"I see," Crestwell said. "And this is very important to you? Do you feel enriched by these challenges?"

"Damn it," Helen said after the phone was securely back in its cradle. "I'm fine." She felt a lump in the back of her throat and tears welling up in her eyes. She tipped her head back so the tears wouldn't mar her mascara, then blinked several times and got back to work.

Chapter Forty

The last meeting of Helen's week was with the attorney in charge of distributing Adrian Meyerbridge's funds. Although distracted by thoughts of the Browns, there was no putting off the meeting. Pittock needed the money fast. Helen met Meyerbridge's attorney in her office. Everyone else had gone home. The attorney spread the paperwork in front of her.

"Mr. Drummond has already signed all the necessary documents," the attorney explained. "You sign here to accept the gift." The attorney handed her a pen.

Helen looked at the figures, and her forehead wrinkled. "Five hundred thousand. Is that all?"

"Is that not the figure you agreed to?"

Helen had never heard the exact figure. Five hundred thousand was a lot of money, but not the kind of money that bought buildings. Helen sighed. Adrian was Drummond's friend.

"I wasn't clear on the details. If Mr. Drummond has signed, then this is the figure."

"It doesn't add up," Helen whispered. She was eating a late dinner at the Craven when Terri called. "Two women. The body. The copycat theory. I don't trust the chief of police." She spoke so softly Terri asked her to repeat. "I can't," Helen whispered. "I'm in the pub."

"And the spies are everywhere?"

"This is not Los Angeles. People here know each other. They listen."

"You're sounding like a conspiracy theorist," Terri said.

The waitress arrived with Helen's deep-fried special. Helen projected her voice into the phone. "The weather's been great here. Just a touch of fall."

"You don't sound okay." The humor dropped out of Terri's voice.

"I'll call you later."

Helen was about to hang up.

"Wait. Can I at least talk to you about some non-privileged information?"

"All right." Helen poked at her food. "You talk. I'll listen."

"I did a bit of research on your Adair Wilson."

"She's not 'my' anything."

"Well she could be. I don't think you have much to worry about. It looks like trouble has a way of finding Adair Wilson, but that's not to say she *is* trouble. The part about her thesis advisor was half-true. They were sleeping together, and her advisor is married to the dean of business. As for the allegation that she blackmailed her advisor to get her first teaching job, I don't believe it.

"First of all, she took a year off after getting her PhD, if you can call working on Broadway time off. At Duke she was hired by a five-person committee and, from everything I gather, they liked her from the start. They were impressed with her work and only let her go because they did not have a tenure-track position open. I don't think her advisor had enough clout to get a whole committee to roll over. She might have wanted to," Terri continued. "Adair Wilson might have pressured her to. But the advisor doesn't have those kinds of connections. No one on the committee knew the advisor personally. And Wilson was at the top of her game. Duke was lucky to get her."

Helen pushed a piece of fried fish across her plate. The breading cracked to reveal white flesh lined with gray veins. She had no appetite.

"What about Marshal and the story about the janitor?"

"That's a harder one. Ultimately, Wilson just backed this woman up. The woman, Anat Al-Fulani, didn't speak a lot of English. Wilson helped her navigate the system. I'm not saying it was smart, but it could have been well-intentioned."

Helen leaned back in her booth. "Thank you," she told her old friend.

"There is one more thing," Terri added. "Most of the news reports say Al-Fulani got deported after the investigations started. Funny thing is, she had just gotten a green card. I called one of the reporters, a woman in Springfield. She saw Al-Fulani's paperwork. Al-Fulani was very proud of it, took her to her trailer and showed her." Terri trailed off.

"What are you saying?"

"I'm asking. Do you like this girl?" He was no longer speaking in the clipped tone of an attorney. "You know you are entitled to have a relationship, Helen."

Helen paused. "It was a mistake."

"College presidents do fall for people. Some

would even say it's important for leaders to have personal lives. I'm just saying, I checked your contract and hers. There is nothing that forbids you from pursuing a relationship with this woman."

"You *are* thorough," Helen said dryly.

"It's my job. Especially when my friend's happiness is at stake. Why don't you go find this woman? Grab a bunch of flowers, tell her she has pretty eyes or whatever you young career women like to hear."

"That's ridiculous."

It was an almost comical scene: Helen with a bouquet of mini-mart roses, telling Wilson she had "pretty eyes." Wilson's white-blue eyes were as beautiful as an avalanche.

"Okay. Take her to a gay bar and get her drunk."

"That's just stupid."

Terri snorted. "I've seen worse."

"I am not going to do any of that," Helen said. "Goodnight."

Still, as Helen mounted the staircase that led from the Craven to the street, she thought she might follow Terri's advice. It was the intuition, groundless but absolute, that if she showed up at Wilson's door, Wilson would be happy to see her—no, not happy, joyful—that made her pause on the last step. Wilson would be waiting for her, *was* waiting for her.

Helen took another step, emerged on the street, and came to her senses. There was someone else she needed to find.

It was odd how ubiquitous the homeless where

when they were not wanted. Now that Helen needed to talk to Sully, the streets were empty. It took her an hour before she found a man with an army duffle bag sleeping on a bench behind the elementary school. She asked if he knew where she could find the fortune teller.

"She's probably at the camp," he told Helen. He gave her directions to the bike path that ran along Crescent Street, past the asylum.

It was after nine and the day had faded to mute blue when Helen found the gravel parking lot the homeless man had flagged as a landmark. Slowly, carefully, remembering the terrifying fall into the asylum spring, Helen crossed the field toward the light of a small campfire. As she drew closer, figures scattered into the darkness.

A toothless man sitting by the fire called, "Are you a cop?"

Someone in the darkness yelled, "She's a social worker. Tell her to buy us some cigarettes."

There was a murmur of laughter.

"I'm looking for Sully the fortune teller."

"You want to hear about tall, dark, and handsome. Sully won't give you that. The hanged man. That's her card." The voice came from the ground. As Helen looked more closely, she saw the sleeping bag near her feet. She had almost stepped on the woman inside.

"You got a fiver?" The sleeping bag stirred, and one dark, boney hand emerged from the covers like something rising from the dead. "You never have a fiver when I need it."

Helen recognized Sully's crackling voice.

Slowly Sully stood, keeping the sleeping bag wrapped around her. In the darkness, she appeared to be more beast—or rock—than human. Her back was humped and the dirty bedding accentuated the mound. Her head seemed to emerge from the center of her chest, like some nightmare creature drawn in the margins of an ancient, sea-farer's map.

"So, you finally want to know? Mrs. Boss, finally came around."

"Can we talk in private?" Helen asked. "I'll pay you, if that's what you want."

Sully extended a gnarled hand. Helen placed a twenty dollar-bill on her palm without touching Sully's skin.

"This way," Sully said.

She shuffled away from the fire. When they reached the parking lot, she stopped and beckoned for Helen to come closer.

"Everybody is listening," Sully whispered.

Helen took a step forward, trying to block out the odor of cigarettes and sweat, so much like Eliza that she watched Sully's face to remind her it was not her sister.

"I need to know about Crystal Evans," Helen said.

"What do you want to know?"

"I want to know if you think she committed suicide. I want to know how she died."

Sully drummed her fingers on the metal guardrail. "So," she said, "they figured it out. They weren't Crystal's legs."

"They think the legs belonged to a student at Pittock. They think she committed suicide."

"And Crystal? What did Crystal do?"

"That's what I'm asking you. They think she committed suicide in the same way. A copycat."

"That was Crystal for you. Always had to be better, always had to tell a bigger story. But she didn't kill herself. No. She wouldn't have done it on the second."

"The second?"

"She had just gotten her Social Security check. She would have blown it first, had a big drink up. At least, she would've cashed it and given us the money. Crystal was like that. She was a good girl." Sully returned her hands to the depths of her sleeping bag, pulling it tightly around her, although the evening was still warm. "You should drain the well before someone else falls in."

"What?"

"I see you in the well."

Sully shifted in her sleeping-bag cloak. The moon had not risen, and the night was suddenly dark. Helen could not make out her sooty face. She was just a voice in the shadows. A voice, and occasionally the glint of yellowed eyes.

"But you didn't want your fortune." Sully spat on the dirt. "You wanted to give me your money. You wanted to give me your charity, but you need to buy the future. You need to know."

"I'm looking for information about Crystal," Helen said.

"You aren't listening." Sully's hands darted out of the sleeping bag and she waved them like airport staff guiding in an airplane. "You don't understand. I am Cassandra." Sully lunged at Helen, grabbing her shoulders. "You don't listen." The smell of Sully's breath was sickening. "I am Cassandra. I see all, and I know you. Mrs. Bosswoman. I *see* you."

For a second, Sully's third eye glowed blue in the

darkness. Then it closed, and she was gone. Only her voice remained, vibrating in Helen's skull.

"Drain the wells, Helen."

Chapter Forty-one

Helen was shaken enough by Sully's rantings, but when she entered the Pittock house that night, she thought she had finally, irrevocably lost her mind. The first thing she felt was a fierce blush spreading across her face. The embarrassment! She had been so distracted she had walked into the wrong house and was standing in a stranger's foyer. Then another thought struck her: there were no other houses near the Pittock house. She had wandered, like Eliza, far from home, and now she stood in this hallway, seconds before discovery. The police would come, and there would be long, quiet conversations to which she was not privy. Drummond would stand up for her, and the homeowners would not press charges. And then?

But no. As she looked around, she saw the familiar layout. The long hall. The parlor. Even the filigreed wallpaper was the same. It was just that everything else had been transformed. On the floor, a white shag carpet ran the length of the hallway. In the parlor, the horse hair sofas, the pram, and the baby doll had all been replaced. In their stead sat a white velvet sofa, white velvet arm chairs, and a white marble coffee table. In place of Jedidiah Pittock's portrait hung an oceanscape. Helen took a step closer. The texture of the paint told her it was no reproduction, and it was gorgeous, all done in hues of white, as though the artist had painted only the light. Totally abstract and yet clearly the ocean at dawn.

On the marble table stood a vase of white lilies. The note below read, "I need you. I love you. You belong in white. Adair."

"No," Helen said. "No. No. No."

She ran down the hall. In the kitchen, stood a white-tiled butcher block table and white stools.

Hands trembling, she was barely able to press Terri's speed dial.

"It's everywhere," she said. She pulled a drawer open and then another. Gone was the cafeteria cutlery. Gone, the dull, wood-handled knives. Gone, the cheap, gas station wine opener. Everything had been replaced. There were instruments in all the drawers—all white. Spatulas, whisks, a carving knife, something that looked like a plastic lemon on a stick, something labeled a micro-planer.

"She's been here. She's touched everything. She could still be here. What am I going to tell Drummond?"

It took several minutes of slamming cupboards for Helen to realize that Terri had been repeating the words "calm down" over and over again. When she finally heard him and stopped, he told her to start slowly, from the beginning.

When she finished he said, "So...do you think she's a stalker?"

"Of course she's a stalker." Helen stared at a cupboard full of white bone china.

"Or do you think she's a wealthy, young woman in love who's not making very good choices?"

Helen could not fathom her motives. She rushed back to the living room.

"I don't know what she did with the portrait of Jedidiah Pittock. It's gone. It's hung over that fireplace for a hundred years."

"From what you told me it was hideous."

"It was an heirloom."

"So call her and ask."

"I can't call her. No one can know about this. If they know about this, they'll know everything." Her mind reeled from point to point: Wilson, their affair, the money it must have cost to refurnish the house. It was all wrong.

"Call her," Terri insisted. "And tell her not to talk. Or go on Twitter. If the students saw someone redecorating your house, they'll accuse you of mishandling college funds while their tuition goes up. Count on it. You'll know who saw what soon enough."

"It's breaking and entering. I should have her arrested."

"Yeah," Terri said in a way that seemed to imply no. "If you feel unsafe," he added, "get a hotel. I mean that. Even if it's just a premonition. But if you trust this woman, call her, make sure she didn't throw the antiques in a dumpster. I bet she didn't. She's old money. They appreciate these things. Then say thank you. 'Thank you for doing something completely inappropriate in an effort to cheer me up.' She sounds rather romantic."

In the end, Helen took none of Terri's advice. She did not call Wilson to thank her or to scold her. Once the initial shock and indignation wore off, she could not work up the energy to care about Pittock's portrait. She certainly did not care about the baby doll. She simply went upstairs, marveled at the transformation there too, and fell into the most comfortable bed she had ever slept in, drifting off beneath sheets as soft as the sky itself.

❧❧❧

In the morning, Twitter was silent on the subject of Helen's décor, as was the newspaper and her voice mail. Still shaking her head at the bizarre transformation of her home, Helen walked across campus and called the DOT office as soon as it opened at 8:00 a.m. The DOT worker was courteous to the point of obsequiousness, but he was not budging on the issue of draining the asylum springs.

"We don't have the budget for it. We've secured the area. Perhaps if there had been some incident, we might be able to move this to a higher priority. But there hasn't."

Helen drew a series of vicious hatch marks on her desk blotter. "Two women were killed in the forest, and their bodies are still missing. That's an incident."

The man on the other end of the line paused, as though leafing through a report. "It says here that the Pittock police did some kind of scope, found nothing in the springs."

"What if I had it on good authority that the scope was wrong?"

"That would be a police matter. They would need to re-scope or order a drain. We deal with accidents. They deal with crimes."

"There was an accident." Helen jumped at the opportunity. "I fell in. I nearly drowned. Is that enough?"

"Can anyone verify that?" The man sounded embarrassed. He thought she was crazy.

"Absolutely. Adair Wilson." Helen gave him the number. "She was there."

A few minutes later, he called back. "I'm sorry ma'am. The woman you mentioned said she had never been in or near the springs with you."

"Look. I'll pay with my own money. I'll mortgage this school. Just do it."

"How are you doing, Helen?" Drummond asked.

He and Helen were sitting on the edge of the fountain in the science courtyard, eating their lunches. The picnic had been his idea. Helen sensed he was trying to comfort her. He was kind. Just beneath the cool, New England exterior was a real affection. He sat very still, not looking at her, yet Helen could feel his full attention.

"You've been through so much recently."

"I'm fine," Helen said. "I really am all right."

Helen hated lying to him. She hated the subterfuge. But she could not share her fears. She made a concerted effort to smile, to dabble her fingers in the water. When he was not looking, she searched his face for signs that he knew about Wilson or that he had guessed her apprehensions about his son. She saw none.

"It's been tough dealing with my sister's death, but I'll be okay." She let her words trail off cheerfully, like the breeze that had kicked up to stir the first fall leaves. There was something brittle in the way it darted, twirled, and then died down. "You know, I've been thinking," Helen added. "You said it was time to start our capital campaign. What did you have in mind?"

"I do like you, Helen," Drummond said appreciatively. "You don't break easily."

Helen smiled. "I'm a tough old soldier."

Drummond chuckled. "That makes two of us."

He took off his Pittock class ring and held it up to the sunlight. The stone glinted, darker than any amethyst Helen had ever seen.

"This was my father's ring. He went to Pittock, and my grandfather went here before him. Institutions like this survive because they plan for the future. We plan for the future. What better way to show that we can weather this storm?"

"That's exactly what I'm thinking," Helen said. As long as she could keep him focused on college business, as long as he thought they were working together for the good of the campus, she could watch Ricky.

"Do you want to hear my plan?" Drummond asked.

Helen nodded

"There is a lot that needs renovating, updating. I'm thinking about something that will make a statement: the old asylum. It's not school property, but it could be. The state has been trying to get rid of it. They can't tear it down because of its architectural significance. However, it's a huge liability and the state does not have the budget to renovate. What if we turned those buildings into student housing? We need it, and they are right there."

"Over two hundred and fifty private rooms," Helen mused, "each with a window. Courtyards, kitchen facilities. We could replant the gardens. It would become a state of the art dormitory. I'm glad you mention that. I've ordered a team to come in and drain the wells."

"You fill the wells; you don't drain them."

Drummond was vehement.

"What?"

"It costs many thousands of dollars to drain a well. It's almost impossible. If you fill them, it's the price of a dump truck and rough fill from the construction site. Oh Helen, call them back and tell them 'no.' We can't afford that."

The breeze had chilled. The sunlight glared in Helen's eyes without warming her.

"I can afford it."

In the distance, she heard a rumble of thunder.

"But why?"

Drummond's patronizing "oh Helen" and her own fear made her angry.

"I saw the figures on Adrian Meyerbridge's estate," she spat out. "We were counting on that money."

"He also donated a quantity of stocks from his portfolio." Drummond did not meet her eyes.

"I went over the figures," Helen said. She was not sure how far she wanted to push. "Give or take, it looks like he could not have left more than half a million, less if the market drops."

Drummond said nothing.

"There are collectors with no connection to the college who would pay at least a million for their name on an administration building." Helen tried to keep her voice friendly. "We may need to think about that in the future."

"I know," Drummond said, still avoiding her gaze. "I wanted Adrian to have that building, Helen."

"What did you tell the board?"

"I told them the truth. The market is variable. The gift was worth more when Adrian first signed."

Helen leaned her head back, resting it against a decorative, stone urn. She closed her eyes to the sharp sunlight filling the quad. She was angry, not just at Drummond and the foolish gift but at the whole town and its old rules. Drummond could give away college buildings like his personal possessions. Hornsby could redact reports and treat the police department like a hobby. Ricky Drummond could mistreat Carrie Brown and then walk away as though he had no part to play in her life. Helen heard Wilson as though she were standing beside her: *You're not part of this place yet. Things disappear here. People disappear.* She could not let Drummond guess her feelings.

"Some things are more important than money," she said without opening her eyes.

The breeze blew a cold spray of water from the fountain. Helen was about to speak, when she heard footsteps. Helen opened her eyes just as Ricky Drummond burst through the arched doorway to the courtyard.

"Dad!" He called as he ran toward Drummond. "Dad, help." He dropped to his knees in front of his father. "Dad, it was awful." There were tears on his cheeks. "You have to come. You have to see it."

Chapter Forty-two

Ricky led them across the Barrow Creek, past the Pittock House, and along the wooded trail that skirted the asylum. The breeze that had riffled the leaves in the courtyard now turned into angry gusts. Trees swayed in the wind. A storm approached, chilling the air. A few drops of rain splattered Helen's face.

When they arrived at the spot Ricky indicated, they found Hornsby and a young officer Helen did not recognize. The two men were wrestling a plastic privacy tarp into place. The young man was trying to stake it at one end, while Hornsby held the flapping plastic from blowing away. Hornsby was yelling at the rookie, berating him for announcing their position on the radio. The young man was holding his ground.

"Police use radios," he yelled over the sound of the plastic tarp whipping in the wind. "If you want to do everything on the down low, you'll have to tell me."

"Use some common sense, boy!"

Several reporters were already at the scene, alerted by the rookie's radio broadcast. When they saw Helen and Drummond, they rushed forward.

"Are you Helen Ivers?"

"Does the body belong to a student?"

"The body?" For a moment Helen was speechless. Then, a few feet away, she heard another reporter speaking to his camera.

"Alerted that well springs around the asylum might cause a drowning hazard, DOT workers were securing the area when they discovered what appears to be a human torso..."

Helen straightened her lapels. Behind the reporters, the police officers still wrestled with the tarp. The smell of putrefaction wafted away from the scene.

"Do you know why it has taken so long to uncover the body?" a reporter asked.

"Do you think this is a serial killer?"

Thunder exploded in the sky above. Helen felt it shake the ground.

"Should students on campus be worried?"

"Has enrollment dropped?"

Behind the reporters, Hornsby lost his grip on the tarp. The younger man let go of the stake in order to catch the plastic. It flew back at him, and he raised an arm to protect his face. The reporters turned. Hornsby barked at them to get back.

For an instant, the tarp flew up and Helen saw the body. The woman's mouth was open in a scream. Her eyes bulged. The lips were bared, the face black and bloated. Helen realized they had drawn the body from the well into which she had fallen. She had drunk that water, breathed it, swallowed it. That water had touched the corneas of her open eyes. That bright water that had fallen from Wilson's body, as if from Poseidon's shoulders. That water had steeped the body of Carrie Brown like a sick, dark tea. That water was in Helen even now, molecules of that tragedy corrupting her body like cancer.

The young officer got control of the tarp to hide the body. It did not disappear from Helen's vision.

Those seconds the corpse had been visible were burned into Helen's memory, melding with Eliza's image. Eliza with her black stare. Carrie with her mouth open. Helen blinked. The image stayed superimposed on the real world, on the faces of the reporters, the bark of a tree. The face was everywhere. Screaming. Bleeding.

The rain broke with a crash of thunder, and Helen ran. She had lost track of Drummond and Ricky but didn't care. She did not care if the reporters saw her flee. She had to escape Eliza's face.

Back at the Pittock house, Helen cowered by the kitchen sink. In the corner, by the broom closet, Eliza stood motionless like a cardboard cutout, her mouth fixed in Carrie's scream. *She's not there. She's not there.* Helen deliberately looked at Eliza, as if a direct stare would dispel the apparition. The hallucination remained in place.

Helen's phone rang. Drummond.

"Are you all right?"

"I'm fine. I had to collect myself."

"You take all the time you need. I'll handle things over here. Get some rest."

Helen turned toward the entrance to the hallway. Silently, instantly, in the time between breaths, Eliza's figure shifted to the doorway. *She's not there.* Taking a deep breath, Helen stepped past the mirage. She sat down in front of the TV. Her own face greeted her, looking poised and controlled in the glare of the camera.

"We have been working closely with the police to affect an immediate resolution to this tragic and troubling situation."

It was like listening to a stranger. She flipped through the channels. Finally she settled on an inane and brightly-colored children's show. The actors bounced around the set, grinning and singing. Helen kept her eyes fixed on the screen, aware of Eliza's form in her peripheral vision. Eliza's face behind her closed eyelids. Eliza's features blended with Carrie's scream.

She was not sure how long she sat in the living room. When she finally moved, her legs were stiff and the room was dark, except for the television. A documentary on bears had replaced the children's show. She was not sure if the shows had followed each other directly or if there had been a show in between. Or a hundred shows in between. She felt like she was living inside someone else's body, as if the real Helen was on television speaking in calm, modulated tones, while she was trapped in the house with her phantasms. Trapped like Eliza had been trapped. In madness.

The thought was even more terrifying than Eliza's apparition. Her heart pounded. Her body shook. Her breath came in gasps. She looked around the room, desperate for some comfort. She focused on her phone. Who could she call? What could she say? And if she did explain, what would be left for her in the world? There was no place for the mad. Eliza knew that. The empty asylum knew that. The well knew. Carrie knew.

Helen looked out the window. The storm had cleared and the moon was high. A row of lights was visible, high above the trees, in the Ventmore theater, where Wilson kept her office.

The theater was empty when Helen entered, illuminated only by emergency lighting and a light high above the stage. In the darkness, Helen could make out Wilson sitting near the front. She turned as Helen approached.

"Ms. President," she said with a slight smile.

"What are you doing?" Helen asked.

"I'm waiting for you. I saw you come across the bridge."

Helen stumbled into a seat behind Wilson. "It was Carrie," she whispered. "I saw her."

"I know."

"Why would someone do that to her?"

"Because he was evil," Wilson said. "Because she was weak."

For a moment, Helen stared at Wilson. Her arms were covered in blood. Helen's body registered terror, before she blinked and saw it was just the pattern inked on the fabric of Wilson's sleeves. Helen reached out to touch the fabric, to differentiate between fiber and flesh, to figure out what was real. Wilson placed her hand over Helen's.

"Why are you here?" she asked.

"I can't stop seeing her." The words came out in a sob. "Carrie. She's everywhere. It was awful. Her face was so… tortured. Now she's in my house. She's in my mind. She's stuck on other people's *faces*." It was impossible to explain. "Like a film. I look at the TV, and I see her screaming. I look in the mirror, and I see her. I see her on my own face."

Wilson took the back of Helen's head in her hand.

"Do you see her now?"

Despite the militant haircut and the smear of

lipstick dotting the center of Wilson's lips, there was something unaffected about her, a kind of simplicity, as though all the world's cheap trappings fell away before the clarity of her gaze.

"No," Helen whispered.

"Why did you come here?"

"I want to forget."

Almost without volition, Helen followed Wilson down the aisle, up onto the stage, and into the forest of dark, velvet curtains. Wilson stepped closer.

"The theater is locked with the master key. No one can come in," she said.

"But I just came in."

"I propped the door. You closed it. I was waiting for you."

Wilson stood so close that Helen could feel her breath. Helen leaned against the curtains, afraid her weight might pull them down. Then Wilson's tongue was in her mouth, her kiss driving Helen back. Through the material of Wilson's jeans, Helen felt a hard prostheses. When Wilson withdrew her kiss, Helen gasped.

"I'm going to fuck you. I'm going to open you, and for one minute…" Wilson drew in her breath and kissed Helen's temple so lightly that she wasn't sure she felt it. "For one minute you are going to forget all of this."

Helen only half heard, aware of the weight of Wilson's body against hers. Wilson spoke again, this time in an even quieter voice.

"Say 'yes.'"

Helen's yes was her mouth seeking Wilson's, her hands struggling with Wilson's jeans, pushing Wilson away just long enough to wrestle with the button. She no longer feared that the curtains could give way; she did not care if the whole curtain fell on them in a pile of smothering velvet. Their crushing weight would be a relief.

Quickly, Wilson pulled down Helen's pants, her underwear. In the dark, Helen could feel the curtains against her naked flesh. Wilson slipped deftly out of her jeans and a pair of men's briefs. In the darkness, Helen saw the silhouette of the enormous prostheses. She clasped Wilson's buttocks, grabbing the leather straps that secured the dildo.

Wilson slid her hand between Helen's legs. Helen closed her eyes. Wilson parted Helen's labia and ran her finger twice around the opening of Helen's vagina. Helen could feel her body's lubrication run down her leg. Wilson guided the top of the dildo inside her. The folds of her outer labia caught on the rubber and pulled painfully inward, then the dampness of her sex released them. Wilson plunged her hips forward, as she pulled Helen toward her. For a moment everything that Helen had ever been dropped away.

The dildo was too large, far bigger than any real man. Helen felt the elastic ring of her vagina stretch as though to breaking, and was certain she would bleed. She opened her eyes and saw only red dust motes, floating in the light beyond Wilson's back. Then she felt Wilson's arms around her shoulders, holding her. Her head leaned against Wilson's shoulder as she gasped. Slowly Wilson moved her hands from Helen's shoulders to her hips. She pulled Helen closer, rocking her hips back and forth just a millimeter, and where that millimeter gave way, pain became searing pleasure. When Helen came, she heard her own voice ring out in the acoustics of the theater, a piercing cry, full of grief. She opened her eyes and saw only the blue light above the stage.

As soon as the orgasm subsided, Helen regained her sense of propriety. The theater was huge, and from where she leaned against the curtains, she could see a hundred dark corners where anyone could be watching. She struggled out of Wilson's embrace and into her clothing, her heart pounding.

"This didn't happen," Helen said lamely. "I'm sorry. I have to go."

Wilson stopped her, her hands on Helen's shoulders. "This did happen. Relax, Helen. I understand. I'm not going to tell anyone. You're the president of the college. Of course I'm not going to say anything, but don't go."

Wilson threw her arms around Helen's waist. She was much stronger than Helen realized as she tried to break free.

"Come back to my apartment." Wilson spoke into Helen's hair. "Let me make you something to eat, get you a drink. Come and spend the night with me. Let me take you home."

Helen felt her muscles release as she sank into Wilson's embrace. There were a hundred dark corners in the theater, but nowhere did Helen see Eliza's face or Carrie's. Wilson dispelled the hallucinations. Perhaps her mind could only accommodate one madness at a time.

"All right," she said.

Chapter Forty-three

Wilson's apartment occupied the top story of the Grandville Hotel in downtown Pittock. When Wilson opened the door, Helen caught her breath. The space was set like the stage for an elegant and understated play. Long scrolls hung from the twenty–foot ceiling. Tall windows opened onto balconies. A spiral staircase led up to a loft, and the rest of the floor plan was open, filled with an arrangement of pale blue leather sofas and white ottomans. Wilson touched a light switch near the door, and several table lamps illuminated the space with a rosy glow.

"Sit down." Wilson gestured to a sofa. "I'll get you a drink."

Helen sat. To her surprise, an enormous dog rose from its place on a white, shag rug. She looked at the creature's flat, black face. The nose almost disappeared into the wrinkles around the dog's eyes. The dog snorted at her.

Wilson returned with two martinis. She put them on the table and nodded toward the dog. "That's Ulysses."

Ulysses ambled over, putting his large, wrinkly, black face on the edge of the sofa.

"I'm going to take him outside for a pee." Wilson patted the dog's head and headed for the spiral staircase that led up to the loft.

"Where are you going?" Helen asked.

"There's a roof top garden."

With Wilson gone, Helen took the opportunity to examine the apartment. On an end table beneath a lamp, Helen spotted Wilson's cubic zirconium studs. She picked them up. It was odd to see this fragment of Wilson's private life, this hint that, behind the bravado and the strange, beautiful face, there was a real woman with earrings and key chains and, presumably, a drawer full of mismatched socks. Just like everyone else. Or not.

Helen held one of the earrings up to the light. White fire sparkled at its center, its brilliance unmistakable. Nonetheless, Helen walked to the window and, in a corner where no one could see, she scraped the jewel along the glass. It left a fine line on the windowpane. A diamond. Helen replaced the earrings on the table.

Wilson returned a minute later.

When they were both seated on the blue sofa, Helen said, "You really shouldn't have done that to my house. You didn't have a right to come into my space like that."

"I always get it wrong."

Wilson looked so crestfallen, Helen wished she could take the words back. Why had she even brought it up? It didn't matter. Space, privacy, rules: what did those mean when a woman's blood had soaked the forest floor, when Eliza's blood had soaked the floor?

"Patrick says I always go overboard. I forget it's supposed to be a gift basket. Was that right?" Wilson's brow furrowed like a student reading bad handwriting in a classmate's notes. "Or flowers."

"Don't worry about it," Helen said. She leaned back against the sofa, her head touching Wilson's shoulder.

Nearby, the dog shook its massive head, distributing flecks of foamy drool across an ottoman. Wilson sat up and wiped it with the sleeve of her shirt. Then she knelt down and put her arm around the dog's neck.

"You're a mess," she said to the beast.

"I'm surprised your landlord lets you have dogs."

As soon as she spoke, she realized how ridiculous it sounded. Ten thousand dollars (or more) worth of diamonds rested on an end table where other people dropped their keys. The painting Wilson had hung above Helen's mantle probably cost twice that.

"The landlord is very lenient." Wilson smiled and looked away. "I own the building."

"You own the Grandville Hotel?" Helen asked.

"It was a present from my family."

Wilson dropped onto one of the sofas and motioned for Helen to sit next to her. "On paper, my family owns it. My dad and my three brothers are all in real estate speculation. That's what rich land barons do when their baby sister gets a job in the wilds of Western Mass. They buy her a hotel." She was neither apologetic nor boastful.

"Where did you grow up?"

"New Hampshire. I'm the youngest. By the time I came around, my father already had three boys groomed for the family business. They figured I would marry one of my brothers' friends, help out behind the scenes, manipulate the wives."

Helen could not help but smile. "How did that work out for you?"

"I manipulated the wives." Wilson winked, but then her face grew serious. "They're good people, my brothers, my folks. When I came out at seventeen, they had no idea what I could do with my life. They could not imagine a life outside marriage and the business. They're very savvy, but they're not modern. They actually had a family conference—just the men, of course—to figure out how much it would cost to support me until death. They figured out life expectancy, ran the actuarial tables, plotted out life insurance plans and divided the cost evenly between my father and my three brothers. They were willing to keep me at home, like back in the 1800s when you had a spinster aunt. Or they offered to get me a flat in Paris. That's where they thought lesbians went."

"And what did you do?"

Wilson's fingers stroked her arm, and Helen relaxed into the touch, listening to the story. It all sounded preposterous, but she was too tired to be skeptical.

"I ran away to the circus."

"Naturally."

"Really. I went into theater off Broadway and then on Broadway. Eventually, I realized I liked teaching more, so I went back to school, got the credentials, and ended up here. How about you? How did you get to be a college president by what… forty?"

"Forty-five," Helen said.

"So? How did you get here?"

Helen gave Wilson a summary of her resume: A BA from Iowa State, a Master's in Public Administration from Harvard, and then a fortuitous teaching assistantship at Harvard that led to a post with the U.S. Commissioner, followed by an assistant deanship at Ohio State. From there, a vice provost at Vandusen was an easy acquisition.

"I read your vita online. You saved Vandusen from losing their accreditation. And now you're the youngest college president in Pittock history."

"I would be at most colleges."

Helen leaned her head on Wilson's shoulder and closed her eyes. Wilson put an arm around her.

"Why so ambitious?" Wilson asked quietly.

"Not everyone has a father who will buy them a building." As soon as Helen spoke she felt bad. "I didn't mean it like that. It would have been nice to get a building. My father was a house painter, and we struggled financially."

Wilson kissed the top of her head.

"So? Why so ambitious?" Wilson repeated. "Every ambitious person I know is neurotic. They're all trying to win their father's love or prove they're not like their mothers. I am too." Wilson chuckled. "Distant father, over achieving brothers, perfect Martha Stewart mother who drank herself to sleep every night. I'm as bad as anyone."

"I'm not that ambitious."

"No."

"Pittock had been trying to recruit me since the last president died. I turned them down. I was used to a big school and a big city."

"But this time you said yes."

"Vandusen restructured."

"And then?"

"They restructured me out of a job." Helen felt a surge of anger, just as she had when she first got the news. "They should have just fired me. There was no restructure in the strategic plan. No one else got let go, nothing changed. A few departments reported to a different dean and one secretary got reassigned. It was just a ploy, so they could let me go and feel good about themselves. They thought they were doing me a favor. We had worked together for years."

"Why would they do that to you?" Wilson searched her face. "It wasn't because of something like this, was it?" She looked frightened.

"No." Helen let out a sad laugh. "If it had been something like this, they would have just fired me."

"Then what was it?"

This is how it ends. If Helen said the words out loud, she could not take them back. She could not pretend it had never happened. She could not reinvent herself.

"My sister, Eliza, was very sick," she began.

"I'm so sorry."

Wilson pulled her a bit closer. Helen paused. "No. She wasn't sick. She was a crazy, awful sister. She used to melt my dolls with cigarette lighters, and then she would scream for them. She would scream, as though she was being tortured, and beg for it to stop. She'd hold the lighter to their faces for so long, it really would burn her. She burnt her thumb so badly one time, it got infected. I could smell it rotting. Once you've smelled that, you will always know. She said she had to sacrifice my dolls so our parents would not die, but I think she killed them in the end. Killed them with worry. Killed them with sacrificing everything to try to help her."

Wilson put her other arm around Helen, in an encircling embrace.

"Even the good times were awful, and there weren't many of them. Occasionally, Eliza would curl up with her head on my mother's lap. Then no one would move, not to change the channel, not to pee. It was like having a bobcat sleeping beside you. You were afraid to move."

Now that Helen had begun, the story poured from her. How she wished her parents had been stricter with Eliza. How she wished they would send her away, and how Helen longed for the day when she could escape the madness of their house and go to college. However, as soon as she left, she began to worry about her parents. Eliza's care consumed them. Helen feared for them: two sweet, simple, gray-haired people, her mother a school secretary, her father a painter. As Helen was finishing her MPA, her father had a heart attack. Her mother followed a few years later, begging from her hospital bed that Helen never let Eliza go into a home. So Helen took the job in Pittsburg. Work was her refuge, and caring for Eliza was her career.

"Eliza kept getting worse," Helen went on. "Instead of hurting dolls or insects or breaking things, she started to hurt herself. She'd wander the city. She didn't bathe. She didn't throw anything away. My parents had owned this beautiful old house, and Eliza filled it with garbage. Whole rooms you couldn't go into because of the trash. Food, trash, excrement and things she bought off TV. I should have put her in a home." Tears slid out of Helen's closed lids. "Instead, I killed her."

Wilson didn't flinch. "Sometimes people don't understand what we have to do."

Helen was not sure if she heard Wilson speak or imagined her voice. Wilson kept her cheek pressed to the top of Helen's head, her voice in Helen's hair.

"How did you kill her?"

"I had just gotten the news of the restructure, and I had a month left at Vandusen. The school was going through another accreditation, and I thought if I could prove that I wasn't distracted, that Eliza wasn't taking me away from work, I could get my job back. I was working twelve hours a day. I didn't have time to take care of her, so I pressured her doctor to give her a dose of haloperidol. Eliza begged me not to. She said she had had it before, and it was awful." Helen pressed her face into Wilson's shoulder. "She said it would hurt so much to sit that she wanted to die. When she stood up it was worse. It hurt to move. It hurt to stand still. She said the Soviet government used haloperidol to torture prisoners. I told her she was crazy. I told her she would take it if she loved me, and she did. A few days later she killed herself."

"How?"

In the low light of the lamps, Wilson's eyes were exactly the color of moonlight.

"She gouged her eyes out with a spoon."

Wilson's face remained motionless. If she had cringed or commiserated, Helen would have stopped talking. Wilson just waited.

"The forensic investigator said it took hours. She probably started by putting the spoon under her lower lid, trying to pry it out. But the optic nerve is thick. She crushed one eye. The other she pulled halfway out of its socket, and then reached behind it with scissors to cut the nerve. There was blood everywhere. You see, she hadn't planned on the scissors. She blinded herself, and then she had to cut the nerve. She was looking for the scissors with both eyes blind. The doctors said schizophrenics can have strange, sick reserves of strength and courage. Sometimes. When it comes to things like this. From what I've read about patients, the wrong dose of haloperidol to someone who doesn't tolerate it...it's just that bad. It's so bad, anyone would put their eyes out, just to stop the pain."

"And she did."

"Yes."

Helen leaned over, clutching her hair in her fists. She wanted to pull it out in searing clumps. She wanted to hurt as much in body as she did in her heart. Then she felt Wilson gently pry her fingers open, and take her hands. Wilson kissed her knuckles, turned her hand over, and kissed the lines in her palm. *I'll read your fortune.*

"It's not your fault."

"Isn't it? I always wanted there to be a silver lining. I wanted Eliza to have a gift, something she gave us, something that made her life meaningful. But there was nothing like that." It was a relief to say it. How many decades had Helen staved off the dreadful sense that Eliza had wasted her own life, as well as Helen's and their parents' lives? Three good people in bondage to her madness. "Sometimes she knew how unhappy she made us. Sometimes, but not often. There was *nothing* remarkable about her, except that she was crazy, and, in the end, she had the courage to gouge her own eyes out. I wanted her dead."

"Sweetheart." Wilson's lips moved against Helen's hair as she rocked her in her arms.

"She ruined my life, and now I'm just like her." The tears had stopped. The worst realization was the easiest to speak. "I see her everywhere, and I see Carrie, and I'm going mad."

Chapter Forty-four

Helen woke early the next morning, wrapped in the sumptuous down covers on Wilson's bed. The sun was barely up and the apartment glowed with a diffuse light that seemed to come from nowhere and everywhere. Helen rolled onto her side. Looking at Wilson, who was still sleeping, Helen felt a rush of sadness. Wilson was gorgeous, unlike anyone Helen had ever seen.

After they had gone to bed the night before, they had made love again, and that time it was so soft and slow Helen felt like every muscle of her body had released, like wine pouring from a bottle. She had explored Wilson's skin with her hands and her lips, and been delighted.

But Wilson was so unsuitable a partner, the very thought of being with her was inconceivable. As Helen watched her, college scandal was not foremost on her mind. She traced Wilson's muscular shoulders with the tips of her fingers. Even if Helen wanted to stay, how long would a woman like Adair Wilson remain interested in her? After the thrill of seducing the college president wore off, after Wilson had won, what would be left? What could Helen offer Wilson with her body like Poseidon and her diamonds?

"I have to go," Helen whispered.

Wilson rolled over, opening her eyes slowly. "Don't go yet."

"I have to."

Wilson's eyes flew all the way open. They were the same color as the morning sky visible through the tall windows. Her lips were soft. Her face relaxed. But Helen could decipher her expression: sorrow. *Another tragedy.*

"You're going to leave me."

Putting her hand on Wilson's cheek, Helen spoke softly. "You're lovely. You really are. But I have to leave."

"No." Wilson drew away, pulling the covers over her chest. "You can't go."

"You are a beautiful, young woman, Adair. You're kind. You're talented." The words sounded paltry compared to the beauty before her. "But I am the president at the college where you teach. I'm ten years older than you."

"And now you're going to say you're not even gay."

"No. I am gay." It was clear now, so easy to discern. All those men: they were simply a punishment. *I killed my sister, and this is all I deserve.* "But I have to put the college first."

"Are you sure?"

"I have to be."

"So this was a mistake?" Wilson clutched the sheet.

"Professionally, yes. Personally, never. But more than this, more than last night, that's impossible for me."

She heard her own voice crack. She wanted to cry for everything that was impossible now. Everything that had been impossible for Eliza; everything Eliza made impossible for her. Maybe in another life she would have fallen for a woman like Wilson. Maybe she would have been a professor, with a cottage on the edge of town. Maybe they would have grown dahlias and kept a cat. Dahlias and a cat and ten thousand dollars worth of diamonds on the end table. No. It would never work.

"I don't think I could be in a relationship with anyone." Helen said to soften the blow.

Wilson turned away, gazing up at the two-story windows.

"Of course. The women I love don't love me." There was no self-pity in her voice, only the cool statement of fact. "I would not have fallen for you if you had not been untouchable. That's my weakness. The unattainable." She turned back to Helen. "That's *my* weakness. Yours is living in the past. Yours is being hurt and not getting help. You probably have PTSD. You know people hallucinate after they've seen horrible things. You could have a normal life if you stopped punishing yourself."

Wilson was angry but not loud. She slipped out of bed and donned an oyster gray kimono that managed to look both militant and feminine. She walked to the edge of the loft and looked down at the living room, her back to Helen.

"My problem," she continued, "is that I fall for the impossible. What else could I do? I move to a new town, and I buy the fucking building I live in. What am I supposed to do now? Date the local librarian? Marry some social worker? When I lived in New York, I auditioned for a part with the Gray Preston Company. Big company. Well established. A lot of grant funding and huge ticket sales. I didn't get the part, and I made the mistake of mentioning that to my brother, Cy. He bought out the stakeholders in the company. Fired the director. Got me the part, and when I wouldn't take it, he ran the company into the ground."

"Is that a threat?"

"I would never let him do that to you," Wilson said, but the words *I could* were implicit. Wilson whirled to face Helen. "I want someone he can't buy and he can't break. I want someone who has played chess with other people's lives. There aren't many people like that, and you know it. That's why you're alone."

"I need to go." Helen rose in one motion. She dressed quickly, tearing the shoulder of her blouse in her rush to get away from the growing desire to give in to Wilson's rhetoric. It would be so easy to fall back into the bed, to say, "You're right. No one understands me like you." Her very bones were languid from lovemaking. Her sex was still wet for Wilson's touch. She threw her blazer over the ripped shirt. When she was dressed, she headed straight for the staircase, glancing only briefly at Wilson before descending.

"Go," Wilson said. Her face registered absolute grief.

She's an actor.

"The garden suggests life and growth," Helen spoke in a sonorous tone.

Before her a group of twenty students and a few professors had gathered to commemorate the Carrie Brown Memorial garden. They stood respectfully still, their hands clasped in front of them. In the very back, a few paces behind the rest, Wilson crossed her arms over her chest. Her face was taut with grief or anger. She tried to catch Wilson's gaze, but Wilson looked away, blinking rapidly.

"It reminds us to look toward the future, not dwell on the past. It reminds us to tend to those we love and to accept the changing seasons and the cycles of life." Helen's voice sounded hollow in her own ears. It was such a cliché. By next year, the commemorative plaque would be overgrown, the garden just a few shrubs on the border of a lawn. Helen stared at the note card in her hands. *We are all actors.*

Helen read, "Seeing you here reminds me that we are not alone. We must turn to each other in times of need. If Carrie had known that, had felt it, we might not be here today."

In the front of the small gathering, a girl began to cry. Helen guessed from her prim, pink sweater emblazoned with the letters "Delta Delta Kappa" that she was not crying for Carrie. Not really. Perhaps the girl wept from some recent heartbreak, the exhaustion of upcoming exams, or just the pathos of the moment. Carrie Brown had died alone. Like Eliza, there had been no one who really cared at that last desperate moment.

Helen finished her speech and moved quickly through the crowd, hoping to catch Wilson—although she didn't know what she wanted to say. The girl in the pink sweater stopped her.

"Thank you," the girl sniffled. "That was such a beautiful speech." The girl threw her arms around Helen, embracing her in a perfumed hug. "That was so sad what happened to Cathy Brown."

Helen returned the girl's hug with one arm as she watched Wilson stride away.

"Carrie," Helen corrected her gently. "It was Carrie Brown."

Helen did not see Wilson for a several days after the commemoration. When next she did see her, Wilson was running across the quad, her boots pounding the ground, sending dry leaves flying behind her. She moved with the adrenaline of someone in flight. Wilson came to a breathless halt before her. Helen's breath seized in her chest.

"Helen," Wilson gasped. There was an autumn chill in the air, and her breath billowed like smoke. Heat steamed off her body.

"What is it?"

"It's Josa Lebovetski. He's dead. You've got to come, Helen. He wasn't in class today." Wilson doubled over like a sprinter at the end of a record-breaking dash, her hands on her knees, her spine heaving. "He hadn't called in sick. The students were looking for him. He's been here forever. Helen..." Wilson gasped. "I love him. He was like a father to me. First you and now him. I can't do this alone." Wilson wiped tears from her cheeks with the heels of her hands. "I can't be *this* alone."

Helen put her hand on Wilson's back, feeling her ribs heave.

"How did he die?"

"I don't know. They just found him in his office. Maybe it was a heart attack. A stroke."

Helen gazed at Wilson and past her to the quad. The view she looked at was also on the Pittock webpage, red leaves on the ground, gold-tinged leaves on the trees. Perfect.

Oh, my darling. She stroked Wilson's back. "Josa Lebovetski was killed."

She knew it with animal clarity. She knew it in her bones.

Chapter Forty-five

Helen felt a sickening déjà vu as she crossed the campus with Wilson in tow. The young police officer who had helped retrieve Carrie Brown's body was standing outside Boston Hall, keeping the perimeter clear.

"The chief is in there," he said.

"What happened?"

The young officer nodded toward Wilson.

"Ms. Wilson called campus security. They checked it out. Office looked like a tornado hit it."

"I think it always looked like that," Helen said. "How did Lebovetski look?"

"I can't say what happened for sure," the officer said. "He was lying on the floor. He looked like he'd been heading toward the door. It could have been natural causes."

"But?"

"But there were signs of bruising around the head," the officer added quietly.

"Why would someone do this?" Wilson dropped onto a bench outside the hall and put her head in her hands. "He was an *old professor*." She said it with the same reverence other people used for children.

Helen sat next to her and put her arm around Wilson's shoulders.

"Come on," she said quietly. "Let's take a walk."

Helen led Wilson away from the police and into

the science quad, where the trellis of wisteria vines hid them from view.

"He was such a good man," Wilson said. "From the beginning when I first got here, and when Drummond wanted to deny my tenure, he fought for me every time. He wasn't afraid of the politics. He just did what he thought was right."

Helen stroked the back of Wilson's neck. She had to find Thompson and Giles and talk to them alone. She had to see inside the office.

"They said his office was a mess. Do you think someone was looking for something?"

Wilson looked up. "No one cared about his research project except him."

"But he thought someone was trying to go through his stuff. He talked to me." Helen hated to confess it, but she had to. "He said someone had been going into his office, going through his papers. I didn't believe him. I just thought he was old. He was getting forgetful. I told physical plant not to go in his office without telling him. I left it at that."

Wilson looked shocked but not accusatory. "You think he was killed for something in that office?"

"I have to find out what it was."

Wilson wiped her eyes. "I can help you."

"I don't want you anywhere near this."

From somewhere in the mesh of wisteria a bird cawed. A breeze rustled the vines, bringing the smell of fall. Before Helen realized what she was doing, her hands were in Wilson's hair and her lips on Wilson's. She could feel the tears drying on Wilson's cheeks, and she kissed her harder for the tears, as though she could drink away the horror around them, as though she could lift them out of the present moment, into a bower where there was only Wilson's skin and their kiss.

"I want you safe. Get out of here. Go home. Go away."

Helen heard Drummond calling for her, and pulled back and stood up. She drew her hand across her lips, as though Wilson's kiss would leave a visible stain. She straightened her ascot and hurried into the harsh sunlight.

It was six o'clock and nearing dark when Helen finally headed back to Meyerbridge Hall. Patrick had gone home and the office was dark, except for the security lighting. Helen rubbed her eyes. At Drummond's request, Hornsby managed to keep the press off campus. Everyone else was in an uproar, waiting for the police report. *Please, let it be a heart attack.* Helen knew it was not.

She switched on the lights in the foyer and then in the hall. Since she had spent the night with Wilson, she had not seen one hallucination. Even outside Lebovetski's building, overwhelmed with the injustice of his death, she had kept her calm, both outside and in. Now, the visions came back with increasing vividness.

In the center of her office, the familiar, horrible stain covered the floor. Blood. She took a deep breath, trying to calm herself. *It's not real.* She took a step forward. Then another. She rubbed her eyes. Blood covered the hardwood. She could not clear it from her vision. Scarlet lapped against the moldings. In the center of the floor, leaning against her desk, Eliza rested, stiff-legged, her eyes turned into gaping holes.

It's only a dream. Helen tried to bring back Wilson's words. *You know people hallucinate after they've seen horrible things.* She pinched the skin on the back of her hand, closed her eyes, and took a breath. The air smelled like drying paint.

"There is nothing there." She spoke out loud, opening her eyes.

The legs. The legs were gone! It was just a torso. No legs. No eyes. Just enough of the body left to know it had once been human.

It's not real. It's not real. The blood was everywhere, reaching for her, growing. Screaming.

Helen ran from the building, stumbling down the front stairs. She was almost to the Barrow Creek when she finally got a hold of herself and sank onto a bench. Lights blazed over the rugby field. The students played a late game. A cheer went up. She took her phone out of her pocket and called Thompson on his personal line. A woman's voice answered. She heard a baby laughing in the background.

"May I talk to Officer Thompson?"

The panic in Helen's voice erased any reservations Thompson's wife might have had about fielding police calls at home.

A moment later, she heard Thompson's voice on the line. "Yes ma'am?"

"It's Helen Ivers. I need your help."

"I'm sorry, ma'am. The chief has unofficially taken me off the case."

"It's not about the case." She told him where she was. "I need to go to the hospital."

Fifteen minutes later, Thompson arrived with a paramedic. The young woman took Helen's blood pressure.

"Are you dizzy? Do you have pain?" The woman wore the serious face of young people with large responsibilities.

"I'm..." Helen hung her head. "I'm seeing things. In the hall over there. I thought I saw my sister's body. She's been dead for almost a year."

"Could you tell what triggered this?" the paramedic asked.

"It's happened before."

"Did you see anything unusual in your office?" Thompson asked.

"There's nothing there." Helen heard her own voice, lost and far away.

"I'll go lock up the building," Thompson said.

The paramedic put a hand on Helen's shoulder and offered her a packet of sugar water. *This was the end.* Helen had feared it would stem from Wilson revealing their sexual encounters, but ultimately the fault was hers. She simply could not hide anymore. She was no better than Eliza.

When Thompson returned, his face was grim. He spoke into a radio on his shoulder. "Chief? Listen, I know you don't want me at Pittock, but I need you over here. By Meyerbridge Hall." To Helen, Thompson added, "I don't know who would pull such a sick prank."

"A prank?"

"You're not seeing things. Someone put a dummy

in your office. Big holes where the eyes should be. Straitjacket wrapped around it."

"But I saw blood!"

"It's stage blood. Halloween stuff."

"How can you tell?"

"Well, it's either so fresh that someone dumped it while I was driving over, or it's drying bright red. Blood dries black. Can you think of anyone who would want to scare you like this? You said you thought it was your sister. Why did you say that?"

"My sister committed suicide, last year, in her kitchen. She put her eyes out, but no one knows about that except..."

Stage blood. Easy access to the campus. Someone who knew about Eliza and was angry with Helen. Someone who played chess with other people's lives.

"This prank, it looks like my sister's suicide. The only person I've told about that is Adair Wilson."

Helen did not want to return to the Pittock House that night, but Drummond—summoned at Thompson's insistence—urged her to go back.

"Escaping to a hotel suggests there's a real danger on campus. We're still not sure there was foul play. We have every reason to believe it was just a heart attack or seizure. If it weren't for the legs, we wouldn't think anything of an old, old man dying in his office. You were right when you went searching for the body," he said. "We can't run away. We have to be here for the students."

They sat in the library, the only building open at that hour.

"I've hired a security guard," Drummond added. "He will patrol the area around the Pittock House. You may not see him, but he'll be there. Are you comfortable with that?"

Helen nodded. She was too tired to complain or appreciate.

"Let's get you home." Drummond checked his phone. "I got a text from the guard. He's in the area."

Chapter Forty-six

A bright moon illuminated his way as he crossed the clearing between the forest and the asylum. In the distance, the Berkshire Western blew its horn. As he approached the main entrance, he withdrew the crowbar from under his coat. This time, the front door was too obvious. Instead, he used a service entrance in one of the smaller courtyards. Ivy covered the plywood door. It was easy to snap the wood, pry the door open, then prop the panel in the tangle of ivy. He switched on his flashlight.

On either side of the foyer, rows of cells disappeared down long corridors, mirror images of each other, except that the walls on one side were a bilious pink and the walls on the other side pale blue.

He took a sheet of heavy vellum from his pocket and shone the flashlight on it. Everyone in Pittock believed the asylum was full of trapdoors. They were the stuff of urban legends: tunnels that filled shoulder–deep with water every winter, the morgue where the asylum staff had left bodies to rot in their steel boxes. Tonight, for the first time, he had the map.

"Too bad, Josa," he said to the ghosts in the silent hall. "You really should have returned your materials to the library when I asked."

He hurried along, careful to walk near the walls, lest the sagging ceilings give way in the middle. Eventually, he came to the end of the farthest wing.

There, he found the narrow staircase leading to the boiler room. At the back of the boiler room was a door. He could still make out faint, red lettering. *Staff Only*. He tried the latch. It opened. Beyond the door, the corridor looked unfinished. Wooden beams were visible in the stone wall, like supports in a mine shaft. The floor was packed dirt.

His flashlight flickered. He hit it across his palm. He could not go back now. He had only a matter of days. Days before Alisha Hornsby arrived at the hospital unexpected, and his power over Hornsby waned. Days, maybe hours, before Helen Ivers put the pieces together. And the need was growing stronger. He had to make her tonight.

He began to run. It had to be there. The doorway and then the staircase. Corridors led off the main tunnel. He thought he made out the word *Laundry* over one passageway. The other side read *East*. A cold drop of water released its grip on the ceiling and slid down the back of his neck. It had to be there! He raced down another tunnel. The light from his flashlight bobbed on the walls. He was panting now, his hands sticky from sweat.

He came to a heavy, wooden door and used the crowbar to pry it open. Beyond, a narrow flight of stairs, barely more than a ladder, led up. He tucked the flashlight under his arm and climbed. At the top of the stairs, another door blocked his progress, but its lock had disintegrated into rust. It snapped like a brittle tooth. He pushed it open, revealing a basement.

A few dusty suitcases lay in a pile on the dirt floor. He picked his way toward another flight of stairs. He put his ear to the door at the top. Nothing. He turned his flashlight off and pushed the door open a crack. It took a moment for his eyes to adjust to the light. He recognized the hallway. Yes. There was the parlor, the long hallway, the filigreed wallpaper.

At the Pittock House, Helen had taken four sleeping pills. For several hours, they cast her into dark dreams. She was in a car that had gone over a bridge. In the water below, she sank and sank, then wrestled with the door, trying to free herself from the black reeds holding her legs.

Suddenly her eyes flew open.

Her heart pounded. The sleeping pills made the covers feel like lead, a childhood nightmare of being trapped in the dentist's chair, the product of some gruesome story Eliza had told. She looked around. Everything was as it should be. The curtains were drawn. Her laptop purred on the desk, a single, blue power light flashing on and off.

Then she heard something: a creaking footstep deep within the house. Familiar panic rose in her chest, and she willed it back. *Go look, there is nothing there.* But there had been something back at Helen's office. A gory scene, staged for her alone. A promise.

She got up and looked out the window to see if she could spot the security guard, but he was out of sight. She pulled a sweater around her shoulders and tiptoed down the staircase. At the bottom, she stopped.

The basement door was ajar. A voice in Helen's mind told her it was a hallucination. It was Eliza, a mirage, a vision. The door opened another inch. *It's not real. It is not real.* Now the door opened fully, a black maw in the filigree of wallpaper. A figure stepped out, dressed in black, the head shrouded in a dark mask. It was all cloak and gloved hands. A shadow moving in shadows. The figure turned.

"Helen." Its voice was low and vaguely familiar.

Terrified, Helen launched herself down the hall. She felt drugged. Every step was a trip. She felt the crack of bone against wood as she fell against an end table. Somehow she managed to keep her balance. There was a pair of slippers in the hallway. She struggled into them. Her heart pounded in her ears.

"Helen, you're mine," the voice behind her growled. "I love you."

Helen flew out of the house and down the stairs.

She screamed for help, and waited for the security guard to call back. There was no answer. She ran to the security phone on the side of the alumni house. Her hands trembled so much she could barely hold the phone to her ear. Nothing. No dial tone.

If she waited for another second, the figure in the hallway would be upon her. She could run for campus. Under the streetlights' high-watt bulbs, the guard would surely see her—if he was nearby. So, too, would the figure in the shadows. She screamed again, but there was no answer.

The only other escape was the path along Barrow Creek. She darted behind the house. The night got darker as soon as she stepped off the path into the forest. Helen considered hiding in the underbrush until the monster had passed her by, but if he could find his way into her house, he would find her in the bushes. *Helen. You're mine.* She ran.

Blackberries whipped her arms, releasing the smell of fruit. Only desperation and speed kept her moving. Each invisible root gnarled across the path propelled her forward. She fell twice but rose again, insensitive to any pain. Blood pounded in her ears. It sounded like footsteps. She did not dare look back. With every step she took, she expected to feel an arm around her neck.

After what felt like a lifetime, she reached the narrow footbridge that Marcus Billing and his friends had crossed the morning they found Carrie's remains. She kept running. Across the silent campus, through the Pittock gates. *I too have seen the angels and trembled.*

The town's main street was empty. Helen intended to flag down the first car she saw, but when headlights appeared in the distance, she ducked into one of the narrow alleyways between buildings. Taking a deep breath, she swallowed her fear. She was about to step out, to wave to the vehicle, when a hand clasped her ankle.

Helen screamed and whirled. Behind her, yellow teeth glinted from a sooty face. The hand that had grabbed her was black with dirt. The figure in the alcove hunkered on her haunches like an animal. Helen recognized Sully, and tried to extract her leg. Sully's grasp was a vise.

"You don't want a ride in that car," Sully said. "I should charge you a fiver for that, but you don't have a fiver. They never do when they need help."

Helen stared out at the street. She heard the car approaching, moving much more slowly than the twenty-five mile per hour speed limit.

"Let me go."

"Not that car."

As the vehicle crossed their field of vision, Sully released Helen. It was not a car. It was a yellow jeep.

"How?" Helen whispered.

Sully sucked her teeth, and then spat at Helen's feet.

"No one believes, Sully. Crazy Sully. But we're all crazy, and we all know." Sully stood up, her face in Helen's. "Now, run!"

Helen did not question. She ran.

Finally, Helen arrived at the police station. She pounded on the locked door, praying the department had enough funding for a third-shift dispatcher, praying it would be Thompson on duty, not Hornsby. *Please be there. Be there.* She fell to her knees. Her breath came in such ragged gasps that she took in no air at all. It was only struggle, not breath. She beat on the door. Inside, the brightly-lit office remained motionless. She heard a vehicle approaching on the street behind her, then squealing to a stop.

A moment later, Helen felt hands on her shoulders. Someone lifted her to her feet.

"Dr. Ivers, are you all right?" The whites of Thompson's eyes stood out against his dark face. "Talk to me, ma'am. Are you injured?"

"Help me," Helen gasped. "He's coming. He's following me."

"Come on. Let's get you inside."

Thompson quickly unlocked the door and guided Helen inside. He locked the door behind him. The front window and the fluorescent lights overhead put them on a stage.

"Let's go into the back room," Thompson said.

Helen was vaguely aware of Thompson radioing Giles and draping a blanket over her shoulders.

"What happened?" he said. "Talk to me."

Helen could not speak. She wrapped the blanket tighter around her shoulders. She was not crying, but she was not breathing either.

"Take your time," Thompson said. "Giles is on his way. We're going to take care of you."

"Someone followed me," Helen finally gasped. "He was in the house, in the Pittock house, in my basement. He called me by name."

"You need to tell me if you are hurt," Thompson said.

Helen shook her head.

"Did he attack you?"

"He was going to. He was going to kill me." The story poured out in a garble: the footsteps, the creaking door, the figure, the knowledge that it was Wilson who planted the dummy, the yellow Jeep gliding past her on Main Street. "It was Ricky Drummond. It had to be Ricky Drummond."

"But you said it was Wilson."

"I don't know. She knows Ricky. She tried to make me think it was him. I don't know." Helen looked up at Thompson. She felt helpless. "I don't know."

"That's okay," Thompson said. "I'll call Margie, our dispatcher. She'll take you home with her. You've got nothing to worry about. She's a tough one. Then I'll get to the bottom of this."

"Where is Hornsby?" Helen asked.

"We'll deal with him tomorrow."

Chapter Forty-seven

The next morning, Helen woke under a faded quilt. Embroidered plaques adorned the walls, promising that Jesus watched over this home. An ancient philodendron hung from a hook in the corner and looped around the walls. Slowly, she rose, donning a robe that someone had thrown over a chair.

"There you are, Hon," Margie said when Helen emerged. She introduced Helen to her husband, a portly man wearing a t-shirt advertising a Baptist summer camp. They both sat at the kitchen table.

"How you doing, Kiddo?" he asked.

Helen attempted a smile. "Better since you took me in."

Margie bustled about the kitchen, fetching Helen a cup of coffee and serving a box of donuts. Helen glanced at the stove clock. It was almost 11:00 a.m. They must have been waiting for her to wake up. Memories of the previous night flooded her mind, and she slumped in her chair.

"You've had a night," Margie said. "You'll be all right now. Bruce here is a Marine. He won't let anyone get to you."

"*Semper fi*," Bruce said, giving the table a cheerful slap.

"Plus," Margie added. "This is the nosiest neighborhood in Berkshire County, and everyone knows it. No one with shady business would come around here."

Helen doubted that but said nothing. She accepted her coffee gratefully.

"What's more, those boys got it straightened out," Bruce added. "Tyron and Darrell. When Margie first told me about them, I thought she was starting a daycare. They're not bad fellows, though. They're green, but they got integrity."

"They got it all sorted," Margie said. "When you get dressed, I'll give them a call, and they can fill you in on the details."

An hour later, Helen was dressed in a pair of Margie's sweatpants and a t-shirt announcing in neon that she loved Cape Cod. Thompson sat in front of her, a glass of water clasped in his fingers.

"After you came to the station last night, we went looking for Ricky Drummond. We found the Jeep at his house, although he was staying in the dorms. I looked up Hornsby's report. Hornsby said he checked the vehicle, but I did a closer search. There were long hairs in the seats. They match Carrie's description. We've sent them off to the lab. Plus, we found some partial prints that matched hers and a bag of knitting under one of the seats. Could be hers. Could be another girl's. Here's the thing..."

Thompson took a deep breath. Bruce and Margie leaned up against the cupboard. They looked concerned, not curious. They had already heard the story.

"I talked to Marshal Drummond again. This time, he wasn't so sure about his son's alibi. He said

Ricky was home that night, but Mr. Drummond went to bed early. He assumed Ricky spent the night at home. However, Ricky could have gone out. Mr. Drummond's bedroom is on the west side of the house, and Ricky had parked on the eastern edge of the drive. Mr. Drummond would not have heard the car if he was awake, and he said he slept soundly, except for an hour or so in the middle of the night."

Helen felt lightheaded.

"Mr. Drummond said he never meant to lie. He just didn't want to raise false suspicion. When we asked to search the Jeep, he said it's been eating away at him."

Helen's heart went out to Drummond. He was so proud of his son. She had seen the light come into his stony eyes when he talked about Ricky. *My pride. My life.*

"Was it Ricky?"

"It looks like it," Thompson said. "At least it looks like Ricky had something to do with it. Maybe Carrie enlisted his help. We don't know yet."

"What does Ricky say?" Helen asked.

"He says he didn't do it, but that's what they all say. Hornsby thinks he did it. He's finally come around. He knows he didn't handle this very well, said his personal life got the better of him."

"They're going to bring in some state troopers," Bruce chimed in. "And the FBI."

"I'm not going to let this get swept under the rug," Thompson said. "There's no denying what's happened, no smoothing things over."

Helen waited for a sense of relief to wash over her. She could go back to work, start the capital campaign and, over the course of the next year or two, watch the campus transformed as new money came in and the students forgot. She could go back to work. The thought gave her pause.

"The dummy in my office… Do you think that was Ricky?"

"It's hard to say, ma'am. Ricky says he didn't do it, but he says he didn't kill Carrie Brown. He's got a good alibi for the night your office was vandalized. He was bar-hopping in Great Barrington with three of his classmates and a girl from town. The bartenders confirmed they saw kids who fit their description, and he's got a couple of Visa receipts."

"What about Adair Wilson?" This was the question that mattered. "Do you think she could have vandalized my office?"

Thompson searched the floor. For a moment, Helen glimpsed the awkward, young man who had first accompanied Hornsby into her office.

"Adair Wilson," he said, as if to confirm he had heard properly.

He liked Wilson. She heard it in the way he cleared his throat. Wilson was certainly not his love interest, nor even really his friend, but they were young professionals in a town ruled by old men and old money. Helen guessed he felt solidarity with Wilson. He probably did not know how much old money Wilson could leverage if she wanted to.

"I'm not trying to frame her," Helen said. "I don't want it to be her, but she's an employee of the college. I need to know if there's any possibility that she was responsible."

"I don't know," Thompson said finally. "You say she's the only one who knew about your sister's death. She says she was home that night, but she lives alone.

No one saw her enter her building. No one talked to her."

Helen felt her heart breaking. "I'll need to call the board and have them put her on suspension."

❧❧❧❧

"So that's it," Terri said. "Case closed?"

"Of course," Helen tried to give her voice the cheer it required. "The judge denied Ricky's bail. Marshal told me he wouldn't pay for it, even if he could. He's the real victim, in some ways."

"Really?"

Helen tucked the phone under her ear. With her free hand, she doodled a tree on the back of a manila folder and then looked up again. Outside, the quad wore the fall colors that made New England famous. A few boys tossed a rugby ball, occasionally tackling each other in drifts of browning leaves. She drew a noose hanging from a lower branch.

"He is sixty–seven. His wife is dead. His son is in jail. At least I had a chance to start over."

"Are you?" Terri asked. "Are you starting over?"

Helen had commissioned an artist to cast a bronze sculpture of Carrie Brown to place in the memorial garden, and she had recently connected with the widow of a wealthy alumni looking to put her husband's name on a building. These were all signs of improvement, and she told Terri about them.

"I don't mean working. I know you're turning that college around faster than anyone expected. I've read the buzz in the alumni quarterly. But are you making friends? Are you getting over this?"

"Yes, Terri. I've been making friends." She

was thinking about dinners she'd recently shared with Drummond. They always met by chance. Their conversations were punctuated by silences, during which, Helen was sure, they both wrestled with their demons. Perhaps that was what she needed in a friend. It was certainly all she could handle.

"What about that woman you liked?" Terri asked.

After a two-week suspension, the faculty association had ruled there was not enough evidence to suspend Wilson. Helen had never confessed their sexual relationship, and now Wilson had good reason to keep quiet about it also. Without that connection, there was little to pin Wilson to the vandalism. After the hearing, Helen had avoided her assiduously, which angered Patrick. He said she owed Wilson a phone call, since Wilson called her office every day. For once, Helen had pulled rank and said no.

"I looked her up online," Terri added. "She's gorgeous."

"It's over," Helen said. "It was a mistake."

"Too bad. You could do worse."

Helen felt like arguing, but it was almost noon, and she had chosen today. She had even put a fake meeting on her calendar so Patrick would not schedule her. She opened her desk drawer and touched the paper that lined the bottom. What Terri did not know, what no one knew, was that beneath that paper lay the prize Lebovetski had died for: a map of the Pittock Asylum circa 1887. It was not an original copy, but it would do.

After the police crew had left Lebovetski's office, she had slipped into Boston Hall. She had skipped the climate-controlled cases. If someone was willing to murder Lebovetski for what he had—and he knew they were after him—he would have sacrificed climate control for security.

Standing in the chaos of books, papers, and blueprints, Helen had despaired of finding anything. How would she even recognize a treasure if she found it? Then she found the poem. It was penned in the spidery hand of an old man, but the lines were straight and the ink dark. He had pinned it on the only section of unobstructed wall.

> Lovely lady of the woods
> who fell as King George fell
> the light caught you like Icarus redeemed
> young lover, be beautiful but remember
> answers are beneath the ivy
> invisible like the dead.

The mausoleum was a stone building on the edge of the asylum grounds, entirely covered in ivy. Helen's hands trembled as she first cleared the foliage, waiting for the horror that lay within. Instead, it looked like a small post office for woodland fairies. In the far end, light from a window illuminated a space the size of a small conference room. The floor was covered with dry leaves and a dun colored bird rested on the window sill. The walls were lined with little plaques identifying the cremains. The inscriptions were innocuous: *Mary Leonara Thompson. 1898—1934. Kind spirit, rest in peace. Ronald Beautress Gill. 1940—1975. Watched over by the angels.* It smelled like damp springtime.

There was no sign that anything had been disturbed for decades until Helen read the inscriptions more closely. Then, in the far corner near the floor, an inscription on a plaque caught her attention. The words shone as though freshly carved, and when she looked more closely, the plaque was a piece of tin foil pressed over the original iron. On it, were etched the words "Helen Ivers. Long live the king."

Trembling, she touched the plaque and then the box behind it. It was like a safety deposit box, long and low with a lid that lifted from the top. She withdrew it from its housing and placed it on the small altar beneath the window. The lid lifted with surprising ease. Helen held her breath, certain that if it contained bones or even the sinister dust of past history, she would scream. Inside was a blessedly familiar sight. Ziplock. The bag held several Xeroxed papers, folded up with a letter.

"Helen," Lebovetski had written, I am sorry I do not know anymore than this, and this is a poor copy. I only guess that this is what they are looking for. If you have found this, I presume I have joined the spirits in the ivy. Please tell my dear Adair to be happy. The spirits have been calling me for many years, I was just waiting to make my grand exit. Drop the curtains on me, my dear girls, and go and be happy for 'no voices chanted choruses without ours, no woodlot bloomed in spring without song...'"

Chapter Forty-eight

She put the conversation with Terri out of her mind as Helen crossed the campus and hiked toward the asylum. Her mind raced. She felt beyond fear. She had lost Eliza. She had lost Adair. She would lose her job, she felt certain about that now. She might even lose her life. This was the end of everything, but before she went down, she would understand the asylum. It would yield its secrets. Ricky would yield up his secrets.

She had just stopped at the edge of the asylum clearing, staring up at the barred windows and cracking bricks, when a voice startled her.

"Over here." Drummond stepped from behind one of the columns that adorned the front entry. His bearing was as elegantly upright as always. Today, his smile was warm and optimistic.

"What are you doing here?" he asked.

For a second, Helen was speechless. "I..." she stuttered. "I was thinking about the renovation, a possible dormitory. I wanted to look around a bit, move forward, make this a site for future hopes, not past fear." Years in administration had trained her to answer difficult questions quickly, and her voice sounded confident.

"A grand idea," Drummond said. His grief over Ricky, however deep, was expertly concealed.

Helen thought how similar they were. "I've

talked to some architects. They loaned me a map." She touched the breast pocket that contained the Xeroxed sheets. "I was going to go in. Does that make me sound like a terrible freshman?"

Drummond shook his head. "I've talked to the police about this. I know where it's safe to go. Some parts of the asylum are falling apart, but the main wards are solid and safe. Let me go with you."

It was strange to see how beautiful the building was inside. The tile floor was cracked. The paint peeled on the walls. Nevertheless, the domed ceiling suggested the elegance of a bygone era. A chandelier still hung from an ornate fixture at the ceiling's highest point. Two spiral staircases curled toward the second story.

"The women were housed in the south wings." Drummond pointed. "The men to the north. Families could visit here, at the center. Sometimes they even had balls and concerts. There is a theater downstairs. We should go look at it."

"It's beautiful," Helen said. "I wish…I wish there had been something like this for my sister."

"Modern institutions are so bleak. Maybe, just maybe, when people see what a beautiful dormitory this makes, they will remember that we used to provide this kind of accommodation for the mentally ill." Drummond put his hand on her shoulder. "I know that is a pipedream, but let's hold onto it. Come, let me show you around."

They bypassed the staircases and walked down the hallway. It was cold and dim. Most of the cell doors were open. Green light filtered through the ivy.

"It must have been terrible to find your sister like that," Drummond said, as though picking up the thread of a previous conversation. "How do you think she found the strength to do that? It is amazing what people can do when they're not tied to reality."

Helen turned from the cell she was examining. "You knew?"

"I'm sorry," Drummond said. "You don't want to talk about it. I shouldn't have brought it up." He held out his hand to Helen as she stepped over a pile of broken plaster.

Helen was about to ask Drummond how he knew about Eliza's death, when a sound at the end of the hallway stopped her. Footsteps pounded toward them. Someone was running. A second later, she recognized Wilson.

"Adair!" Helen exclaimed.

"Marshal, don't move," Wilson yelled, raising the Glock toward Drummond's head.

For one surreal moment, Helen remembered all the "Weapons on Campus" seminars she had mandated. There was always one well-meaning counselor in Birkenstocks who lamented that students turned to violence because they thought it made them powerful. "Real power," the counselor would expound, "can only come from the within. Guns don't change anything."

This gun changed everything. The air crackled around the weapon. The light from the windows disappeared into its black barrel, leaving the room darker. In the dim light, Wilson looked ten times more beautiful and infinitely more dangerous. She trained the gun on Drummond, her arms steady, her eyes as white as burning metal.

"Get down on the mother fucking floor, Marshal!" Wilson's voice was as deep as a man's and full of rage.

Without thinking, Helen stepped between Drummond and Wilson. "Adair. No! What are you doing?"

"Helen, step away. It's him. It's not Ricky. Marshal killed Carrie Brown, and he's going to kill you."

Behind her, Helen heard the provost's voice, calm and paternal. "Adair, I know this has been hard on you. I know you cared about Carrie, and that you want to do something, but you already have. You led us to Ricky. I was blind. We all were. Put down the gun."

"Listen to me, Helen." Wilson's eyes remained focused on Drummond, the gun trained on his head. "I talked to Sully and the men at the homeless camp. They've seen Drummond in the woods. They're afraid of him. They call him the surgeon. And I asked Lebovetski's students. I figured out what he had. It's a map, Helen. It's got to be. A map showing the underground passageways from the asylum to the warden's house. The warden's house that is now the Pittock House. Lebovetski had borrowed the map from the rare book room at the library. That's what Marshal was looking for when he broke into Josa's office and killed him."

Helen stared into the barrel of the gun. She did not need to see a bullet to know it was loaded. Helen turned toward Drummond. It was unthinkable. "Marshal?"

"I've walked these woods a hundred times. Of course they've seen me," Drummond said. "However,

I did not kill two women and Professor Lebovetski." He held out his open hands. "Nor do I know anything about a map. Adair, this is ridiculous."

Wilson continued as though Drummond had not spoken. "You know what else, Helen? The Pittock House belonged to the asylum warden. It was built with an underground corridor that led into the asylum. That way, the warden could travel quickly to and from his work in the winter when it was snowing. That's how Marshal got into your house. That's why he needed the oldest map."

"It was Ricky." Drummond's voice had lost its paternal warmth.

There was only one person Helen knew for certain had been in the Pittock house without permission.

"I talked to Ricky in jail." Wilson's eyes darted toward Helen, then quickly returned to her target. "He did slash your tires. He followed you to the Cozzzy Inn, and he slashed your tires because he thought his father was having an affair with you. He had followed his father to the Cozzzy Inn before, and he was angry that Marshal would date another woman so soon after his mother's death. Only it wasn't you."

Helen felt Drummond's hand on her shoulder.

"It's okay," he whispered.

"It was Carrie. All those nights Marshal was out of the house, it was Carrie Brown he met at the Cozzzy Inn. The clerk said an older man met a young woman with a leather jacket. He said he thought it was probably a college girl, that they always paid cash. Marshal lied about Ricky's alibi. Ricky was home the night Carrie was killed. It was Marshal who wasn't."

"Adair, give me the gun," Drummond said. He reached around Helen toward Wilson.

"Move and I will blow your fucking head off."

"You don't want to do that," he said. "Just give me the gun."

Wilson said nothing. She squeezed the trigger a fraction of an inch. "Put your hands on your fucking head, Marshal. Walk back out that hallway. One stupid move and I swear to God I will kill you," Wilson yelled.

I want her. Even now, I want her. Helen drew back, straightening her shoulders. She could not let desire sway her judgment. She could not let beauty decide, at this last instant, whom she trusted. She knew what was right. She knew where the path diverged, where she and Eliza parted ways. She had stood on that crossroad, and Eliza had called to her from a distance, from the shadows, from among the beautiful, horrid things that lived on the dark side of the mind. Beautiful like Wilson, with her wild eyes the color of ozone. So beautiful, even now, she took Helen's breath away. But Helen had survived at that crossroad because she took the other path. It had to be Wilson who was mad, not Drummond. Wilson with her gun and eyes ablaze.

Drummond looked at Helen. "Do something," his eyes pleaded.

"Give me your gun." Helen's voice was cool. "You trust me. Drummond trusts me. Let me hold the gun and walk us out. We'll walk outside. You can talk to me. I'll listen. Just hand me the gun."

Wilson's eyes were wide. If she let Wilson keep the gun, someone would die. Helen took a breath.

"I love you, Adair," she whispered. "Trust me. I'll protect you. I'll protect us." She took a step forward. "Give me the gun, and we'll be together. We'll walk outside. We'll call the police. You and I will be together. Always."

She could see the muscles in Wilson's arms begin to tremble.

"No," Wilson said. "You'll never love me."

"You have to give me a chance." Helen held out her hand. "Give me the gun."

The gun was lighter than Helen expected, like a terrifying toy. She held it awkwardly, pointed downward. She did not know what would happen if she accidentally bumped the trigger. She wanted to release the magazine and drop it on the floor, but she did not know how. Her heart raced. She gasped.

Drummond took a step closer.

"Helen, watch out!" Wilson yelled.

Suddenly, there was an explosion. Reeling in the empty seconds after the blast, Helen could hear nothing. She felt agonizing pain in her left ear, as though someone had stabbed her eardrum. Her hand was empty.

Wilson lay on the ground, her legs and arms shaking in hideous, stiff, rapid-fire jerks. The floor around her was wet with urine.

In the other ear, she heard Drummond hiss, "Fucking dyke."

He grabbed Helen by the elbow. He was holding Wilson's gun. He had wrenched it from her hand in the time it took Wilson to say, "Watch out!"

Now he pointed the gun at Helen's head. "One move, one word, and I blow your fucking head off."

Despite his warning, Helen reeled toward Wilson. She opened her lips, although she did not hear the scream issue from her mouth. Wilson was motionless. Helen tried to run to her side, to press her hands against Wilson's chest.

"You killed her!" Helen sobbed.

The enormity of the situation gripped her. "Marshal?" Helen pleaded. "What are you doing?"

Helen felt the butt of the gun crack against her temple. She dropped to the ground. The pain was excruciating. She could see only red. She felt Drummond grab her arm, and half-walk, half-drag her down the hall, away from Wilson's body. Then she passed out.

Chapter Forty-nine

When Helen woke, she was strapped down. Her legs were bound together, her arms fastened to her sides. Above her, the ceiling was low. Droplets of water clung to the rough surface. She turned her head, wincing at the pain in her temple. The walls beside her were carved out of stone, like the root cellar in her grandmother's New Hampshire home. On the other side of the room, a propane lamp rested on a metal cart. Beside the lamp lay an array of objects, the flotsam and jetsam of the asylum. An old saw. A syringe. Then it hit her: they were not refuse. They were tools, carefully laid in a row.

"You're awake," a familiar voice said from behind her head. "What a quick recovery. You must be in very good health."

Drummond moved into her line of sight. He looked like himself, handsome and composed, his salt-and-pepper hair neatly shaped around his face. His sport coat hung on the back of a folding chair. His shirt was spotless.

"What are you doing?" Helen asked. She tried to shake free of her bonds. She surmised she was on a gurney. The flimsy metal rocked with the motion of her body, but the restraints held her tightly. "Let me go!"

She screamed for help, expecting Drummond to silence her with a fist.

Instead, he simply regarded her, his expression thoughtful.

Finally, he said, "Josa Lebovetski would be so unhappy. I haven't kept it at the right temperature, the right humidity. It's not archival at all." He stood up and took a folded piece of paper out of the pocket of his jacket. He unfolded it and held it over Helen's face. "No one knows where this room is. Scream all you want. You're twenty feet underground."

"You can't do this to me. Someone will find me."

"They won't be looking. You were so traumatized by that little stage production in your office, you ran away." His voice was conversational, almost friendly. "We talked about it for a long time, you and I. And you wrote such a nice resignation letter, complete with a forwarding address. Someplace much nicer than that slum Carrie rented."

"Marshal, you can change your mind. You're not well. This isn't your fault. You don't have to do this."

Helen's mind raced. She briefly entertained the notion of a hallucination, but this was nothing like the visions of Eliza. The pain in her head told her this was real.

"You don't even know what I have in store for you," Marshal said. He moved in front of the table with the lantern, casting a shadow that engulfed the room. "Carrie was so sweet." He spoke like he was only half-aware of being overheard. "She had such pretty breasts. Young women always do. I bet Adair's are starting to sag, aren't they?" He turned to face Helen again. This time his voice was hard. "What is she, thirty? Thirty-five? She's nothing now, though. She's dead. Your little dyke lover. I could have told everyone, Helen, but I didn't. It didn't even matter. You were so discreet, slipping away to her house after you fucked in the theater."

Helen felt a deeper chill run through her bones. He had known. He had watched. He had been in the theater. In her house.

"Don't look surprised. There are many ways in and out, if you know the campus." He had been toying with something in his hand. Now he lifted it up. A syringe filled with milky liquid. "Carrie wanted it. You never understood that. You were so sad that she died. Poor little Carrie, but she wanted it." He held the syringe up to the light.

Helen had to keep him talking, anything to stop the syringe in his hand.

"You'd be surprised what you can still find in here," he went on. "Drugs. Tools. Equipment. When they closed down the asylum, they ran. No one would stay here if they didn't have to, not even the doctors."

"Tell me about, Carrie," Helen said. "I want to understand."

Drummond snorted. "She was a whore, but she wanted it like I did." He took a step closer, the syringe still in his hand. "She wanted to cut her legs off. She'd been fantasizing about it since she was six years old, rubbing her twat and thinking of cutting off her legs. Ricky knew it, but Ricky is weak. He said it was weird. He said it scared him."

In the shadow cast by the lantern, she could no longer see Drummond's face. Terror gripped her. He was probably going to torture her, and then he was going to kill her, There was nothing she could do. Even when she saw Eliza lying in her own blood, her eyes ripped from their sockets, she had thought to stop the bleeding, to find a towel, to call someone. There had been a possible action and then another, to carry her from the horrifying discovery into the bleak busyness that follows a tragedy. Now, there was nothing.

Drummond laid the syringe beside her. The glass rolled against her leg.

"I was going to take her to South Africa. Other countries understand. They're honest. Money buys everything here, and it buys everything there, but in Africa you don't have to negotiate so much. I found a doctor who would take off her legs for a price, send her back once she healed. She wanted to do it."

Helen watched him turn back to the table and pick up the saw. The teeth glinted in the lamp light. She thought she might be crying, but couldn't tell. The terror was so intense it ripped her mind from her body. *I'm not here. I'm not here.*

But she was.

The part of her mind that could still reason, forced the words out of her mouth, "Why didn't you send her to South Africa? Why kill her on the train tracks when she wanted the same thing you did?"

"You were so weak." The comment seemed directed at Carrie. "You wanted your forum, your friends. You wanted to be normal. Body Integrity Identity Disorder. Ha! You were just as sick as I was. You weren't normal. We can never be normal." Drummond refocused on Helen. "I wanted to fuck her stumps." His face contorted. He no longer looked recognizable. "She wanted to live with it, with her legs and her need. But I can't live with it."

"What can't you live with?" Helen asked.

"I need it." He was breathing through his mouth. "I needed her stumps." He stood, slamming his fists down on the gurney beside Helen's head. "Father can't hurt me anymore." He paced the small room, muttering.

Helen tried to see how his distraction could work to her advantage, but her arms and legs were fixed. She tried to jerk her body enough to throw the syringe to the floor. It didn't move.

Drummond's pacing slowed, then stopped. "Now I have you. No one can stop me, and nothing can take you away from me." He picked up a band of surgical rubber from the table. "After I cut off your legs, I can keep you alive for days… maybe years."

"No, you can't," Helen said. "They're going to remodel this building. They're going to find me. Dead or alive. They will find me, and they'll find you. It's not worth it. If you let me go, you've only committed one murder. The courts will look at it like that. Only one. You can stop right now."

Drummond picked up the band of rubber and slid it under one of Helen's legs and between her bound thighs. He tightened it and tied a knot. He pinched the fabric of her pants above her pubic bone, laughing to himself. Then he reached for the other band.

"No. I couldn't stop at one. I couldn't stop at Anat. She's just like you, only I didn't think to tie off her legs. She bled out in minutes. Carrie. Lebovetski. And don't forget my loving wife. It was so sad how that trailer fell on her. Ricky still hates me for not catching it, not warning her, not knowing it was going to tip. But I *pushed it*. And then of course there were all those whores. No. I couldn't stop at one, and the courts won't give me any reward for good behavior."

Helen felt the rubber cords cutting into her legs. Her feet were already numb. Drummond picked up the syringe again, held it upright, tapped the air bubbles and pulled back the plunger.

❧❧❧❧

With all the strength she had, Helen wrenched her body in its bondage, rocking the gurney just enough that for a second her hand touched the wall. She pushed off with her fingertips, praying she'd have enough strength to topple the gurney. It swayed. For one heartbreaking moment she felt the wheels reclaim their place on the floor. Then one of the wheels hit an uneven spot. The gurney tipped. Helen slammed to the floor, still tied down. She collided with Drummond's legs, sending him sprawling. The syringe shattered against the floor.

In the silence that followed, Helen heard a voice so faint it could have been in her head.

"I could read your fortune for a dollar."

A second later, another voice hushed the first.

Then, "She's down here. I saw him take her down."

"Where?"

The second voice sounded like Thompson. She screamed. Drummond leapt to his feet and reached for the gun, but Helen didn't care if he shot her. She screamed and screamed, drawing the voices closer.

With a crash, the door swung open. From one side of the frame, Helen heard Thompson's voice, clean and loud this time.

"This is the police. Drop your weapon, and put your hands on your head."

"Sully, get back upstairs." It was Giles, hiding on the other side of the open door. He raised his voice. "We're prepared to shoot. We *will* open fire."

Helen looked up. She could not turn her head

far enough to survey the whole room, but she could see Drummond's feet. His stance was rigid. He had not moved.

"He has a gun," Helen cried out.

"Put your gun down," Thompson yelled. "If your hands are not on your head when I enter the room, you're dead. You can't escape. The building is surrounded. Marshal Drummond, you have a chance to save your own life. Walk slowly out of the room with your hands on your head."

"I'm coming out." Drummond's voice held the calm of a college provost. "Please, don't shoot."

As Drummond took a step forward, he came into her line of sight.

"He's still armed," she yelled.

Drummond took one more step forward.

Thompson and Giles appeared simultaneously on either side of the door. Drummond raised Wilson's gun. Gunshots reverberated against the stone walls. Drummond dropped to his knees. For a moment, he froze in that position like a penitent sinner. Then he fell, face forward, onto the floor.

Giles pointed his gun at Drummond's head, while Thompson kicked the Glock away and put handcuffs around Drummond's wrists.

"Is he dead?" Giles asked.

"He's going to be if the paramedics don't get here fast. I'll stay here," Thompson said.

"Come on," Giles said to Helen. "I'll get you out. You're going to be all right. It's over."

Helen felt the rubber tourniquets released from her legs, then the cuffs that held her legs and arms. Giles did not even offer to let her walk. He picked her up in his enormous arms, and carried her like a child.

Chapter Fifty

Giles accompanied the ambulance to the hospital, asking repeatedly if the paramedic could give Helen something.

"Not until we check for neurological damage."

"Are you sure?" Giles kept asking. "Look at her."

Helen was aware of someone sobbing breathlessly, but it didn't feel like her. Maybe it was someone who looked like her or maybe there was someone else in the ambulance.

At the hospital, the staff protected her from the barrage of reporters. The doctor gave her a battery of tests, and then a painless injection that sent her into deep sleep. She dreamed of Eliza, not the horrific tableau of her suicide, just Eliza as she remembered her from their young adulthood, a sullen, stringy-haired woman drifting through life. In the dream, Helen called out to her. Eliza kept drifting, like a piece of gray cloth carried along by a current. Helen tried to run alongside her sister. Her legs were heavy and Eliza kept gaining ground, growing father and father away. "I have to find Adair," Helen kept saying. "Where is Adair?" In the dream, Eliza knew, but was too preoccupied to tell her. Helen felt waves of despair as Eliza drifted father. "You have to help me. I've done *everything* for you!" Helen screamed. "I gave you my whole life!"

In the dream, it was cathartic. *I've been waiting years to say that.*

When Helen woke, pulled to consciousness by a nurse checking her blood pressure, she felt none of the relief from her dream world. Eliza was dead. Adair was dead. Both of them were dead because she hadn't listened. She sat up.

"How are you feeling?" The nurse had tiny, nimble fingers, no thicker than the fine cornrows arranged across her head. "Can I bring you anything?"

"What time is it?"

The woman checked a small, digital clock mounted on the wall beside Helen's bed. "About 10:00 a.m. You've been here overnight."

"Am I hurt?"

"The doctor wanted to keep you for observation."

"Can I go?" Helen asked.

"Lie still, and I'll get the doctor. He'll clear you to go home."

The nurse disappeared. Slowly, Helen assessed her body. Her head still pounded and her temple was painfully tender. She felt stiff and bruised but nothing more. She lowered one of the bed rails and swung her legs off the bed. Glancing around, she saw that someone had brought her clothing. It was probably Margie. The sweatshirt on top of the pile bore a puff–paint likeness of the statue of Liberty. When she unfolded it, she read "God Bless America." There was a small bathroom off her room. Helen stepped inside and changed.

When she came out, she found her wallet, keys, and phone in a plastic bag by her bed. The phone had suffered no damage. She turned it on, and sat on the edge of the bed. She should call Terri, but couldn't bear his sympathy at the moment. He would offer to fly to Massachusetts. She didn't deserve it. What she needed was a ride home and someone to explain the previous night in a way that told her what to do. Did she have to leave Pittock? Did the police know Drummond had taken Wilson's gun from her hand? There would be questions, an investigation. The board would ask her to resign. She didn't care. She just wanted someone to move her through the day, and the day after it, and the day after that, until... what? She had wanted Adair. She loved Adair. And then killed her. At the end, whom could she call when she was beyond pity?

Patrick arrived at a run, his round face flushed, his words coming out in a jumble. Dropping into the chair beside her bed, he clasped her hands. "Oh, my God, Helen! I was so worried. Are you okay? Of course you're not okay. What am I asking? You're alive, at least."

Helen closed her eyes. She didn't want sympathy.

"Can you get me out of here, Patrick? I want to go home." At the word "home," her throat constricted. *Let me take you home,* Adair had said, and in the twelve hours she spent in Adair's condo, Helen had felt more at home than in any house she had owned or rented. Behind her closed eyes, she saw Adair in her gray kimono, her eyes full of grief.

Helen leaned her head against the car window as they flew down the Mass Pike.

"How did she know I was in there?" she asked, staring at the fall colors flashing past in a blur of yellow, blood, and ocher.

"I'm sorry," Patrick said.

"Sorry." The words floated in the air, like a language half-understood. "For what?"

"I told Drummond where you were going. I was worried. You didn't seem right."

"What about Adair?"

"We went out to lunch. I was telling her what you were doing, telling her about Drummond going after you. We were sitting outside the Craven, and that crazy woman, Sully, came up to Adair and started raving about killers and madmen. She kept saying, 'He has your lover under the grate' and then something about an isolation ward. I was about to call the cops to get her out of there, but Adair jumped up and headed off like there was a fire. I'm sorry. I never liked Drummond, but I didn't think he was a killer."

"They've got him in the medical ward at the state psychiatric hospital. Six bullets but he survived. And Hornsby confessed. Drummond was paying him off from the beginning."

Helen barely listened. She wondered how many of the cars on the road belonged to tourists, come for the fall colors. Had they heard the news about Pittock? Did they turn back and head home, or had it simply added a thrill to their pleasant vacations. Would they say, "Remember that time we drove out to the Berkshires, and we had the good sirloin, and that woman was killed by her provost?"

"I know it's hard to believe," Patrick said, as though Helen had spoken. "But you knew it. The Meyerbridge donation. We both thought it was too small. Even for broke-ass Pittock, even if Meyerbridge was Drummond's friend, no one sells a building name for five hundred thousand dollars. Turns out

Meyerbridge gave the school about 2.2 million, but Drummond gave half of it to Hornsby. I don't know how he managed it. That'll be someone's job to find out. I'm guessing he's been skimming for years.

"Anyway, after Thompson and Giles took you to the hospital, Hornsby called Thompson and told him everything. Drummond had offered him money to keep things quiet. He said no. Then Drummond came back with this story about a cancer treatment in Switzerland. It could save Alisha, his wife, and Hornsby went for it. Only, when he finally got in touch with the hospital, they said there was a serious protocol for getting into the test study. It wasn't proven, and Alisha wasn't a candidate."

"He tried to arrange something for Carrie," Helen said, still staring out the window. "He was going to send her to South Africa to have her legs amputated."

"Well maybe in South African you can buy a doctor for a price. The Swiss aren't so flexible. Alisha Hornsby died. She got an infection while she was there. The Swiss doctors took good care of her, Hornsby said, but she didn't make it. She was glad to see the Alps before she died. Hornsby turned himself in. The money doesn't mean anything without her. He only did it for her."

Patrick's small sedan rattled noisily. A rip in the cloth of the ceiling revealed yellow foam.

"I guess Adair was right about the theater budget," Patrick nattered on. "She'll probably make you give her back-pay for all the years she was supposed to get funding. Not that she needs it. She's so fucking rich, but she loves to make a point."

Helen waited for Patrick to catch himself. *She'll make you give her back-pay. She loves to make a point.*

Adair was dead.

"They airlifted her to New Hampshire in a private helicopter," Patrick added. "Her brothers are scary. Two of them came down to get her. It was like the NRA meets the GOP meets the mafia. I thought they were going to open fire on Thompson when he said he wanted to keep her in Pittock."

Patrick had pulled off the Mass Pike, and they were winding through the Berkshire hills. Helen closed her eyes. She held her body very still. She wished she could stop breathing.

"You okay, Dr. Ivers?" Patrick asked.

Helen nodded. She didn't want to cry in front of him. Her grief was too big and too full of her own guilt.

"Why did Thompson want Adair's body?"

Helen's eyes flew open as Patrick veered onto the gravel shoulder. The car stopped with a screech. He turned to Helen, grasping her arm.

"Helen." He didn't sound like a chatty secretary anymore. "Adair's not dead."

Helen opened her mouth, but no sound came out.

"Did someone tell you she was dead?"

"I saw her," Helen whispered.

"Oh, God, Helen!" Patrick leaned over the gearshift and hugged her. "You thought she was dead?"

Helen sobbed.

"She was wearing a vest," he said, still squeezing her. "That gun–nut brother of hers bought her a whole paramilitary outfit. She got four cracked ribs, and they were worried she might have punctured a lung, but she didn't. As soon as her family heard what happened, they sent the helicopter down to get her. She's taking a leave of absence, and her father is threatening to sue the college, which will probably bankrupt us, but she's alive. She's fine."

"I saw her." Helen clung to Patrick. "I saw him shoot her."

"She said it was the performance of her life," Patrick said, his voice full of pride. "She knew if Drummond checked on her, he'd shoot her in the head. She said she even pissed herself to make it look more realistic. She hoped he'd think it was blood."

Helen couldn't tell if she was crying or laughing. She pulled away from Patrick and wiped her eyes.

"I thought she was dead. I thought I killed her. She gave me her gun. I talked her into giving me her gun, and then Marshal grabbed it. I wasn't even paying attention. She warned me." She stopped. "Patrick, I love her."

The engine was still running. Except for its intermittent rattle, the car was quiet.

"I guessed," Patrick said. "She told me there was a woman. Addie and I have been friends for ages, and this was the first time she wouldn't tell me who. She said she couldn't. She was protecting someone. She said it was someone powerful. And I saw the way you looked at her."

"She didn't tell you?" Helen was touched.

"She said you didn't want people to know, so she wasn't going to tell anyone until you were ready."

"I have to see her."

Patrick looked away, biting his lower lip. "You'd better. She's pissed."

Chapter Fifty-one

Three days later, her head still aching from the blow of the gun, Helen found Adair's ancestral house in the hills of New Hampshire. A footman in full uniform opened the wrought-iron gate that led to the driveway. Another attendant took her keys, as though the idea of leaving a car parked in the circular driveway was abhorrent. Slowly, Helen climbed the marble stairs that led to the front door. Yet another servant, this time a woman in a black suit as elegantly tailored as Helen's own, greeted her.

"I'll ask Miss Wilson if she is expecting you," the woman said.

"She's not," Helen tried to explain, but the woman was already speaking into a small phone she had withdrawn from her pocket.

"She'll just be a moment. Wait here."

Helen surveyed the foyer as she waited. While Patrick had described Adair's family as a paramilitary organization, the house offered nothing but subtle good taste. Everything from the terracotta tile, to the large abstract paintings, to the restored antiques, exuded masculine elegance. Helen tried to imagine Adair growing up in this palatial hall. No wonder she had such confidence.

A few minutes later, the woman ushered Helen into a parlor decorated in rich, red leather furniture. A fire burned in the fireplace, half hidden by an intricate metal screen. The windows looked out on an expansive deck and, beyond that, rolling fields and forest. Helen did not have time to appreciate her surroundings. Seated, half-reclining on a sofa in the center of the room, Adair sat wrapped in a fur throw. She wore a skirt and a cashmere sweater of a rich raspberry color. She'd smoothed her hair into a gold streak across her forehead, more Princess Diana than lesbian radical.

Adair was flanked by three men. On one side, stood a slender, gray-haired man, about Helen's age. In another life, she would have found him attractive. He had Adair's vitality, her pale blue eyes. He introduced himself as Monty. On the other side of the sofa, stood a stocky man with a chest like a granite slab. Helen guessed this was Cy, the gun aficionado. He said nothing, his mouth set in a scowl that was all the more sinister for his round baby face. Next to Cy, the patriarch of the family sat in a heavy, carved-oak throne. Arthritis gnarled his hands, but his back was straight and his face steely. In their center, Adair leaned her cheek against the leather sofa and stared out of the window.

"I… I've come to speak to Adair," Helen said.

"Go ahead," Monty said. Then to Cy he whispered. "Prichard let her in. I told her not to." He meant for Helen to hear. She was not welcome and they weren't leaving.

Helen took a step closer.

"May I sit here?" She gestured to the sofa next to Adair. Adair shrugged and winced. Helen reached out to touch her shoulder, then stopped at the edge of the fur throw.

"Adair, I'm so sorry." The words were inadequate and she knew it.

Cy's eyes bored into her.

"I know that's not enough." Helen tried to think of what to say. It was all so clear now. She had thought Adair was a wild-child, while she herself was established and powerful. Too conservative for Adair. Or so she had thought. Now she saw Adair in her natural surroundings.

Once again, Helen was a shabby girl from Pittsburgh's working class, her suit the same grade as the door attendant's. She should have been proud to be Adair's lover. She was now. She didn't care who knew, and if acknowledging it meant starting life over, she could do that. The position at Pittock had meant nothing in the bleak hours when she thought Adair was dead. "I love you," she wanted to say. The stern eyes of the men stopped her.

"Why didn't you believe me?" Adair said quietly.

Helen could feel the men glaring at her. "Adair, I'm so sorry."

"I told you everything," Adair said. "From the first moment I knew anything, I told you. I told you about the legs, about Anat. I told you about Carrie." She stopped, as though just speaking these words had exhausted her.

The men's eyes cut into Helen's scalp.

"I know," Helen said. "You tried to warn me."

Adair said, "I was wrong about, Ricky. I thought he was the murderer. It all fit together, but I didn't feel it inside. Is that why you left me? Because I got it wrong about Ricky? Why, Helen? Why would you take my gun? How could you choose Marshal Drummond over me?"

Helen wanted to say that she had not chosen Drummond, that she had just handled a difficult situation the best way she could. But it felt like a lie. In that last instant before she took the Glock, she had disbelieved Adair and chosen Drummond.

"I was just so wrong."

"I trusted you to protect me, Helen."

"Please come back to Pittock."

"Why?"

Helen hesitated. "We need you. The students need you."

Adair closed her eyes, and Monty took a step toward Helen. "My sister is tired."

She was being dismissed.

"Adair please."

It was too late. Monty was moving her toward the door, politely but irrefutably. He ushered her into the hallway, putting his hand on her shoulder in a gesture simultaneously patronizing and dismissive.

"I can understand why a woman in your position would not want to align with Adair's lifestyle. Naturally, it's not what we would have chosen for her either. But here in New Hampshire, family is very important."

Here in New Hampshire. Helen almost laughed. The Wilsons' mansion had as much in common with New Hampshire as the Taj Mahal.

"Here in New Hampshire, we stand by our own," Monty continued. "We believe family comes first. Always. We expect that of our friends too."

Helen stepped away from his touch.

"What I am saying is that we could buy your little college or bankrupt it. Whichever." He tucked his hands in his pockets and stared over Helen's shoulder, out the window at his estate. "Adair does not need you. We will support her in the manner to which she has a right to be accustomed." He turned his gaze back to

Helen. "I'm saying, don't contact my sister again. She has been through enough. She deserves someone she can count on, someone she can 'go to the well with,' as my brother Cyrus would say. Naturally, we'd all like this to be a man, but lacking that, we'd like it to be a woman with balls."

Helen was still speechless as the front door closed behind her. The instant she turned, her car appeared, driven by a liveried valet. Dazed, she got in and drove a few miles down the road before pulling into the parking lot of a small country store. The letter board out front advertised "organic meat" and "fine wines." Clearly, the grocer knew his clientele. Helen turned off the engine and called Patrick

"What do I do?"

"You've met the dragon brothers, haven't you? Those men give me nightmares."

"What should I do?" she asked again.

"Do you love her?"

"I do."

"Tell her and don't worry about the rest. Adair is the best friend I've ever had, but she's a princess. I won't lie. She flies up to New Hampshire every time something goes wrong. A performance flops; she gets a bad review. She sulks for a day or two. Her brothers threaten to buy whoever upset her, buy them and ruin them. Then she comes home."

"This is more than a bad review."

"So maybe she'll stay for a month. I know Adair. Optimism and women: those are her weaknesses. If she thinks there's a chance with you, she'll come back."

Helen paused. "If her brothers are so rich, why didn't she just ask them to rebuild the theater? Why is she even at Pittock?"

"Ultimately?"

"Yeah."

"She doesn't want them to fix her life. That's why she's not in the family business. That's why she didn't marry some lesbian heiress—there are plenty in her circle. Or a gay politician, who needs a cover and is willing to pay for it. Adair could have had it a lot easier, but she wants to be her own woman, make her own decisions. It's hard to be strong when you've always had that kind of money, but she is. She really is. Don't worry too much about her brothers. Just make sure she knows how you feel."

Helen said goodbye to Patrick and dialed Adair's cell. The voicemail answered immediately, and Helen did not hesitate.

"Adair, I love you. I should have said that to your face. I should have said that in front of your brothers, but I won't lie. They're terrifying. I don't know how to say I'm sorry for what I did because you could have died. I thought you died, and when I did, I didn't care about anything else." She went on until the voicemail cut her off.

She didn't know how many messages to leave. She spoke until she couldn't think of anything more and she began to repeat herself. After a few seconds of silence, she pressed END.

Dimly aware of the parking lot, she saw luxury cars pulling in and out of the gravel. Funny how the rich liked to play at having a humble life. She saw that now; Adair had been playing. Playing the hard-working professor. Pretending outrage over the theater budget. Feigning a life of work and salary and paycheck. Playing and not playing. Playing but also making a life of her own. It was something Helen had not even considered when Eliza was alive. A life of her own. It was time. The autumn was just beginning. The leaves were a tableau of scarlet and gold. The sun was so high, it cast no shadows. And it was a new year. For the students. For Pittock. For Helen.

Helen jumped when a black limousine pulled up next to her car, spitting gravel as it came to a stop. After the events of the past days, even the click of a stop light, turning from red to green, invoked a jolt of fear. The driver's window glided down. An Asian man sat at the wheel in a starched uniform with a stony frown. He pointed toward the tinted window behind him.

Helen looked. The back window retracted.

Adair still held her phone to her ear.

"You may get in on the other side," the stern driver said. "The Wilsons will arrange for your car."

He said "arrange" the way someone might say "decommission," but Helen didn't care about the car. She only cared about Adair and getting into the limousine before Adair changed her mind.

Helen had ridden in limousines before. There was always a lingering smell of prom, as though someone had quickly wiped up the cheap liquor. Adair's limousine, like her house, was amazing. The leather seats were as smooth as butter and blacker than night. Adair had rolled her window up, and once Helen closed the door on her side, daylight disappeared behind the silky black windows. Adair sat in a pool of light from an overhead lamp, recessed cleverly in the ceiling. The whole interior was dark, except for Adair's face.

"I'm so sorry," Helen said.

Adair turned away.

Helen did not hear the engine but the limo was moving again. An opaque window separated the passengers from the driver.

"I love you," Helen tried again. "I didn't know what to think. I saw Marshal every day, in his office, on campus, in meetings. If I had just had a second longer to think… It was just that Marshal was so dull. He was so stiff and sad. I couldn't imagine how he could do those things."

"Did you think *I* did them?" Adair asked without turning.

"No."

Maybe. She hadn't thought that Adair killed the women in Pittock. It was just that Adair was so rare, so wonderful. If someone was capable of ending the world or creating it, of opening up a fissure in the fabric of the universe – for good or evil – it was Adair, not stuffy Marshal Drummond.

"My sister always hallucinated," Helen said, "ever since she was a child, and by the time she was sixteen or seventeen it terrified her. But I remember, when she was little, she'd occasionally see something she called 'Alma' or 'The Friend.' She'd look up, as though someone had come in the door and just beam. It was the only time she smiled."

Adair turned, reached across the seat and took Helen's hand.

"When I saw you in the asylum…" Helen clutched Adair's hand. "Part of me was thinking, *what if she's not real?*"

"Come here," Adair said, gesturing for Helen to slide across the seat.

Outside, the trees passed in a blur.

Helen moved across the seat, and Adair drew her into a kiss. Helen wanted to squeeze her with the strength of her passion, grief and guilt. But she remembered the broken ribs and touched Adair with trembling hands. Only her lips and tongue conveyed the intensity of her feelings. They kissed for a long time. Helen only stopped when she felt tears on Adair's cheek.

She drew back, touching Adair's face tenderly. "I'm so sorry. Are you okay? You shouldn't even be out, should you?"

"I feel like hell." Adair whipped her eyes with the heels of her hands. "But I'll live. That's not it. I just..." She took a shaky breath. "Don't leave me again. Don't go away. Or, at least, if you're leaving, tell me now. It's the hope that kills me. Patrick says I'm a fool. I always think it's going to work." She laughed sadly. "But he's got his husband and his happy life. What does he know?"

"I'm not going anywhere," Helen said.

She put her arm around Adair and drew her close. It felt wonderful to hold her, to smell a hint of her cologne, to feel Adair relax into their embrace. She kissed the top of Adair's head.

"But..." Helen added. She felt Adair stiffen and held her closer to comfort her. "Just out of curiosity, where are we going?"

Adair sat up a little and Helen kissed her gently. "Not that it matters. I'll go with you."

"I thought we could go somewhere. New York. Provincetown." Adair said, "We have a few houses up in Kennebunkport. No one could expect us to go back to work after what we've been through."

"No one would expect you to work after seeing your family's house," Helen said, cupping the back of Adair's head in her hand. "Yes. Any of those."

Adair touched a button in the wall of the limo. "Ubol, please take us to the airstrip."

The voice of the driver came through a crystal clear sound system. "Yes ma'am. Destination?"

Adair looked at Helen. Helen shrugged.

"How about the Cape?"

"Yes ma'am."

That night, they ate dinner in Provincetown. The season was changing and the patio restaurant had put out heat lamps to warm the diners, but the planters around the restaurant were still full of late-blooming flowers. The narrow streets were still full of tourists. Music poured from a few waterfront dancehalls. Beyond, the ocean was calm. For the first time in months, Helen felt genuinely hungry.

Over dinner, they discussed everything that had happened at Pittock, putting the pieces together one by one. The clues. Their guesses. Their first uncertainties.

"When they first discovered the legs," Helen said. "Marshal said he was glad the media wasn't tying it to other events. I didn't follow up on what he meant. I should have."

"You shouldn't have to ask. You trust people will tell you things like that, and when I did, I came at you too hard. I should have made an appointment, like Patrick said. Gone through proper channels."

"No. You were right. Do you remember when you said, 'there is no procedure for this'? Of course there's not."

They spoke in low voices, leaning toward each other. Helen's mind still reeled. She was trying to find a place for everything that had happened, a way to understand it and still have faith in the world. At the same time, she felt a strange giddiness that was not tinged with anxiety. Adair was right there. When she touched Adair's hand, Adair smiled.

After dinner, they strolled down to a bar overlooking the water and ordered a bottle of wine. There, as if by silent agreement, they did not resume their conversation about Pittock and Marshal Drummond. Instead, they talked about Adair's family, what it was like to grow up in a house ruled by men and money. Adair talked about how her brothers had protected her over the years. Their willingness to support her. The good they did in their community. And how hard it was to make friends when she came from such extravagant wealth.

Helen told Adair about Eliza, about the hard times and the sacrifices. Eliza's wild flights of fancy and inappropriate behavior.

When the bottle was empty, Adair led Helen back to a bed and breakfast at the end of the main drag, set above the other buildings on a slight promontory. One of the Wilsons' assistants had made the arrangements. It was clearly the grandest accommodation in Provincetown.

"Don't turn on the lights," Adair said, when they entered. She crossed the dark room and opened the curtains.

Beyond the window, the ocean spread to the

horizon without a single distraction. Helen knew there were buildings below them, but the height of the room hid these. Helen followed Adair and put her arms around her. Adair leaned into her embrace and wrapped her arms across Helen's as they both looked out the window. The water was very still and the moon hung, almost full, near the horizon.

"I wanted you from the first moment I saw you on campus," Adair said. "So stern. So upright. But it was when I saw you at the crime scene…you cared. You were the only person there who showed any…grief."

Helen swallowed. "And I thought I was holding it together."

"You were. That's not what I meant."

Helen kissed the side of Adair's neck where her neck curved into her shoulder. Then she turned Adair toward her and began to unbutton her shirt.

"Wait." Adair stopped her hand.

Helen froze.

"I…" Adair began. Then she quickly unbuttoned the shirt and dropped it to the floor, her eyes closed, as though awaiting criticism.

A dark bruise covered Adair's left side. It started below her collar bone then traveled over her breast and across her ribs.

"I'm so sorry." Tears pushed at the back of Helen's eyes. She blinked them away, trying to speak with a steady voice. "He could have killed you."

Adair nodded.

Helen reached out to touch Adair, then pulled back her hand. "I don't have the right, do I? This is all my fault."

Helen looked up, meeting Adair's pale eyes. Adair looked uncertain, shy even.

"I'm just asking you to be gentle," Adair said.

Helen began to cry and kissed Adair through her tears.

They did not draw the curtains as they shed the remainder of their clothes. Instead, Helen led Adair, naked in the moonlight, to the four-poster bed. She pulled back the cover and nestled Adair in the sheets. Then she kissed her, starting with her eyelids and moving down her throat, along her undamaged side, across her belly, and down the silky skin of her thighs. When desire tightened Adair's muscles and Helen heard a plea in her ragged breath, she gently parted Adair's legs and licked the moisture from her body. Finally, when she worried that the tension of waiting to orgasm would hurt Adair's fragile ribs, she pressed her kiss to Adair's swollen clit.

When Adair came, her cry was as wild and open as the seagull's cry above the ocean. Helen pressed her kiss to Adair's body until the tremors subsided. When she looked at Adair again, Helen thought she saw the whole ocean in Adair's eyes.

"I love you," Helen whispered.

Adair ran her hand through Helen's hair, drawing her up.

"I've always loved you." Adair spoke into their kiss. "I've always been looking for you."

Adair rolled Helen onto her side, her hand gliding down Helen's belly.

"You don't have to," Helen said.

The bruises on Adair's chest cast her perpetually in shadow although the moonlight was bright enough to read by.

"Shh," Adair said, propping herself up on her good side and slipping her fingers between Helen's legs.

All thought of protest left Helen's mind as Adair gently stroked the folds of her sex.

"When I'm better, I'll make love to you properly." There was a wink in Adair's voice, perhaps because Helen was already straining against Adair's hand, already feeling her world distill down to the orbit of Adair's fingertips and to her own imminent release.

When they were spent, they lay in each other's arms, the moonlight washing over them.

"What happens after this?" Helen asked.

"My brothers want me to go back to the estate to recuperate for a few weeks. They insist. And then I want to come back to Pittock, to you...if you want me."

Adair hesitated as though she could imagine a world in which Helen did not want her.

"*Of course* I want you." It was so simple. All those years that Helen had thought love was impossible, they had melted away like snow thawing. She smiled. "We could get a little cottage on the edge of town and plant dahlias."

Adair chuckled. "If you want."

Helen closed her eyes, dreaming of the dahlias Adair might plant: ruby-crusted petals, plate-sized blooms so luscious the neighbors would turn away blushing. It was hard to imagine a normal life with a woman like Adair, but it was not hard to imagine love.

Epilogue

Marshal woke in the medical ward of the state psychiatric hospital. His arms were cuffed to the rails of his bed. Pain, unlike anything he had experienced, screamed in his right leg, as though it was being pulverized and burned.

"Oxycodone," he gasped. "Morphine."

The guard, who had been reading a magazine by the door, glanced up. "I'm not your nurse."

"Get me some fucking drugs!"

"Hmm," the guard said, and turned back to his reading.

Marshal shook his restraints, rolling from side to side against the bed rails. The pain writhed in his leg, not just a sensation but an entity. "Help me!"

Finally, a man in a white coat walked in and stood over his bed.

"My leg," Marshal said through gritted teeth. "Give me something."

"A bullet exploded in your leg," the doctor said. "It shattered the bone, the muscle. I could give you a sleeping pill." The doctor looked at his chart. "Marshal."

"I don't need a sleeping pill." They were torturing him. Dumb mules! They didn't understand. "I'm the provost of Pittock College. The provost! This is all a mistake. Get me some drugs, and get me out of here."

"Oh, I don't think that's going to happen, Mr. Provost," the doctor said. He wasn't much more than a boy, probably a medical student.

"I'll have your license," Marshal screamed.

"Threats aren't going to get you anywhere." The doctor turned to go.

The pain shot up through Marshal's leg and into his eyes. He gagged. "I'm sorry. I'm sorry. Just give me something."

"We'll see what we can do. I don't think we'll be able to give you much relief, though. That's the problem with phantom pain. It's a memory, not a nerve impulse. Your body remembers the pain of trauma, but we can't go back in time and take that memory away. And we can't numb the nerve impulse for a limb that's not there."

For the first time, Marshal looked down at his right leg…at the flat white sheet below his knee, the hideous lump where his thigh ended.

"No!" he screamed. He tried to kick his leg, but there was no joint. He was helpless. He couldn't move. Even if they released his hands, how would he walk? The pain was excruciating.

"You're an educated man, Mr. Provost," the doctor said, clearly enjoying himself. "You can appreciate the irony." He glanced at his watch. "Ah. My shift is over. It seems like yours has just begun. Looks like it will be a long one."

The doctor was right. It felt like a lifetime. For days, maybe weeks, Marshal lay in sweating agony, drifting in and out of consciousness, but never escaping the pain. Then, in the middle of one night, he woke and his mind was clear. Father had always said prison was for the poor; madness was for the weak. He would escape. Somehow. And the pain in his phantom leg would be the torch that lit his way back to Helen Ivers.

About the author

Karelia Stetz-Waters is an English professor by day and writer by night (and early morning). Her work includes the thriller, The Admirer, and a YA novel, Forgive Me If I've Told You This Before (coming Fall 2014). She lives with her beloved wife, Fay, her pug dog, Lord Byron, and her cat, Cyrus the Disemboweler. Her interests include large snakes, conjoined twins, corn mazes, lesbians, popular science books on neurology, and any roadside attraction that purports to have the world's largest ball of twine. She would love to hear from her readers.

More at

Home page: www.kareliastetzwaters.com

http://kareliastetzwatersauthor.wordpress.com

The Purveyor:

Beatific conjoined twins Charity and Prudence Kimball have refused a scholarship that, if they accept, could prove lucrative to Pittock College. College President Helen Ivers sends Professor Adair Wilson to speak to them, but what begins as a routine college recruiting mission turns deadly when the twins are abducted. Convinced their abduction is her fault, Adair sets out to find the twins, embarking on a mission that pits her against a ruthless human trafficker known as the Purveyor.

To learn more about the author or the sequel, visit

www.kareliastetzwaters.com
or
http://kareliastetzwatersauthor.wordpress.com/

CPSIA information can be obtained at www.ICGtesting.com
Printed in the USA
BVOW07s0321050115

381907BV00001B/42/P